PW-1

A Novel by

SPENCER R. SCARCELLO

Rae-Jak Publishing
Newport Beach, California

Published by Rae-Jak Books
A division of Rae-Jak Publishing, LLC
220 Newport Center Drive, Suite 11
Newport Beach, CA 92660

ISBN 978-0-9831536-3-4

ACKNOWLEDGEMENTS

I truly believe this novel was divinely inspired, so I would like to thank God for giving the idea to me, and all the help thereafter. Each person that assisted me along the way is a Christian, not by design; it just worked out that way.

My wife Carol Scarcello, friend Marty Enniss, and her husband Pastor Gary Enniss were key in encouraging me to write the book.

Authors Norma Roland, William H. Reagan, and John Andrews helped get me started, teaching me what I needed to know and how to go about the whole process.

Our dear friend Lynne Jonsson painted the cover art.

Best selling author Jack Peterson mentored me through the editing and publishing process.

MY SINCERE THANKS TO YOU ALL.

CHAPTER 1

INTRODUCTION

My name is Ralph Diamond. My wife Tina and I live in Spruce Valley Lake, Central California, and this is my story.

I woke up early on the morning of July 18, 2023 and rushed out to the garage to see the results of my experiment. As I looked at the four five-gallon buckets on the floor, I was ecstatic and let out a loud scream. My experiment had been a success. My wife Tina, who was brushing her teeth at the time, dropped her toothbrush, burst into the garage, and asked: "Ral, are you okay? I heard screaming!"

She looked as if she were foaming at the mouth from the toothpaste, so I jokingly said, "You look like you're more excited than I am." She gave me a puzzled look, then I pointed to the buckets, and *she* started screaming. We embraced each other for a long time, and we both had tears of joy in our eyes. *This could truly change the world!* I was testing a formula which when added to water will germinate seeds in a matter of minutes, and plants would grow to full maturity in a matter of hours.

The night before around 11 p.m., I filled each bucket halfway with water and added one drop of the formula I was testing. Next, I added just a squirt more of water from the garden hose to fully dilute the formula. I then added a few radish and carrot seeds to the first bucket, string beans in the second, corn in the third, and tomato seeds in the fourth one.

The first bucket now was nearly bursting with beautiful firm radishes and carrots, each much larger than normal. I tasted them, and they were more flavorful than any I have ever eaten. The string beans in the second bucket were also fully developed. They had risen out of the bucket and were sprawled about six feet across the garage floor. There were more beans on each plant than I had ever seen before. In bucket number three, there were four corns stalks about five feet tall, filled with more ears than I had ever seen on corn before. Bucket four had three tomato vines that had grown nearly halfway across the garage floor, with hundreds of blossoms on them.

I wanted to test the formula both indoors and out using various types of lighting and water. I contacted my friend Duke Holdman who was vacationing at a new seaside RV park near San Francisco. I asked if he would be kind enough to bring me back five gallons of sea water. He was just getting ready to return home and was glad to oblige. Over the next several days I tried every combination of water, lighting, and location I could think of. It didn't seem to matter which type of lighting I used — fluorescent, incandescent, LED, halogen, or sunlight — the results were always the same. I tried everything from tap water to ocean water; again, there was no difference.

I grouped the various seeds I had purchased into categories and compiled a chart of how long each type of seed took to grow to a fully mature plant. I found that simple plants such as herbs grew very quickly in about two to four hours. Vegetables such as peas and beans required four to six hours. Larger plants like sweet corn grew to ten feet in height in twelve to fourteen hours, and tomato plants stretched an amazing thirty-two feet around the garage floor in sixteen to eighteen hours with hundreds of large luscious tomatoes on them. The only additional task was adding more water to the larger plants as they grew.

I had to sit down at the end of my experimenting and let the gravity of this breakthrough sink in. *My God!* I thought. *This could mean the end of world hunger and possibly the beginning of world peace.* I felt I finally had all the information I needed to go to the next step — contacting the media.

We live about an hour outside Sacramento, so I called the Channel 19 news department, the largest in the area, and explained what I had in my possession. They took my name and phone number and told me they would call back. About two hours later I received a call from a man who introduced himself as Robert Ulson, the head of the Channel 19 news department. He seemed cautiously interested in what I had to say, but I could tell he was very skeptical. He thanked me for contacting them and said he would send someone to check it out.

A few hours later my gate bell rang, and I pressed the button to open it. An older model sub-compact pulled up in the driveway and a very attractive young lady exited. She extended her hand and said, "Hi, I'm Misty Lane. I'm an intern from Channel 19 news here to follow up on your phone call."

"My name is Ralph Diamond," I said. "Everyone calls me Ral."

"It's a pleasure to meet you, Ral," she said.

When I looked at her I was kind of disappointed as I was expecting a reporter and a news van, not an intern.

I took her into the garage to show her why I contacted them. By now nearly the entire garage was filled with plants of all types; they covered almost the entire garage floor, with some climbing up the walls nearly to the ceiling.

"Wow," she exclaimed. "When did you plant these?"

"Some about a week ago and others around twenty hours ago," I replied.

She immediately began taking pictures with her phone and said, "I'll need to document this from the very beginning."

"I thought as much," I said. "If you will help me throw this stuff away, we can get started."

She was more than happy to oblige, as I told her she could take whatever she wanted. "I'm going to let you do the experiment yourself to assure you there isn't anything deceitful going on." After the garage was back to its normal condition, I told Misty to take four buckets and fill them halfway with water. She did, asking, "What's next?" I handed her a small eyedropper of the formula and told her to add one drop to each bucket, and then add a squirt of water from the hose to mix in the formula. Next, I gave her a plastic storage box, which held about a hundred seed packets.

"Pick four of anything you like and put three seeds of each type in a separate bucket," I directed.

"Okay," she said. "What now?"

"Now we wait," I replied.

I grabbed a couple of folding chairs from the house, brought them into the garage, and sat down. She took a few pictures and sat down beside me. I showed her the chart I had compiled, and she was flabbergasted. "You mean all these grow from seed to full maturity in just hours?"

"That's right," I said, "and it takes far less water than growing them in the ground." We made small talk for about half an hour, and then I told her to check the buckets.

"OMG! (Oh, My God)," she shouted. "They are all germinating....This is incredible!" She snapped more pictures and moved her chair right in front of the four buckets so she wouldn't miss a thing.

A short time later, my wife Tina returned home from grocery shopping. After putting the groceries away, she came into the garage and joined us. I introduced her to Misty, and they struck up a conversation. As it turned out, they are both from Cleveland. They talked about where they each lived and all the places my wife had remembered visiting when she was a little girl. Misty filled her in on how things have changed since then. The two very much enjoyed talking to each other, and Misty, I think, was feeling a little homesick.

My wife excused herself and went into the house to get something for us to snack on along with some lemonade. As the hours passed, and in between taking more pictures of the plants' progress, the conversation became a bit more personal. Misty, feeling quite comfortable with Tina, began sharing her childhood memories.... They were not good ones. Her mother and father were both drug addicts, and her father was sent to prison for killing a man over a drug deal gone bad when she was only five years old. Her mother was in and out of jail numerous times and was never really there for Misty. As a child, Misty suffered child abuse at the hands of her mother's boyfriends and was raped on several occasions. At one point, when she was around twelve years old, her mother began pimping her out to earn money for drugs.

Misty said her only saving grace was Jane Flynn, a girl who lived next door to her in Cleveland. Jane was six years older than Misty and quickly became her mentor. Jane guided Misty through all the horrible times in her life and convinced her to stick it out until she could graduate high school. If not for Jane, Misty would have run away on several occasions. As graduation time drew near, Jane called Misty over to her house to talk. Jane had graduated college with a bachelor's degree in business and had been looking for a job, preferably in California. She told Misty to sit down. Jane then informed Misty that she had sent out several résumés over the past few months and had received a job offer from Channel 19 news in Sacramento, California.

"I have accepted the offer," she said, "and I will be leaving for California next week."

Misty was crushed and began sobbing loudly. Jane was her only friend and confidant; how would she survive without her?

Jane said, "You only have three months until you graduate; you can do that standing on your head. Here's what I have in mind," she continued. Jane handed Misty a cell phone and said, "Call me whenever you want. We will stay in contact regularly, and when you graduate, I will send you a plane ticket to Sacramento, where you will move in with me." This greatly lifted Misty's spirits, and the two hugged and cried together.

The day soon came when Jane would be leaving; Misty went to her house to say goodbye. The two talked for a long time about the past, and Jane reiterated her promise to Misty. "Your new life is about to begin," Jane said. "Hang in there a few more months; everything is going to be fine, I promise." Jane's taxi pulled up outside, and she left. Misty returned home and balled her eyes out. The next three months passed very slowly, and Misty marked off each day on the calendar in her room. She and Jane spoke frequently on the phone, and Jane would give Misty updates on her status. Jane had moved into a two-bedroom apartment just outside Sacramento. She said, "I have a room all prepared for you, and I think you are going to love it here; I am so anxious to see you again."

True to her word, after graduation Jane sent Misty a plane ticket to Sacramento. Misty gathered up her things, wrote her mother a scathing letter containing everything she had wanted to tell her for years, laid it on the kitchen table, and left. Jane picked Misty up at the airport, and they went back to the apartment. It took a few days for Misty to get settled and familiarize herself with the area. She was happier than she had ever been before. She took night classes at the local college along with a few more online. She had always dreamed of becoming a news anchor, and with Jane working at a news station, there might be a real possibility of her dream coming true. After a few months of waiting tables at a few different restaurants, Misty got a big break. Jane told her the station was looking for an intern, and the job was hers if she wanted it.

"The pay is not much, but it's a foot in the door toward your dream," Jane said. Misty was thrilled and took the job.

"That's how I got to where I am today," she told us.

My wife and I were both very shocked, hearing of the horror Misty had gone through. She, on the other hand, had a big smile on her face. "That part of my life is over, and I'm not looking back," she said.

"We are both very proud of you," I said, which was strange because we had just met the girl. Several hours had passed by now, and the plants were well on their way to maturity. Misty excitedly called her boss and sent him the pictures she had taken. "It's for real!" she exclaimed. "I can't believe it!" I could only hear one side of the conversation, but I got the idea he was as excited as she was. He was asking her a lot of questions she couldn't answer, and she said, "Hang on. I'm going to put you on speakerphone."

"Hello, Mister Diamond. It's Robert Ulson….We spoke briefly this morning."

"Please call me Ral," I said.

"Wow, Ral! It seems you have something here that could change the course of history."

"I hope so," I replied.

"With your permission, here's what I would like to do," Misty's boss continued. "I will send out a reporter and film crew tomorrow morning about 7:00 a.m. They will need to have constant access in order to document everything from start to finish. Is that okay?"

I responded, "The reporter is already here — just send a film crew."

"With all due respect, Ral, Misty is not a reporter; she is an intern," came the reply.

"If you want the story . . . she's the reporter," I insisted.

Robert conceded, saying, "You heard the man, Misty. Get yourself a motel for the night, charge it to the station, and be back there to meet the film crew in the morning. This is your big break, kid. Make me proud."

Misty hung up the phone, threw her arms around me, and said, "Thank you so very much. . . . You have no idea what this means to me."

"You certainly deserve it," I said.

"OMG! I have nothing to wear!" she exclaimed.

My wife said, "Come on, honey. Let's go to the mall and get you something beautiful for your big debut."

"But I don't have any money," Misty said.

"That's okay kid. This one's on us," I said. "Besides, this will make a great story when you are world famous in a couple days."

Just then the whole thing sunk in, and Misty had to sit down. "That's right," she said. "This will go worldwide within days. This is too much. I can't believe it."

After a few minutes, she regained her composure and started to leave with my wife. I said she could spend the night with us if she wanted to, and she replied, "Thank you so much, but I think I had better do exactly what my boss told me to do."

I agreed. "Good thinking, Misty."

While the girls were shopping, I ordered us all some pizza and made reservations for Misty at the nearby motel. The next morning she arrived about a half hour before the film crew. She looked fantastic! She helped me hang some sheets on the walls of the garage so no one would recognize our house. After the crew got set up, she started to interview me. I had told her beforehand that I wanted to remain anonymous for now. She asked all the questions you would expect, and then she ended by asking me what I wanted to do with the "Food Formula," as it had quickly became known. I said I was hoping to hear from some large chemical company that might be able to put this on the market as soon as possible. My hope was to get this to all the starving people around the world. That part of the interview ended, and we started with the actual planting, which took only a few minutes.

Misty and the crew, Don and Skip, knew they were in on what could be the greatest story in modern history, and the excitement was palpable. As the plants continued to grow, Skip and Don — the cameraman and the sound engineer — began telling us stories of events they had covered in the past. They were both seasoned professionals in the news game, and the stories they told were both heartbreaking and amusing. They finished up around 3:00 a.m. and headed back to the studio. My wife and I had very much enjoyed their company and couldn't believe it was so late.

About 9:00 a.m. we were awakened by a phone call from Robert Ulson, who said the story was ready to air and wanted to touch base with me first. They had shot my in profile in the dark to hide my identity as requested, and they also disguised my voice. He said it would be the lead story on the *News at Noon*. My wife and I anxiously waited as the time drew near: Misty came across as a real professional. We were getting very attached to her as all our kids were in their forties and fifties and had long since moved away. She was like a recently discovered relative, and we were very proud of her.

The story was on nearly every station and channel within minutes. It had gone worldwide by early evening. The next morning I received another call from Ulson who said, "The station manager wants to talk to you. Her name is Alex Thorne. Thank you again for letting us break the story."

And with that he put me through to Alex, who said: "Hello, Mister Diamond. This is Alex. Our phones here have practically been smoking. We have received 129 calls from chemical companies around the world wanting to manufacture your formula. To show our appreciation for letting us break the story, I would like to offer you the services of our legal department. With your permission, we will act as a

11

liaison between yourself and them. We can weed through all the legal stuff and narrow the field down to just a few for you to choose from."

"Thank you, that's very kind," I said. "I'll call you in a few days, and bring you up to speed on where we are." Then she hung up.

Three days later Alex called as promised, informing me, "We have been working on this around the clock since I last spoke with you. We have received all sorts of offers, but one stands out over all the rest. The Able Chemical Company, the largest in the U.S., has offered to patent the formula in your name. They have worldwide distribution capabilities, and they are offering you a two hundred fifty thousand dollar signing bonus. That money is yours no matter what happens with the formula. You also will get a fifteen percent royalty on every drop sold.... That is a fantastic offer," she asserted.

"Sounds great to me. What do we do next?" I asked.

"I will have the contracts drawn up, and we will submit them to Able and yourself; if all approve, we'll have a signing party and celebrate."

A few days later, my wife and I went to the station to seal the deal. After the signing, no one was sure exactly how long it would be before the formula hit the market. It had to be patented, extensively tested, and the FDA would probably have to approve it.

As this process continued, Misty was doing updates nearly on a daily basis due to the extreme interest in the story. I give her a lot of credit; she had stories such as how this formula would produce as much food in a one-acre warehouse per month as a hundred-acre farm would produce in a full growing season. It would also be able to produce year-round and use one thousand times less water. She did all the research herself and was turning into quite a reporter.

Able Chemical had purchased a large manufacturing plant and began renovations. They wanted to be as prepared as possible when final approval comes. The process dragged on for months, despite the "rush" status given it by everyone including the President of the United States Clayton James. Four and a half months later I received a call from Alex Thorne.

"Carol Avery, the executive producer of *Hard Facts*, called me this morning," she said. "She would like you to call her as soon as possible."

Hard Facts is the most popular TV magazine show in the world. "Do you know what she wants?" I asked.

"No," came the reply, "but I think you should call her."

"Thank you. I certainly will."

When I reached Carol, she informed me that the Food Formula had finally been approved. Able Chemical is expected to begin production in about two weeks, and it should hit the world market within a month.

"Fantastic!" I shouted. "This is wonderful."

"*Hard Facts* would like to do a one-hour special on you and the formula," said Carol. "We have been researching the story from its beginning and have about forty-five minutes of air already taped. Of course we want the story to include the man behind it all. We are offering you one million dollars for your exclusive interview, but you will have to reveal your identity. Do we have a deal?" she asked.

"The story you want to do is only a tiny part of a much larger one," I said.

"You're kidding; what is that?" she asked.

"I'm afraid that is something I can't discuss over the phone."

"Please give me your address and phone number, Ral. I'll be on the next flight out of JFK and call you when I get to California."

Carol called around 3:00 p.m. the next day and said, "Hi, Ral. I'm here and at the same motel where Misty stayed. Would you and your wife please come join me for a drink? As you know there is a great watering hole right next door."

We met her around 3:30 p.m., and after getting to know each other for a while, she asked where we lived and if she could come over the next morning at about 8:00 a.m.

"That would be fine," I said.

CHAPTER 2

THE AMAZING STORY

As my wife and I drove home, we were discussing how Carol didn't seem to fit our stereotype of a corporate executive. She was a smaller woman, soft spoken, and extremely polite; we were pleasantly surprised. The next morning Carol arrived right on time, as expected. We met her in the driveway and invited her in. After sharing some coffee and small talk, she said, "Well, let's get down to brass tacks — shall we? What's this incredible story you have to tell?"

I showed her some pictures I had taken and began to tell and show her all about my amazing experience. I don't think her mouth closed once during the entire three and a half hours.

"I don't know what to say," she said. "That is the most amazing thing I have ever seen. If you could please give me a few minutes, I have some phone calls to make."

"Tina and I will be out on the gazebo," I said. "Please come join us when you're finished."

After about twenty-five minutes, Carol came out. "I spoke with the folks at headquarters, and here's what we've come up with. We want to do two specials, each two hours long. The first hour of the first show will deal with the Food Formula, and then we will introduce you as the person behind it all. We will begin the second hour with you telling 'the rest of the story,' as they say. Headquarters wants to send out one of the corporate jets to pick up you, Tina, and myself the day after tomorrow. We will fly directly to New York, and we will set you up at a nice hotel for a week," she continued. "We are prepared to pay you two million dollars per two-hour show. Now all of this is tentative; it depends on scheduling, and so on. What do you guys think?"

"Sounds good to me," I said. Turning toward my wife, I asked, "What do you think, honey?" We both agreed.

Carol then said, "Great, I'll be in touch," and with that she left.

My wife and I sat back down in the gazebo and began discussing the whole thing; we were both very excited.

Carol called the next day and said everything was a go. "We leave from Lakeview Airport at 7:00 a.m. tomorrow morning. I will drive us all to the airport and leave my rental car there. My P.A. will meet us at JFK and take us to the hotel. Is all this okay with you guys?"

Tina and I nodded in agreement, said goodbye, and started packing.

"Do you believe all this?" I asked my wife. "In a week we are going to be millionaires?" The whole thing was hard to imagine, and neither of us got much sleep that night. We had never been on a corporate jet before; this was going to be exciting. The experience was totally different than flying commercial. We were both treated like royalty. Carol went over the revised contracts with us, and we had a small signing party right on the plane.

Meg, Carol's personal assistant, met us at the airport. She was young, bubbly, and extremely efficient. She immediately filled Carol in on all the details as we walked toward a corporate limousine. We got in and Carol introduced us to Meg. While shaking hands, she said, "It's a real pleasure to meet you both. If you need anything — and I mean anything — call me."

She handed us a cell phone to use while in New York with all the pertinent phone numbers already programmed in. We soon arrived at one of the top hotels in New York. My wife and I looked at each other and couldn't believe we would be staying there. A hotel concierge welcomed us, opened the door for us, and retrieved our luggage from the trunk as we followed him into the hotel.

"Would you like me to drop your luggage off at your condo?" Meg asked Carol.

"No thanks, Meg," she replied. "I will be going with you shortly."

As we entered the lobby, up stepped the hotel manager who said, "Hello, Miss Avery. It's so wonderful to see you again." He turned toward my wife and me, saying, "Please allow me to show you to your room."

The hotel did a lot of business with *Hard Facts*, and they always provided very personal service. We soon arrived at our room, and as he opened the door, my wife and I locked eyes. "My goodness," she said.

"This place is awesome." It was a very large suite with windows everywhere to take in the view of the city. We were looking around like two foreigners who had never been to the big city before.

"Why don't you both get settled," Carol suggested, "and I will come back in a couple of hours to take you out for drinks and dinner."

"That would be great," I said. "Thank you."

"Please help yourselves to anything you want," she offered. "The bar is over there; they have a pool, spa, gym, sauna — you name it. And room service can get you anything you want. Make yourselves at home ... please. Just sign everything off to the room, and we will take care of it."

After Carol left, Tina and I looked around the many rooms and were amazed. Everything was first class — right down to the gold-plated faucets in the two bathrooms. The place was huge!

Carol returned around 6:30 p.m. We all sat down, and she said, "Let me give you a quick rundown of the next few days. Tomorrow is Sunday so we will not be doing any taping. With your permission, I would like to pick you both up at 8:00 a.m., we'll go out for breakfast, and then I'll show you around New York. We have some amazing places to eat, as well as a number of places I think you will enjoy seeing. We will begin taping around 9:00 a.m. Monday and should finish sometime Thursday. Joyce Aims will be conducting the interview. Any questions?"

We both shook our heads no, so Carol said, "Well then, let's go have some fun."

We went down several floors to the Caribou Room. The restaurant was decorated in an African theme, and everything was done to perfection. We were escorted to a booth and ordered drinks. It seemed all we had been doing since yesterday was drinking, but we both were so excited that partying seemed very appropriate.

After an incredible dinner, Carol said, "I'll pick you both up at 8:00 a.m. tomorrow." As promised, Carol was right on time. After an amazing breakfast, she chauffeured us around to many of the wonderful sights New York has to offer, and the meals we had were fantastic.

Tina and I got up early Monday morning, went downstairs for a quick breakfast, then walked out front to wait for Carol. The traffic on the street was something like we had never seen before. The limo arrived a couple of minutes later, and Carol and Meg opened both doors, each saying, "Good Morning."

My wife and I entered and sat down; Carol pointed at me and said, "Well, it's time for you to go to work." Then pointing at Tina said, "It's time for you to go out and have some fun. Meg has kindly offered to show you around the city."

Meg leaned in toward my wife and whispered, "More like begged." They giggled and smiled at each other, and I knew my wife was going to have a great time.

We arrived at the SBS (Star Broadcasting Systems) building a few minutes later. It was the newest of all the buildings in New York and took up an entire city block. Though not really a skyscraper, it was twenty-one stories and what it lacked in height was made up for by its appearance. It was all glass, particularly the bottom floor; you could see right through to the street on the other side. There were four lobbies, one on each of the four streets surrounding the building. The driver opened the door, and Carol and I exited. I leaned into the limo and kissed my wife goodbye; then she and Meg drove off for the day.

SBS has four main divisions and each had its own lobby. The one we entered was absolutely beautiful. The reception desk was extremely large with wooden and colored glass inlays; I had never seen anything like that before. The entire floor was a combination of marble, granite, and other natural stones all laid out in an intricate pattern to exactly copy an impressionist painting by the famous artist Rodolfo Panini that hung over the reception desk. It was magnificent! The exterior glass tinted automatically when hit by the sun; there were no window coverings at all.

The chairs in the lobby were leather recliners, with a built-in TV set and a phone. Carol and I went directly to the security office to get me a visitor badge. My picture and fingerprints were taken, along with a retinal scan. They were extremely efficient, and the entire process took only a couple minutes. We stepped into the elevator and went up to the twenty-first floor. When the elevator doors opened, there was a large TV screen that displayed "WELCOME TO HARD FACTS, SECURITY LEVEL PLATINUM."

There was a male guard seated behind an ultra-modern desk who said, "Good morning, Miss Avery."

"Good morning. How are you today, John?" she inquired.

"Just fine, ma'am. I see you have a guest today."

We both signed in, and Carol looked directly into a camera and said, "Carol Avery," followed by the time and date. I repeated everything she had done, and then she walked over to a section of the wall and placed her index finger on a small square piece of glass. She looked directly into some sort of scanner, and a voice said, "Carol Avery . . . welcome." She stepped back, and I again followed her lead.

We approached two large metal doors with no visible handles or hinges. "HARD FACTS" in very large 3-D gold letters was displayed over them. The doors parted by retracting into the walls. As we entered and walked down the hallway toward her office, "Good morning, Miss Avery" or "Good morning, Carol" was uttered by a number of people. I could tell she was very well liked by her fellow workers.

We walked into her corner office. It was incredible! Two walls were all glass with a spectacular view of New York City. "Please sit down," she said. "Can I get you anything — coffee, pastry, water?"

"No, I'm fine," I said. "Thank you."

"It shouldn't be long now before they're ready for us," she continued. "Just think, Ral, in a couple weeks you will be known around the world."

She may as well have hit me with a ton of bricks. It all suddenly sunk in. I am about to be interviewed by Joyce Aims, quite possibly the most famous news anchor on the planet and nearly everyone in the world is going to see this. I suddenly began to feel ill. I was sweating and shaking, and I felt like I was going to throw up. "Ral!" she exclaimed. "Are you okay?"

"No," I said. "I'm not sure I can do this; what if I look stupid or say something wrong."

Carol walked around behind me, leaned over, placed her hands on my shoulders, and said, "You're just having a panic attack. Take a few deep breaths and calm down." She leaned in further and in a very soothing voice said, "This is not live TV, just a taping. We are all here to see that you come across as intelligent and well spoken. If you make a mistake, and we all do, you just say, 'Can we do that again?' Joyce very rarely gets through an entire interview without having to redo something. . . . No one is perfect."

She then wrapped her arms around me, placed her cheek next to mine, and gave me a big hug.

"I feel better now," I told her. "Thank you very much."

Carol responded, "It's me who should be thanking you."

"Why's that?" I asked.

"Have you ever heard of Marty Talbert?"

"I *love* that guy," I said. "I watched him for years on the six o'clock news."

"Everybody loves Marty," she said. "After many years as a successful anchor, he left to create *Hard Facts*. He held the position I have now," she explained. "The show was number one in the ratings for that time slot and category, a whopping thirteen years in a row. Marty was amazing. He could get an interview with anyone: presidents, kings, movie stars. You name them and Marty could get them. He decided to retire a couple years ago, and I was promoted to the position. I worked my butt off seven days a week, called in every favor I could, but I just couldn't measure up to my predecessor's work.... Do you believe in God, Ral?"

"I've been a Christian since birth," I answered.

"Me too," she said. "And I believe you are the answer to my prayers.... I don't know how to thank you."

"The four million works for me," I joked. We both laughed.

CHAPTER 3

THE TAPING

Someone peaked their head in the door and said, "They're ready for you guys."

"Tell them we will be right there," Carol answered.

"One last thing," she said. "Joyce thinks you are here solely for the Food Formula interview. I told her after she introduces you to ask how you came up with the formula. I know this seems a bit sneaky, but we want to get her reactions on tape when you tell your amazing story. Stuff like that is pure gold!"

We entered the studio by going through another security point. Joyce immediately came to meet me and said, "Of all the stories I have done over the years, this is the most exciting. I am truly very pleased to meet you."

"It's my pleasure," I said.

"Let me introduce you around," Joyce offered. She knew everyone's name and all about them — the camera people, sound engineers, everyone. The studio was state of the art. Other than the cameras, sound equipment, and monitors, I didn't recognize anything. We sat down at a solid glass table with the most comfortable chairs I had ever been in.

"In a couple minutes we'll be starting," Joyce said. "Pretend it's just you and me having a conversation over drinks. If you need a break or want to answer a question differently, just say, 'Stop.' We are very informal here and want you to feel as comfortable as possible."

The lights suddenly went up, and from behind me I heard Peter Fallon, the director, say: "Okay, places everyone. At this point we will have just aired about forty-five minutes of the Food Formula story, and Joyce will introduce our guest, Mister Ralph Diamond. In three...two...one..."

He then pointed at Joyce, who said, "Welcome back. Now the moment we have all been waiting for. It is my distinct pleasure to introduce the man that will end world hunger, Mister Ralph Diamond."

"Thank you, Joyce," I said. And as I thought of how much money people are paid for these types of interviews, I suddenly realized why everyone always says, as I did, "It's a pleasure to be here. Please call me Ral."

After a few get-to-know-you-type questions, she asked, "How did you come up with this formula — are you a chemist?"

"Let me tell you a story," I started. "My wife and I live on forty acres of wooded land in a rural area of Central California. I love riding around our property on my ATV and was doing so one day when I saw this." I opened a large envelope and slid a photograph across the table to Joyce.

I continued, "As you can see, there is a large elliptically shaped translucent object sitting right in front of a fenced-in storage area. Since you can see right through it, notice the fence poles behind the form. They are ten feet apart and five feet high. Using them as a gauge, the object appears to be about fifty-five feet wide and fifteen feet high.

"I shut off my ATV and just sat there for several minutes trying to remember every little detail I possibly could. I had no idea what this thing was. I thought perhaps it was a methane gas bubble that came out of the ground, but it didn't move or change shape. Then I thought it might be something experimental from a nearby military base. I had seen on TV where the military was experimenting with invisibility, and perhaps this was some type of flying craft, or even a UFO," I concluded.

"Were you scared?" Joyce asked.

"No, just curious. I decided to go back to the house and get my camera. I had seen enough UFO documentaries to know you need to have evidence. Nothing is more frustrating than hearing someone say, 'My son Billy and I watched this huge thing over our house for an hour and a half, then it just took off at a tremendous speed.' 'Damn!' I would say to myself, 'Didn't either of you think to go in the house and get a camera?' I was not going to be that person," I said.

"I started up my ATV, turned around slowly, and headed toward the house, almost as if I thought I might scare it away with the engine noise. I returned, camera in hand and took a few pictures." Then I paused, adding, "Well, perhaps this will explain it better."

I put my index finger up to the side of my neck, pressed down, and removed a small round disk that was a brilliant greenish color and roughly the size of a dime.

"My God!" Joyce exclaimed. "Did you just pull that out of your neck? What is that?"

"It's a recording device," I replied.

"May I see it?" she asked.

"I'm afraid not," I said. "I was warned by the people who gave this to me that this device was tuned to me and me alone. No one else can operate or even touch it without becoming violently ill. Let me show you how it works and everything will become clear."

I set it on the table and touched the top of it with my index finger. A thin beam of white light shot up about three feet, stopped, and slowly came down while expanding outwardly into several colored concentric rings. Each was about two inches wide and spaced about an inch apart; there were ten rings in all. The outer ring was about three feet in diameter with the rest getting progressively smaller toward the center.

"That is absolutely beautiful!" Joyce said.

I glanced over at her face, and she had one of those looks of amazement that Carol had hoped to capture on tape. "It's not just a lovely centerpiece," I said jokingly. "It contains recordings of everything that happened to me from the time I took that picture until they brought me back."

"You lost me," Joyce said.

"I'm going to play the first recording and you will see what I am talking about," I explained. "I have to warn you, though. This is like nothing you have ever experienced before. You will think you are actually there. You won't be able to see anything you see now;

we won't even see each other. You will, however, be able to look all around, including up and down as if you are actually there.

"The recording will fill this entire studio, so I want to caution everyone not to try to walk around, as you might fall over something. If anyone feels uncomfortable or overwhelmed for any reason and wants me to stop the recording, just say so."

As I reached forward with my index finger, the outer ring stretched out to meet me. With that touch the first recording began to play, and everyone in the studio gasped.

"Everything inside the craft looks dimly lit because of a power problem. Off in the distance you can see me taking pictures. I'm sure by now you have noticed the five beings standing inside the craft looking out at me. The recording is being made by something inside the craft — I have no idea what — but it is so far beyond anything we have. You can see me getting off my bike and walking toward the craft," I continued. "I'm now about ten feet from the edge of the object, and I am reaching down to retrieve a small rock to lob at it, as I still don't know if anything solid is actually there."

I went on, "As the pebble contacted the top of the craft, it made a strange low-frequency humming noise, something like I had never heard before. Now I know there is definitely something there. As you can see, I'm turning my head and covering my eyes with my arm while reaching out with the other arm to try and make physical contact with it. I have no idea if it has an electrical charge or something else that may cause me harm, so I am being very careful.

"After several cautious swipes, I made contact. Thrilled I was still vertical, I put both hands on the surface. I am searching for telltale signs such as rivets, welded seams, or screw heads that would tell me that this was a terrestrial object. I found nothing; it was perfectly smooth. It felt like my hands were on a large pane of glass."

"Cut!" Peter said in a loud voice. There was a collective "Oh, no" from everyone else in the studio.

"Take thirty people," and looking at Carol, he said, "We need to have a pow wow."

"Did I do something wrong?" I asked.

"Not at all," he said. "You're doing a great job. The problem is that there are six camera persons and only one of me. I can handle two or three, but there is so much to see here, and I don't want to miss anything. Usually, I know exactly what is going to happen next and can plan accordingly. With this, I have no idea what's coming. We need two more people to help direct the other cameras. In my opinion this will have to be shown in a split-screen format at least some of the time. It's your call, Carol."

"I agree with you one hundred percent, Peter. Let me see what I can do." Carol got up from her chair and walked out of the studio.

As everyone left, I said, "Peter, can I see you for a minute?"

"What's up?" he asked.

"Let me show you something that might help." I reached down and turned the disk on again. After the rings had all formed, I pointed toward a small white dot on the outer ring. "See that?" I said. I placed my finger on the dot and moved my hand backward. This created a viewing area about six inches in diameter. "If I move my finger to the right, you will see the recording begin to play within the viewing area. The further I move to the right the faster the recording. Conversely, moving to the left goes in reverse. If you would like, you can preview what's coming up so you know where everyone needs to be."

"Wow!" he exclaimed. "That's fantastic! When we snag two more bodies, you can show that to the three of us, and we can plan the shots accordingly. Thanks. Come with me, I want to show you the break room."

We left the studio and walked down the hall to a glass-enclosed room that was actually a restaurant; it was beautiful. I was expecting a typical lunchroom atmosphere with a refrigerator, sink, and vending machines, but this place was incredible. I was kind of hungry and ordered a sandwich and iced tea; Peter ordered a salad.

"This is on me," I said.

Peter responded, "Everything here is free."

"Still on me," I said. He smiled. The food was amazing — with giant proportions and large drinks.

"You guys are so fortunate to have such a nice place right here on the same floor."

"Yes we are," he said, "but it isn't just a wonderful gesture on the part of management. Most of the stuff we do here is 'hush hush,' and they prefer we don't mingle with others in the building for security reasons." Makes sense, I thought. He continued, "Besides, under 'Platinum Security' we are not allowed to leave except for emergencies."

"Where is everyone?" I asked. "I thought the rest of the gang would be in here."

"They are all trying to find the two extra people I asked for," he said.

"Wow, now that's teamwork," I replied.

"Everyone here was hand picked by Marty Talbert when he started *Hard Facts*; they are all the best of the best. If there is any sort of problem, regardless of whose area of responsibility it falls under, we all pitch in to find the solution.... It's very effective."

The gang all came into the lounge together about ten minutes later, with two additional people — problem solved. Only fifteen minutes had passed and everyone was anxious to get started again. Unfortunately, that wouldn't be the only problem that day. No one had ever tried to tape this kind of recording before and being coupled with an interview, a number of technical problems had to be solved. For instance, studio cameras are meant to record on a fairly level field. They will tilt up and down but not much. There were things directly overhead and straight down that needed to be captured as well. Peter asked for yet another two people from the news department with hand-held cameras. Now there were a total of eight cameras trying to capture all the action.... This was unheard of. After all those problems were solved, we had a power outage due to an overload from all the additional equipment that had to be brought in.

I was extremely impressed by the professionalism displayed by everyone. There was no cursing, dirty looks, or someone blaming someone else for a particular problem. In fact they repeatedly apologized to me for the delays. With what they were paying me, I didn't care if it took five years to finish. The day was more than half over, and we had accomplished very little. Peter got everyone's attention and told them to stand by. He and the other two directors asked me to show them a preview of what was coming up. They decided collectively it would be best to preview a section, tape it, and move on to the next preview, tape it, and so on. After the entire recording was taped, Joyce and I would do a one-on-one interview, and she would have a better idea of what questions to ask. I resumed playback just where we left off.

I continued to feel my way along the object, and when I was about one-quarter the distance around, I suddenly found myself inside. There was one alien being in front of me, and four more about ten feet behind him. "You boys aren't from Spruce Valley Lake, are you?" I jokingly asked.

They all looked nearly identical, about four and a half feet tall, average in stature with very long arms, having three long fingers and a thumb. Their heads were the same size as mine, which was large for their bodies, with faces that were very childlike...actually cute.

They looked to me to be about twelve years old; their noses, ears, and mouths were smaller than mine, with much larger eyes, which was their only distinguishing feature. The pupil was black like mine, but outside of that, the color(s) completely filled the eye socket ... no white at all, and the eye colors were amazing. Some had a solid color, while others had many patches of color; they reminded me of those paintings that were so popular in the seventies of children with very large eyes. Their skin was kind of pinkish-gray, completely smooth and blemish-free, and they had no visible body hair whatsoever. They were all wearing identical light, yellow-green, one-piece suits with no sleeves, and metallic-looking shoes. Underneath the suit was a transparent garment that covered everything but their heads.

The one closest to me said, "Please do not be afraid; we mean you no harm. In fact we desperately need your help. I am Zo-L. We are travelers from another planet and have come here simply to observe your civilization. We have lost all main power, and our auxiliary power is nearly depleted as well. We have been stranded here for six of your Earth days. Will you please help us?"

"Yes, of course." I said, "What can I do?"

"We are in need of sodium chloride and oxygen," came the response.

"By sodium chloride do you mean salt?" I asked.

"Yes," he said.

I then asked, "How much do you need?"

"100 kilograms."

That's about 220 pounds, I thought. "I have that; now as for the oxygen, I have a small tank that is part of my welding outfit. Will that work?"

"Where are these items located?" he asked.

I turned around, pointed, and said, "Over there in my house."

I said to Joyce, "I'll have to pause at this point and explain a few things."

Everything was frozen for the time being, and everyone got a chance to look around and see all there was to see without being distracted by doing his or her job.

"First of all, Zo-L can read my mind so he knows what I am going to say before I say it. Also, everything you are about to see occurs in real time. Nothing has been cut out; what you see is as it happened. Finally, the recording you see inside my home is taken by something on or in his uniform. You will see everything around him but will only see his arms or legs come into the frame occasionally."

I continued the playback.

"May I see these items?" Zo-L asked. As the word "Yes" came out of my mouth. We were both standing in my living room.

"Wow! You'll have to tell me later how you did that," I said. I knew he was in a hurry, and probably scared to death, so I quickly said. "The salt is in the laundry room. Follow me." I lifted the top off my water softener to reveal the salt tank, and I reached in and grabbed a pellet and handed it to him. "The tank holds 350 pounds of salt; there's about 300 pounds in there now. Will that work?"

He raised the pellet to his mouth and tasted it. "This will do nicely," he said.

"The oxygen is in the garage," I said. Then I opened the door. There are two steps down entering the garage and as I pointed to them I said, "Be careful." He didn't respond, and I thought to myself, hmm — no sense of humor.

My welding outfit was behind some other stuff, as I rarely use it. I pointed to it and said, "Let me get it out and by the gauges we can tell how much oxygen there is left."

"No need," he said. "I can see how much is in there." I was amazed. It's a steel tank and the valve was closed so the gauges were at zero. "May I have these items," he asked.

"Before you do anything, please wait," I said. "Of course the answer is yes, but I would like to ask a favor of you. Will you please allow me to take a few pictures of you and I together, and then take me back into the ship with you so I can take a few there as well?"

"Yes," he said. I quickly raised my camera and took two pictures. Moving beside him, I stretched out my arm and took a couple more of the both of us.

"I'll get some buckets and a scoop and start loading up the salt."

"No need," he said, and with that, we were back in the ship, which had become even darker than before as the power continued to wane. If power is completely lost, the ship will loose its invisibility cloaking and will become a solid object to be seen by all. The salt and oxygen were on the floor next to the wall between the four chairs the Travelers use. Zo-L has a separate chair a few feet in back of them. I wasted no time and began taking pictures using my flash hoping my battery would hold out.

The salt was just standing there in a perfect column as if it were still in the tank. It should be on the floor in a pile, as they are individual pellets. Both the salt and the oxygen tank moved slowly forward and went right through the wall, as if it weren't there. The room was completely silent; I don't believe they were even breathing. Everyone's eyes were transfixed on the large section of wall just in front of the four chairs. The wall went all the way around the inside of the ship but there was a narrow shelf protruding underneath this particular section. I figured this must be the ship's bridge or control center.

I said a silent prayer for the Travelers as we all waited for something to happen. After what seemed like forever, the wall section and shelf lit up brightly with all sorts of colored symbols on them. The room also became brightly illuminated, although there was no visible light source. The ship was now totally transparent except for the control area. The boys went crazy! They were hopping from side to side on one foot, then the other. They had their arms extended in the air and were making a whooping noise repeatedly. I dubbed this "The Happy Dance." They then all began hugging each other while continuing to jump around — it was fantastic!

Zo-L suddenly turned in my direction and flew at me so fast I didn't have a chance to react. He threw his arms and legs around me and hugged me tightly. The other travelers suddenly stopped moving and became quiet, as if frozen in place. Zo-L then released me and quickly retreated back to where he was. They all acted as if he had done something terribly wrong. I smiled at him, extended my arms, and said, "Come here, you."

He immediately resumed hugging me as everyone smiled. I again extended my arms and beckoned the others to join us ... they did. I was now holding five alien beings in my arms, and it was great. They can levitate themselves, so I felt no extra weight at all. When they hug you, there is a physical feeling attached. For want of better words, I would call it love, and it increased as each one joined in. I had never experienced anything like that before; it was truly beautiful.

The four travelers soon returned to their chairs and seemed to be checking the status of everything, as I continued to take more pictures. The inside of the ship was perfectly smooth; there were no switches, knobs, screwheads, or fasteners of any kind, nothing I was expecting to see in a spacecraft. Everything flowed together; the chairs seemed to just rise out of the floor with no seams between the two. It was as though the entire inside was one continuous piece.

Zo-L looked at me and said, "You must come with us to our planet, Ar-Z, so we can tell Overseer and our people what you have done for us. I know they will want to meet you." I immediately began thinking of Einstein's theory of general relativity, which states, "Nothing can exceed the speed of light." The nearest star, Alpha Centauri, is nearly four and a half light years away, which means I would not be back on Earth for nine years. Not good.

Zo-L, reading my mind, responded, "Your science is very young. What does the time piece on your arm say?"

I lifted my arm up, looked at my watch and said, "It's 10:30 a.m., Saturday, July 15, 2023."

"I promise you, Ralph Diamond, I will return you here before four Earth hours have passed. It will still be Saturday, July 15, 2023."

"Well, you've never lied to me before," I joked. "So yes, thank you. I'd love to come with you."

He laughed and said, "Good one. That was even better than the stair joke. See ... we do have a sense of humor."

Abruptly Peter yelled, "Cut! That's enough for today, people. Good job, everyone. Back here tomorrow — 9:00 a.m. sharp."

I turned off the recorder, and everyone in the room came over to see me. They expressed how blown away they were with what they had just seen, and how proud and happy they felt to be included in such a history-making story.

"What was the stair joke?" someone asked.

I said, "As Zo-L and I were walking into the garage, I pointed down at the two stairs and said, 'Be careful.' I was referring to how ridiculous it would be for a person that had just transported himself and me from inside a spacecraft to inside my house to fall down two stairs and end up lying face down on the floor."

"Oh," came the response. "I completely missed that one." Everyone laughed as they exited the room.

As Carol and I waited for Meg and Tina to return, she said, "Let's go to my office." We sat down and she leaned over and opened her desk drawer and removed a bottle of 20-year-old single-malt scotch. She said, "This is just for special occasions, and they don't come any more special than this." She poured us both a glass, and we toasted our first day of taping. "Here's to changing the world," she said.

"I guess we're quite a bit behind, huh?" I asked.

"Not at all," she answered. "This is an open-ended taping; we have the studio for as long as it takes. You can't rush something this big."

By the time we were notified that the girls had arrived, we were both in full party mode. Carol summoned the limo to take Tina and me back to the hotel. As she walked me down to the lobby and out to the limo, she said, "Good night, you guys. Have a great evening, and I'll see you same time tomorrow."

On the ride to the hotel, Tina told me what a great time she and Meg had.

"Where did you go?" I asked.

"Shopping, of course," came the answer. She showed me a couple outfits she had purchased and said, "I'm sure I'll be able to wear these, as Meg said they are going to take us to some nice places." She mentioned that Meg had thanked her several times for affording her this "mini vacation," as she put it. "After a while I got the feeling that maybe she was not completely happy with her job," Tina continued. "I asked her what it was like being a PA."

"She answered, 'Well ... Carol is the third boss I have worked for. Generally speaking, you really don't have much of a personal life; you're on call twenty-four-seven and if anything goes wrong, you generally get the blame.'"

"'Is Carol like that?" I asked.

"No," came the answer. "She is a sweetheart. She even took the blame in a meeting once for something *I* did. I didn't find out about it till two weeks later."

"Everyone here is so nice," Tina said to me.

"I know," I responded. "It's wonderful."

We entered our room and both went to lie down and rest for a while. We got up about an hour later and showered, then Tina said, "I have got to take you to this Italian restaurant Meg and I went to today. You are especially going to love it." (I'm full-blooded Italian, but my grandfather Americanized our last name when he came to America in the 1930s.)

After dinner, we walked around awhile. The sights and sounds of New York were a far cry from the quiet rural life we're used to. We took a cab back to the hotel. We were still a bit jet-lagged and exhausted from the day, so we retired early. The next morning we tried a new little place down the block for breakfast. The cleaning lady had highly recommended it, and she was sure right.... It was great! We waited in front of the hotel again for Carol and Meg to arrive, which they did a few minutes later. We entered the limo and after the usual "good mornings," Carol leaned toward Tina and me and said, "I have to tell you; I am a bit disappointed with you two."

"What's wrong?" my wife asked. "I checked with the front desk this morning, and it seems you two haven't so much as charged a phone call to the room." Carol continued, "I thought I told you guys to have a good time! Money is not a problem."

"We're not the kind of people to take advantage of a situation," I said.

"I know you're not; that's why I brought this." Reaching into her purse, Carol then handed Tina an envelope and said, "Here's a little WAM.... Please use it."

Carol then immediately turned to Meg to ask her something, and my wife leaned over toward me and whispered, "What's WAM?"

"Walking around money," I answered.

Tina smiled at me and said, "Well, you heard the lady; if I have to, I have to. Thank you very much Carol. You're very kind."

Traffic was lighter that morning, and Carol and I arrived in studio about 8:15 a.m. Much to our surprise, everyone was already there. "You guys are sure early," Carol said.

"Everyone can't wait to see what happens next," said Peter. "I don't think any of us has talked about anything else since yesterday."

"I hope you mean with each other.... Remember, you have all signed 'non-disclosure' forms," Carol reminded them.

"Yes, of course," came the reply from several people in the room.

"Well, we're all here. Shall we get started?" Peter asked. Everyone responded with an enthusiastic "Yes."

"Okay, places everyone," Peter directed.

"Oh damn!" I said. "I don't have the disk." The entire room fell completely silent as I patted my pockets looking for it. After a brief pause I said, "Oh, that's right." I pushed my finger into my neck and retrieved the disk. "Here it is.... Damn, you guys are easy!"

"Good one," came a remark from the back of the room. Everyone burst into laughter except Peter. I think the poor guy was about to have a heart attack. He looked at me with sort of a half smile on his face, pointed at me and was shaking his head from side to side.

"What?" I said. "I was told you 'show biz' people always like to start with a joke."

Someone else said, "Good one," and the place erupted in laughter again.

"All right, you clowns. I expect this from you all, but not the new guy," Peter said, referring to me. It felt great to be fitting in with the group.

Peter continued, "Okay, everyone, today will be the beginning of the second hour of the first special. We have gone over the preview, and we are good to go. Joyce will welcome everyone, bring the audience up to date with a brief recap, re-introduce Mr. Diamond, and then we will resume the playback. Any questions?"

CHAPTER 4

VISITING Ar-Z

Peter began his countdown as usual, and Joyce said, "Welcome to *Hard Facts*. I'm Joyce Aims. For those of you just joining us, let me bring you up to speed." Since this recap was just going to be a replay of prerecorded information, Peter yelled, "Cut!" And they were ready for me.

Joyce re-introduced me, and I began to explain, "I am about to take an amazing journey with the Travelers to their home planet of Ar-Z. I would like to remind everyone that this recording is in real time and has not been edited unless otherwise stated."

I reached over and touched the disk to begin playback. Peter wanted me to back it up to the point where Zo-L had asked me to go with them.

As I was looking around for a place to sit, I realized there wasn't one. Having recently had a knee-joint replacement, I was concerned because I have trouble standing for extended periods. Suddenly, the ship went from transparent to opaque, then back to transparent in the blink of an eye. As I looked out I thought, "We're not in Kansas anymore," quoting a famous line from the "Wizard of Oz."

I said, "There is so much here to see, and everything happens so quickly, I'm going to pause the playback so I can explain a few things.

"Look around," I continued. "Believe it or not, we are at a spaceport on another world. . . . Ar-Z is its name. When we left Earth, just a few seconds ago, it was not even 11:00 a.m., and the sun was shining brightly. Here it appears to be dusk. There were dozens of spacecraft: every shape and size you can imagine, some just hanging in mid air."

"Look up," I said. "About five hundred feet above us was a drinking straw-shaped vehicle so long you could not see either end. They call that Ki, which means new beginning. They can move five hundred thousand people at one time anywhere in the galaxy — instantly."

I waited a few more seconds to allow the camera people time to take in everything they could.

"Pay attention to the Traveler on the far left; he is going to say something audibly to someone at the base. That person will, in turn, notify everyone else at the facility mentally that the Travelers have returned. Everyone is extremely concerned about them, as they are long overdue." I then resumed playback.

After the Travelers' brief conversation, people began to appear in front of the ship. They formed a line of about hundred people in just a couple of seconds. . . . They just appeared out of thin air. Then another line appeared just behind the first and about one foot higher, then a third, and so on.

"Zo-L, who are all those people?" I asked.

"They are the 2,028 that work here at the Research Center," he replied. Zo-L then turned to me and said, "If it is okay with you, I would like for the other Travelers and I to exit the ship and tell everyone what happened and how you helped us. I will then motion for you to come out and join us."

"That will be fine," I said.

He continued, "When the door opens there will be an exchange of atmospheres between your planet and ours. Our atmosphere is also much heavier than yours, so you might find it a little more difficult to breathe at first. You will acclimate very quickly and find you need to breathe less often. You may also have noticed that our gravity is considerably less than you are used to."

With that, he turned and exited the ship behind the other Travelers. A million thoughts were running through my head. "What do I say? How do I act? Should I bow, wave, or what?"

I was wearing an old dirty pair of sweat shorts and old sneakers. Everyone else was dressed in uniforms, which were neat and spotless. I figured I had several minutes before I was asked to come out, so I would just observe how the Travelers acted and do what they did. I was representing my entire planet, and I didn't want to do anything that would be taken the wrong way. For all I know, a wave to them might be the same as giving someone the finger on Earth.

As soon as the crowd saw the first Traveler come out, they erupted in celebration. They were all doing The Happy Dance and whooping so loud it actually hurt my ears. When the Travelers stopped in front of the crowd, the celebrating ceased. I figured this is when Zo-L would begin to explain where they had been, the *problems they had, and how I was able to help. Much to my surprise he immediately motioned for me to join them. I found out later that they communicate mentally not just with words, but they can send images as well. It took less than one second for Zo-L to show them mental images of the entire situation. First, the ship having power problems, me coming down the hill to investigate, Zo-L and me in my house, and finally another of us in the ship with the salt and oxygen restoring the ship's power.*

As I appeared outside, I received the same wonderful greeting, as the Travelers — The Happy Dance and all. After several seconds the celebrating stopped. Zo-L turned to me and said, "They want to give you a hug."

I certainly didn't want to offend anyone, so I said enthusiastically, "Sure. How is this going to work?"

"Just take a deep breath, keep your arms at your side and close your eyes."

I did as Zo-L asked, and I was thinking... this is going to take a while. I was really anticipating that wonderful feeling of love you get when they hug you. As they began, it felt like there were several powerful fans around me, all blowing from different directions. The hugs were incredibly fast, so the feeling of love with each embrace was small; however, they were cumulative. It only lasted about fifteen seconds, then it stopped, and everything went completely silent. The "love" feeling was so overpowering, I had tears streaming down my face; it was unlike any experience I've ever had. As I opened my eyes, Zo-L was looking at me very strangely, and there was no one else there but him and me. I found out later that the Ar-Zians do not produce tears when they cry and that accounted for the strange look I received.

"Where did everyone go?" I asked.

"The workers returned to their jobs, and the Travelers went to their homes," he said.

Zo-L turned around and began walking toward a rather small craft, which looked to me like a big snow globe. "I'm headed home myself," he said. "Would you care to join me?"

"You're my ride home," I said. "I'm not letting you out of my sight."

He raised his arm with his index finger extended and declared, "Good one!"

"This was quickly becoming our thing," I thought. This is so great!

"Do you live nearby?" I asked.

"Yes, I live on PW-1, a planet just the other side of our sun."

"Incredible!" I thought to myself. They hop around planets faster than I go from room to room at home.

As we approached the snow globe, it opened as though it had a slice cut out of it. As we entered, I had to slump over a bit to fit. Zo-L touched a few symbols, the door closed and immediately opened again. As we walked out it was still dusk. I didn't understand how we could be on another planet, and it would still be the same time, but I hadn't understood much of anything thus far.

We walked up to a huge dome-shaped object. It looked like a giant half bubble, which was a beautiful neon blue color. Zo-L walked right through the wall, and I followed. Once we were inside, in a near panicked voice he said, "Please excuse me."

I sensed something was wrong, but I had no idea what. Zo-L shot across the room instantly and disappeared behind a wall that jutted out from the other side of the dome. Perhaps he has to use the bathroom, I thought; I didn't see one on either ship.

As I entered the dome, which appeared to be about a hundred feet in diameter and fifty feet tall, I felt something brush against my leg. Looking down I saw my camera case lying on the floor and noticed I was completely nude. My sweat shorts and shoes had disappeared, and my entire body was now perfectly clean. Earlier at home, I had been working on the car, trimmed two trees, and repaired a broken sprinkler pipe. I had mud, grease, sawdust, glue, and pine sap on me, but now I felt cleaner than I ever had before. There wasn't so much as a flake of dead skin on me. "The room was also immaculate," I thought to myself. If I remember correctly we humans lose about 315,000 skin cells per minute. I hope whatever is keeping me clean is familiar with the Peanuts character Pig Pen 'cause that's gonna be me. The old saying, "This place is so clean you can eat off the floor," came to mind...and it was actually true here. I looked around for something to wear but saw nothing.

The room was illuminated, but there didn't seem to be a light source. It was as if the air itself was glowing, and there were no shadows anywhere. As I looked out, I could not tell there was a wall there; you could see everything outside very clearly. I tried to feel the wall with my hand, but it went right through. It felt as if I was putting my hand through a microscopically thin sheet of water. I noticed that none of the light from inside was cast on the ground outside...strange!

I began walking around to have a closer look at the few things that were in the room. "This can't be his home," I thought. There's almost nothing here — no kitchen, no electrical outlets, and almost no furniture. This must be some sort of warehouse. I noticed a small shelf to my right that appeared to be hanging in mid-air; I surmised it was probably attached to the now-invisible wall. When I got closer, I could see there was a small object about the size of a toaster sitting on it. It was oddly shaped, with a hole in the center, and something sticking out that looked like the end of a clarinet. There was also a tabletop and two chairs without legs just hanging in mid-air. "Gravity seems to mean nothing to these people," I thought. I took a couple pictures, and quickly moved on to conserve my battery life.

About fifty feet away there was what looked like an ultra-modern floor lamp. It had a wide round base, which quickly narrowed as it went up about five feet, then curved ninety degrees to the right and flared out like a bell.

I walked over to the wall that Zo-L had gone through; it was about ten feet high, twenty feet long, with an adjoining wall on each end that connected back to the dome wall. On one of those walls there was something similar to the control station on the ship. A chair was floating in front of a large screen area on the wall, and there was a narrow shelf at the bottom.

There was still no sign of Zo-L, and I was becoming a bit anxious. I turned around and began walking back to where the snow globe was. As I was about halfway across the room, I heard loud screaming. I quickly turned around to see a naked woman flying toward me *at a tremendous speed. The next thing I knew, I was falling backward, and she had both arms and legs wrapped completely around me. Now I'm not sure what the proper etiquette is on PW-1, but I imagine it is frowned upon to be in a naked embrace with another man's wife, regardless of what planet you are on. Due to the lower gravity and heavier atmosphere, we fell slowly backward. When my back was about one foot from the floor, we stopped. She was crying hysterically, and saying something to me I could not understand. She suddenly stopped talking, and I could feel her place her hand on my head.*

A few seconds later, she began speaking in English. "Ralph Diamond, Ralph Diamond," she kept repeating. She was still crying, as I felt the two of us returning to an upright position.

She let go of me, moved back a few feet, and slowly descended to the floor. Even though she had been crying, there were no tears.

"Why are you crying?" I asked.

She said, "You have no idea what you've done — do you?"

I was panic-stricken and asked, "Is Zo-L alright? Have I done something wrong?"

"No." She explained: "Zo-L is responsible for the safety of the Travelers, and if it weren't for you, there is no telling what their fate might have been. When he arrived home, he was overcome with emotions and wanted to lie down for a while to compose himself. Will you sit and talk with me?" she asked.

"I would like that very much."

I saw her glance over at the two chairs, which began moving toward us very quickly. One of the chairs was getting larger as it came to a stop next to me. She levitated and gently lowered herself into the chair.

As I looked at the S-shaped object, I wondered if this was going to be like getting into a hammock, and I might soon be face first on the floor. She must have sensed I didn't know what to do, and I was gently levitated and placed in the chair. It formed itself to every curve of my body; it was extremely comfortable.

She moved her chair next to mine so we were side by side facing each other. "May I hold your hand?" she asked. I stretched out my arm toward her, and she gently put her two hands around mine. She ran her thumb and index finger over the joints in my finger and asked, "What are these? Are you injured?"

"No," I said. "They are joints so I can bend my fingers." I lifted up my hand and made a fist to show her. I then noticed her fingers had no joints; I'm sure the Travelers must be the same, but in all the excitement, I hadn't noticed.

"How do you bend your fingers?" I asked. "You have no joints."

She lifted her hand and rolled up her fingers as if you were rolling up a sleeping bag.

I grimaced and exclaimed, "Oh, my God!" She then straightened them back out and rolled them up again... this time backward. As she looked at my face, which was still in shock, she began to giggle; she was just adorable. As she examined my fingers more closely, she asked about the ridges on the tips.

"Those are called fingerprints," I said. "Each of us has a unique set."

"What do they do?" she asked.

"You know . . . I'm not really sure. I think they make it easier to pick up things, and they can be used to identify us. I have a million questions I would like to ask you," I said.

"If I may touch your head again, I can give you some information that might answer some of those questions."

"That would be wonderful," I said.

She reached out her hand, spread her fingers, and placed them on my head as before but in different locations. There was a wealth of information being downloaded into my brain as if it were a computer program, and I was the computer. It only took a few seconds, and when she was done removed her hand.

I said, "Oh!" I now understood the gravity of what I had done.

She asked if she could retrieve some information from me.

"Sure," I said. She placed her fingers on my head, and she began to cry again; this time I knew why. I could see the images she was retrieving, and they were not good ones. There was war, famine, hatred, murder, natural disasters, slavery, and all the other terrible things that happen continually all around us. I could see the look of horror and disbelief as she saw images of us watching television programs about murder, assault, rape, and other crimes against humanity as entertainment. It was somehow okay to view these horrible things, but sex and nudity is considered obscene; the dichotomy was impossible for her to understand.

"She is absolutely right," I thought, "I know lots of people who have sex, but I don't know anyone who has committed a heinous crime."

There were good things as well, but the bad ones really affected her. When she removed her hand, she was badly shaken. "I'm so very sorry," I said.

"It is I who feel so sorry for you and your people."

I replied, "Thanks to you, I now know a lot about your planet, and your people, but I don't know your name."

"I am Zo-L's wife, Ra-L, and you are Ralph Diamond — correct?" she asked.

"Yes," I said. I noticed that they call each other by their full name ... even husband and wife. I gathered that is why they have such short names.

She then glanced upward, where a small Orb about the size of a golf ball suddenly appeared.

"What is that?" I asked.

"It's a message for Zo-L from Overseer," she answered. Zo-L came out from behind the wall to join us. Strange as it sounds, I was pleased to see that he was naked as well. As he glanced at the Orb, a person appeared on the floor directly in front of him. He was so real looking, but it was just some kind of projection. He spoke to Zo-L, and he spoke back when Overseer had finished. It was not a conversation, just an exchange of information.

Overseer and the Orb soon disappeared.

Zo-L looked over at the floor lamp gizmo, which thanks to Ra-L, I now know is called a "Mass Integrator-Disintegrator," or MID for short. Another chair was being created right before my eyes. It was absolutely amazing! It took about five seconds, and there it was. Zo-L rose off the floor then gently lowered himself onto the chair.

He informed me that Overseer had a message for me. "He wants to meet you, and thank you in person for what you have done for us. He also informed me that you have a number of medical issues, and arrangements have been made to remedy those issues at our Medical Research Center, if you will allow us to do so."

"How does he know that?" I asked.

"Our ships constantly monitor the health condition of everyone onboard."

"Wow," I said. "I would love to take you up on that offer . . . thank you. Do we have to leave right now?"

He said, "No, we have plenty of time." He then hesitated, acted a little embarrassed, and added, "I have to apologize for intruding on your thoughts earlier. The Travelers and I were afraid we might never return; so we had to resort to drastic measure....Please forgive me."

"Is that how you learned to speak my language — by reading my mind?"

"No, I learned it from Life Center. The information had been gathered by the Probes we sent to your planet for observation. I retrieved that information from the Probes through Life Center. We were all amazed to learn there are over 6,900 different languages spoken on Earth, so I learned the three most popular: Chinese, English, and Spanish.

I hate to ask you for yet another favor, but would you mind if some of our family members joined us? When I told them how you saved us, they cried and asked if it was possible to meet you."

It didn't even dawn on me that after such a traumatic experience; he would definitely want to have his family around. "I would love to meet them," I said, "just not in the nude."

They both laughed, and then levitated themselves and me back to a standing position on the floor. "Strike this pose," Zo-L said. He was standing with his feet about one foot apart, and his arms were held a few inches away from his body.

I did as requested, and suddenly we were being clothed. Zo-L and I had on the greenish uniform, but it covered our entire bodies. Ra-L had on a silver colored uniform....It seemed backward to me. It took less that ten seconds, and we were fully dressed.

The uniform was like a second skin; you literally could not tell you had anything on. When you moved there was no binding or pulling as with my normal clothing. The only difference between the men's and women's uniforms, besides the color, was a codpiece in the crotch of the men's to protect their genitals. Ra-L looked as if she was one of those supermodels you see occasionally in ads, where their clothing is painted on.

The Ar-Zians can mentally communicate with any one individual, or group of individuals, instantly anywhere on the planet. They can also appear anywhere instantly. As soon as we were dressed, a large group of people appeared; I would guess around fifty. It was like looking at a herd of penguins; they all looked exactly alike. Of course the men and women were wearing the two different colored uniforms, but other than that... all the same. The men were about one-half inch taller than the women and slightly stouter. The women were all made from the same mold, including large breasts, a narrow waist, and very shapely hips; the men, on the other hand, were less defined but nonetheless identical. Neither men nor women have any body hair at all and no teeth.

As they each came up to me, they said. "Thank you so much," and gave me a hug. As I mentioned earlier, they have the most incredible eyes, their only defining feature as far as I could tell. The various colors and combination of colors were astonishing, many of which I had never seen before. Since their eyes are so large, it made the colors even more pronounced. After the hugs were over everyone left; the whole party lasted only about five minutes. It seems they do everything at a very rapid pace....I was very disappointed to see them leave.

Zo-L then pointed to the shelf that held the toaster-looking device, which I now knew was called a "Nutritional-Integrator-Disintegrator" or NID. "Those are for you," he said.

I walked over to have a look. "Oh my gosh!" I exclaimed. There were about fifty precious stones there including diamonds, emeralds, rubies, and ones I had never seen before.

"Those have some meaning to your people, right?" he asked.

"Absolutely," I answered. "These are worth a lot of money; I can't accept these."

"They are worthless rocks here," he said. "We do not even have a monetary system. When I asked my family members to each bring one with them, they thought I was joking."

"Thank you very much; this means the world to me," I said. Then I gave him and Ra-L a big hug.

I pointed to the NID next to my newfound wealth, and asked, "What is this used for?"

He explained, "That produces the food we eat. We insert a finger into this hole, and it can tell the entire state of our health. It can determine what nutrients are in need of replenishing and provides us with morsels containing them. Let me show you."

He then inserted his finger into the hole and pulled it right back out. In just a few seconds, a small bowl was being created, then filled with small pieces of food. It kind of resembled a small bowl of fruit cocktail, only with more different shapes and colors.

"Where is your drink?" I asked.

"The morsels contain all the liquid we need; we do not sweat, cry tears, urinate, or defecate, so we require very little water."

I thought to myself if they don't sweat, that's the reason they don't need eyebrows or eyelashes. The bowl had two small pockets on the brim, and he explained they were used to place a piece of something you either like or dislike. If you like the flavor of something, you place a small piece of it in the first pocket, and NID will be programmed to serve you that flavor more frequently. The opposite is true with the second pocket.

He said, "Give it a try." I inserted and extracted my finger as he did, but the machine seemed confused and produced only four tiny pieces.

"Your physiology is different than ours, so it produced only the things it could measure," he said. I picked up one of the pieces and began to chew it. "Just let it melt in you mouth," he said. I had forgotten that they have no teeth, and of course that is how they would eat it. The flavor was absolutely incredible and

lasted a long time. It was like sucking on one of those butter mints: the candy that looks like little yellow pillows. The other pieces were equally delicious; all the flavors were like nothing I had ever tasted.

"There are over one million flavors to choose from," he said.

"How do you select?" I asked.

He picked up a small flat wafer from on top of NID and said, "You place this on your tongue, and NID will begin producing flavors in broad categories. If you like a particular category, you just think positively and that group of flavors will be added to your favorites. If you do not like a category, you think negatively, and none of the flavors in that category will ever appear in your bowl. If you are not sure about a category, you can ask to taste each flavor inside the category."

"What if you are still hungry after eating everything?" I asked.

"You can ask for a bowl of what you would call snacks," he said. "They are just flavors and have no nutritional value at all. You can snack all day if you want."

"Oh man," I said. "If you only knew what trouble we go through on Earth trying not to overeat."

We then walked over to the MID, and he said, "This is why we do not have a monetary system; this can produce anything we want."

"Anything?" I asked.

"Well, it has to be something that is programmed into it, or it can scan an existing item and reproduce it. May I see your timepiece?" he asked. I handed it to him, and he placed it in a tray on the side of the MID. A small ball of pink light rotated around my watch several times rapidly, then disappeared. Zo-L removed my watch, and another one was created in a matter of seconds. It was an exact replica, scratches, dents and all. "Unbelievable!" I said.

"Some mornings Ra-L and I will want to play Jai, which is a game of strategy using large game pieces. As we eat our morning meal, we will instruct MID to create the game. It takes only a short time. Here, let me show you."

I watched in amazement as lines began to appear in the middle of the floor. Then large geometric shapes began to take form; it reminded me of a giant chess set. In no time at all, a beautifully colored array of sculptures was all over the floor, about twenty-five I guessed. "How does it work?" I asked.

"Everything in the universe is made up of particles of energy. MID takes those energy particles from the air and arranges them into whatever atoms are necessary to reproduce the item you select," he explained.

"So you don't have to purchase anything?"

"No," he said, touching MID. "It's all right here." Looking back at the game he said, "When we are finished playing, I mentally instruct MID to disintegrate the game like this."

As I watched all the pieces and lines on the floor seemed to vaporize and instantly disappear back into the air. "This is what happened to your clothing and shoes; you may have noticed at that time, your body was perfectly clean as well. MID also keeps us and the room completely clean at all times." As he said that, I remembered having looked down at my naked body and even the dry patches of skin were gone.

"So when you enter the room, MID removes your clothes and anything else not supposed to be on your body?"

"That is correct," he replied.

We next moved on toward the wall outside the end of their bedroom. This is where I had seen the unit that looked like the bridge of the ship.

"This is Life Center," he explained. "It is used mainly for learning, and communicating, similar to your computer and television combined. Learning here is quite different than your planet. If I wanted to learn all that is currently known about our galaxy, I would wear this headset, inform Life Center of what I would like to learn, and it would download that information directly into my brain."

"How long would that take?" I asked.

"We do not track time as you do; days and years are all we measure," he explained. "To answer your question, let's try it. Using your timepiece let me know when you are ready, and I will start the learning process."

"Okay," I said. "Now." I started the stopwatch feature, and Zo-L put the headset on. It took exactly forty-two seconds, and he was done.

"You actually know all there is to know about the galaxy now?" I questioned. He began reciting the learning experience, word for word, to me. "Okay, okay, stop — show off!" I said.

He laughed and said, "Good one."

"Is this how you teach your children?" I asked.

"Yes. When a child is born, Life Center begins to monitor its every move. At certain points in

62

development, Life Center downloads information to the child, much like your children learn going to school."

"So they can learn a whole year's worth of information in just seconds as you just did? That is incredible; sure wish we had that when I was growing up."

"Life Center also functions as an entertainment center. Let us sit in the middle of the floor, and I will show you what I mean." As we sat down he explained that our galaxy was being mapped using Probes similar to the Orb I had seen earlier, only much larger.

"There are thousands of them out there," he said, "and each one searches a tiny sliver of the overall galaxy for things of interest. They can completely analyze a planet or moon's chemical and mineral makeup from many light years away. They can also tell if any form of life exists. If a Probe sees something interesting, it moves in for a closer look. If it detects life — being plant or animal, not microbial — it flies overhead mapping and taking recordings. If the life is of significant interest, it will land and do a more comprehensive investigation. When it has completed its mapping assignment, it returns and the information is reviewed. If there is evidence of advanced life, or life forms that we have not seen before, we will send Travelers to investigate.

"Let me show you one of my favorite Probe recordings," he said as he mentally instructed Life Center to begin. We were suddenly in outer space viewing everything just as the Probe sees it. You could look in all directions, including down, just as if you were floating in space. The Probes must have a phenomenal number of cameras onboard, I thought, as you could see it zoom in millions of times magnification, in one spot then another all around. It must have detected something interesting, because instantly we were orbiting a planet. It looked to be just a "Gas Giant" similar to Jupiter; you couldn't see anything except vapor. Charts and symbols appeared to the left of the planet, and Zo-L explained they were results of various chemical, mineral, and atmospheric analyses. He began to tell me what each one meant, but it was way over my head....I just wanted to see some cool stuff.

I soon got my wish; the opaque surface of the planet suddenly became transparent. Seeing right through the entire planet, you could tell there was no surface at all. There was an entire ecosystem floating around in the gaseous atmosphere. The Probes can analyze the tiniest of objects from thousands of miles away without interfering with them at all. It zoomed in on various creatures as they traveled about. Most of them were translucent like jellyfish, with only a hint of color. Some were gigantic, hundreds of feet long, others very tiny. They all had wings or sails of some type to navigate the surroundings. Most roamed about freely, while others were tethered together in sort of a communal arrangement. I could have watched this all day, but Zo-L had promised to return me to Earth within four hours, and I knew no matter what, he would be true to his word. He turned the recording off, and we got out of our chairs.

"Well, would you like to have a look around outside?" Ra-L asked.

"Very much so," I replied.

They stood on either side of me, locked arms with me, and the next thing I knew we were about 500 feet in the air. I would be lying if I said I wasn't scared. Looking down I could see other blue domes miles away from each other. It was eerily silent because there are no animals, no traffic, or any other noises at all. Sound does not even penetrate their domes. There can be loud activities taking place inside, and you would not hear a thing even if you were standing right in front of the dome. There were trees everywhere, with plants in between. All of them glowed brightly in the dimly lit evening with unbelievably beautiful colors emitting from all of them. The leaves on some trees were huge; some of the trees had only one color, while others had many different colored glowing leaves. Smaller plants filled the areas between the trees and were also illuminated with large gorgeous flowers; and there were winding trails everywhere. The ground cover was nothing like I had ever seen before. It was very soft and made of thin tufted plants that varied in color from patch to patch. It was like walking on thousands of small pillows and there were no weeds anywhere.... Every plant was stunning.

The next thing I knew, we were over a beach. The water was so clear that it took me awhile to realize it was even there. Clusters of plants that were under the water were luminescent as well. As the waves lapped the shore, they transmitted the various colors from the plants through the water. They mixed together as the waves broke, producing a spectacular array of colors. As I looked out at the horizon, you could not make out the curvature of the planet as you can on Earth. I began to wonder more and more about this new world I was experiencing.

Sensing my curiosity, Zo-L said, "PW-1 is approximately ten times larger than your Earth. In fact so is our solar system. Ar-Z and PW-1 are just under three light hours away from each other with the sun in between. Our days are thirty-two Earth hours long, and one revolution around the sun takes approximately ten of your Earth years."

I was then taken to a place where the plants were more tropical. There were several waterfalls all around us that formed large pools. Again the vegetation was incredibly striking. We must have traveled quite some distance as it was light out and we were on the ground. I now had a chance to see things close up. Looking at some of the plants, the flowers were as big as my head and smelled wonderful, aromas I had never experienced before. I was taking pictures everywhere we went; I am going to have quite a story to tell when I get home. Time was running short, so we soon arrived back at Zo-L and Ra-L's dome, and I thanked them many times over.

"We should leave now and go to the Medical Research Center," Zo-L said. I gave Ra-L a big hug and said goodbye. I felt like she had become a very dear friend even though I had only known her for such a short time. I felt very sad, as I knew I would never see her again. Zo-L had MID create a container around the gemstones and handed it to me. I was so excited about my experiences so far that I had completely forgotten about them.

"Oh my gosh!" I said. "Thank you so much! I would have killed myself if I had forgotten these." He looked at me strangely, and I said, "It's just a joke."

"Not really a good one . . . is it?"

"No," I replied. "They can't all be winners."

We walked out to the snow globe and entered. When the ship became transparent, we were high above the planet. "It is so beautiful," I remarked. Zo-L began circling the planet, pointing out its various features.

"Below," he said, "you can see a 51,000 mile wide swath of land that circles the planet; 2,571,323,431 Ar-Zians live here. Above and below that, there are 603,021 small islands dotting the oceans. Also, you see some of the 1,001,321 rivers, lakes, and other bodies of water. The oceans above and below meet each other in several places."

We went completely around the planet in about one minute; that's 250,000 miles . . . unbelievable! The craft went opaque then transparent again, and we were just outside the Medical Center on Ar-Z. We exited the craft, and when we did, it became a solid object again. As I looked to my left, I saw something.

"Is that Ki?" I asked, referring to the people mover I had seen earlier.

"Yes," Zo-L said. "The Spaceport is over there. This entire Research Center is about four miles square in Earth terms. It contains the Spaceport, Medical Center, Space Probe Development Center, and so on. This is where the 2,028 people you met before perform tasks. The Research Center is the only place on either planet where people have tasks. There is a long waiting list of people that would like to contribute time here, and they are rotated in whenever possible."

I asked, "You mean out of the billions of people on the two planets, only 2,028 have to work?"

"Yes," he answered. "But we do not consider it work; completing tasks and contributing to our society is an honor and a privilege."

As we walked toward an enormous dome, I saw a man and woman. They must be the Medical Researchers who are here to help me, I thought. They met us just outside the dome, Zo-L introduced us, and we followed them inside. There was equipment everywhere, and I did not recognize any of it. The two researchers and Zo-L spoke briefly, and then he turned to me and said, "They want to do a few tests to see what health issues you have, and correct them."

I turned to them and said, "Thank you. That is very kind of you." I was asked to stand in a spot marked on the floor. An open-ended clear cylinder about three feet in diameter descended around me.

My uniform disappeared, and a bright yellow ball of light about the size of an orange appeared at the top of the cylinder, and it began to rotate around the inside. It was about a foot above my head and was picking up speed rapidly. The light then began to descend slowly while rotating around me. In less than a minute it was at the bottom and disappeared. I saw the researchers looking at a couple pieces of equipment, checking the results, I surmised. Then, as before, another light appeared; this one was red. When it reached the bottom, the cylinder rose up and moved away.

"How do you feel?" I was asked.

"Fantastic!" I exclaimed. "I haven't felt this well since I was a teenager.... Thank you so much!" I asked *them what they had found, and if they were able to remedy everything.*

Through Zo-L, they replied, "We found a lot of things we were not expecting: teeth for instance, and also a number of organs that differ from our own. To answer your question more directly, your arteries were very clogged, and there were three screens in your heart. We removed all of that including the screens (stents). Your bones had many deposits on them (arthritis). We removed all that and also your artificial knee. We replaced it with new bone and cartilage and did the same for your other knee. You had a breathing problem and two aneurisms, which were repaired. We also removed all scars, blemishes, and wrinkles from your skin, and we eliminated a number of harmful viruses and bacteria."

I didn't know what to say — I was speechless. I walked over and gave them both a big hug. I then looked down at my body, and there wasn't a blemish anywhere. I have always been very active and had a number of scars from accidents while building two houses, working with power equipment, and so on. Even my knee replacement and appendix surgery scars were gone. Not so much as a freckle, or wrinkle ... not too bad for a 68-year-old man. I was anxiously looking around for a mirror; I wanted to see what my face looked like.

"What are you searching for?" Zo-L asked.

"A mirror," I replied, "something that will show my reflection so I can see what I look like."

"Trust me. ... You're just lovely," he joked. "We have no such device, but I will show you the recording."

Everything here is recorded, every minute of every day, everywhere...I'm not sure why or how. The room suddenly filled with a blown-up image of my naked body. I looked closely at my face and said, "You're right, Zo-L, I am quite lovely." We both laughed.

We began talking about how our bodies were different. The researchers pointed to a diagram of an ArZian body they projected in mid-air, and I walked over to have a look. The head and brain were very similar to mine. I saw two lungs and a heart. Okay, I thought, that looks right. The stomach below was very small with only a tiny section of bowel. No small intestine, no colon, rectum, or anus. I saw something that resembled a liver, but that was it. No kidneys or bladder. Then I noticed their skeleton was all one piece, all made of cartilage. No wonder they were so flexible.

Zo-L and the researchers locked eyes, and I could see them all smile. I looked at Zo-L and said, "What?"

"How would you like a few enhancements?" he asked.

"I'm not sure what you mean," I said.

"Your brain is identical to ours; through many years of genetic engineering and cloning, we have been able to increase our brainpower to hundred percent of its capability. We can open up new pathways in your brain, which will give you abilities such as doing difficult mathematical calculations, increase your memory, and telekinesis among others things."

If I remember correctly, telekinesis is mind over matter: the ability to affect matter, time, and space — using your mind. I excitedly said, "Yes, please!" A helmet-like device then lowered around my head. I was asked to remain as still as possible.

A few seconds later it was raised off of me, and Zo-L said, "That's it....Try to lift yourself off the floor."

"How?" I asked. "Just imagine yourself off the floor," he replied. I did as he suggested, and there I was, floating in mid-air. It startled me so much I began flailing my arms and legs around as if trying to regain my balance. Everyone began laughing hysterically. I immediately imagined myself back on the floor, and realized I would have to practice doing that later.

Zo-L then said, "Mention a complex math problem out loud and try to solve it in your head."

"What is the square root of 26?" I said. Then I immediately answered, "5.0990195." Zo-L then said something to me in Ar-Zian, and I understood him.

"You can now speak and read our language as well," he explained. I was beside myself with joy. My vision was vastly improved, I could magnify images hundreds of times, I could adjust the volume of my hearing, and I could also sense things around me, even behind me....It was astounding.

"We must leave now, and introduce you to Overseer," Zo-L said. I turned and thanked the two Researchers repeatedly. As luck would have it, Overseer is located right there at the Research Center. Zo-L transported him and me to another location, and we were standing right in front of him. He had a very impassioned look on his face, as he gave me a long and tight hug. He was visibly shaking as he told me how much he appreciated what I had done for all Ar-Zians. He explained to me that they have not had a single accidental death in over 125,000 years, and it was a Traveler.

"There was a terrible accident while trying to explore a black hole. Three Travelers were seriously injured and one passed away. This is why what you have done is so important to us." He told me they wanted to plan a celebration in my honor and asked if I would return as their guest.

"I would be very thrilled to attend; may I bring my wife?"

"Most definitely," came the response. "Zo-L will give you the details when he returns you to your home."

Overseer handed me a small bottle and said, "This is for the people of Earth." He also handed me a tiny disk and asked me to hold it between my index finger and thumb. As I did, he touched it with a small wand, and I felt an ever-so-slight shock on my fingertips. "You and you alone will be able to operate this device. Anyone who tries to touch it will become temporarily very ill." He then took the disk from my hand and placed it against my neck, and I felt it bury itself under my skin. He bid me goodbye and disappeared.

We reentered the snow globe and returned to the Spaceport. As we exited, a new crew of Travelers greeted us. Everyone seemed so genuinely happy to meet me — I felt like a movie star! We were escorted to a new ship and were soon back on Earth. I was thrilled to see my ATV outside and knew that time had not passed me by. Zo-L transported us back inside my house and we both sat down on chairs with actual legs ... pretty mundane, I thought. He asked me to retrieve the disk from my neck by placing my index finger over it. When I did, he touched it with another small device, and explained, "This is an update to the recording of everything that happened since Overseer gave the disk to you."

He asked me to set the little bottle that was given to me on the table. He explained to me that this was a formula for producing food from seeds in a very short period of time. "We haven't grown food in 102,321 years; NID provides it all for us. This should end your food production problems here on your planet. Touch the top of the bottle."

As I did, the chemical recipe appeared in the air; even though it was in Ar-Zian, I could read it. "All these ingredients are available on your planet. Just follow the preparation instructions, and you can make as much as you want."

Now it was I, not Zo-L, who was completely overcome with emotions. My voice was cracking, and I was trembling. "I don't know how to thank you," I said. "You have probably just saved millions of lives."

We hugged for a long time, and then he said, "You will receive a message from an Orb, much like the one you saw at my home. When it sees you, it will call out your name. Just say yes and the recording will begin. It will inform you of the upcoming celebration and the arrangements that will have been made. If you have any questions, ask them when the recording finishes, and you will soon receive a response."

"Do you have any idea how long it might be before the Orb arrives?" I asked.

He answered, "I think Overseer is planning something big, so I would expect it might be quite some time; it's hard to calculate."

Zo-L stood up, and said, "Goodbye, my friend."
We hugged again, and he disappeared.

Peter yelled, "Cut! Nice job everyone." I stopped playback and turned the recording off. As I looked around, there wasn't a dry eye in the studio. Peter looked over at me and smiled; he nodded his head and said, "That concludes this portion of the show; from here on it will just be a one on one with Joyce and Ral." He then named off only the people who would be needed for the interview, thanked everyone else, and dismissed them all.

Peter, Joyce, and Carol then came over to me and sat down. Peter looked at the disk and said, "Please turn that on again."

"Why?" I asked.

"I'm curious about something," he responded. "If I remember correctly, there are ten rings: Red, Green, Light Blue, Purple, Orange, Pink, Yellow, Dark Blue, Burgundy, and Light Green — in that order. As you played each ring, it moved to the inside and the next ring became the outer one. If I am correct, you have played only two recordings.

"Oh my God!" he exclaimed. "You've been back! Haven't you?" My silence gave him the answer. Peter and Joyce both looked at Carol, as if to say, *Please get us that interview!*

We all exited the studio, and Carol looked at me and said, "I want to take you and Tina to the Chaparral Lounge for dinner tonight."

"I was told that is the ritziest restaurant in the tri-state area and nearly impossible to get into....How did you manage that?" I asked.

"We have a lot of notables on the show, so we have a standing arrangement with them," she answered. "In case you haven't realized it yet ... *you* are one of those notables." She walked me down to the lobby as usual, where Meg and Tina were waiting for us. We said hello to each other, and Tina and I entered the limo for the ride back to the hotel. "I'll pick you up at seven!" Carol shouted. I waved my hand in the air to let her know we heard her.

I asked Tina if she and Meg had a good time today. "OMG," she said. "We had a fabulous time."

"You're even starting to sound like her," I joked.

"Do you know what was in the envelope?" she asked.

"What envelope?" I inquired.

"The WAM envelope Carol gave me . . . ten thousand dollars!" she said loudly.

"Wow!" I said. "She really does want us to have a good time. Is there any left?" I asked jokingly.

I hope you don't mind, but I have been using it to buy Meg a few things as well.

"I think that's a great idea, honey." Carol picked us up right on time, and we were out for an evening on the town.

The restaurant was incredible! We were seated in our own little room, and Carol ordered three Prairie Dogs, the restaurant's exclusive drink. They came in very tall fluted glasses and were flaming. The waiter gently smothered each flame with a small gold-plated Stetson hat. They were fantastic! Shortly thereafter, Carol ordered another round.

The drinks were pretty strong, and we were having a wonderful time. The meal seemed to go on forever, course after delicious course. Three hours later we were on our second after-dinner liqueur. We were having the most incredible time.

I looked at Carol and said, "Well, isn't there something you want to ask me?"

With absolutely no hesitation, she leaned toward me and in a soft voice whispered, "Are their really more recordings? Did you really go back to Ar-Z?"

"Yes" and "Yes," I answered. She dismissed the waiter who had been in the room with us the whole time, so we could have complete privacy. "What do you plan to do with them?"

In a loud obnoxious voice I joked, "Why, whatever do you mean, Carol?"

She laughed and said, "Come on! Don't keep me in suspense!"

"Relax," I said. "The interview is yours if you want it."

She slumped back in her chair, smiled greatly, raised her glass to toast me and said, "Thank you very much."

"You're welcome, Marty. I mean Carol." She got very emotional when I compared her to Marty. "See," I said. "You're every bit as good as your predecessor!"

Carol's eyes got as large as saucers. "I just thought of something," she said in a loud voice. "We will have much more on tape than the two specials will hold. I can set you up with an agent who can get the whole thing put on DVD. SBS owns JK Sterling Corporation; they are the main competitors of Sony. Do you remember the *Alien Autopsy* TV special?" she asked. "After that aired, they sold a ton of VHS tapes of the show and then DVDs. You could make a fortune.... What do you think?"

"I think since JK Sterling is owned by SBS, you should act as the agent and get the commission yourself," I said. "I don't think it will be a very hard sell — do you?"

"Do you know what you are saying?" she asked.

"Yes, you could make a boat load of money," I answered.

"You guys have got to be the nicest people I have ever met....Thank you so much!" she exclaimed.

"Now you're one up on Marty," I said. This of course called for another round of drinks. I've got to give Carol a lot of credit; she can drink Tina and me under the table.

The next morning came all too early, but we made it out front on time to be picked up. In studio, I saw Carol talking to Peter and Joyce. They both were grinning from ear to ear, so I figured Carol must have told them she had sealed the deal. I could tell they were both very proud of Carol, and that made me feel great. She was finally filling the big man's shoes.

CHAPTER 5

ONE ON ONE WITH JOYCE

Peter said, "Places, everyone." Although I felt quite comfortable with everyone, I was still a little apprehensive about the interview. I had never done anything like this before.

"In 3...2...1..." came the countdown, and Joyce began. She gave the usual greeting to the audience, introduced herself, and gave a quick recap. She turned to me and said, "Welcome back, Ral. Let us begin with Ra-L screaming and running into you, knocking you over. Weren't you scared?"

"Well, she didn't actually knock me over," I said. "Ar-Zians can travel very quickly; their mind also speeds up so they are very aware of what's around them. They slow down considerably when they get about a foot from where they want to end up. In her excitement, she slowed down a bit late, and the buildup of pressure in the atmosphere in front of her pushed me backward." As for my being afraid, I said, "When a well-endowed, adorable naked lady comes flying at you, if she isn't carrying a weapon, that's a good thing. That's fantasy, not fear."

Joyce laughed. "What information was exchanged when she touched your head, and what was that like?"

"The first time she touched me on the floor was to learn my name and language. The second time, in the chair, was as though a hundred voices were all speaking to me at the same time, very rapidly, almost like fast-forwarding a CD. Somehow though, I was able to understand each individual voice and remember everything they said. It was a wealth of information."

"What was it that prompted your look of understanding and you to say, 'Oh,' as though you had an epiphany?"

"I learned that the Ar-Zians live an amazing 7,216 Earth years. No one dies before that time."

"How can that be?" she asked.

"Let's consider what caused our demise here on Earth: accidents, illness, natural causes, murder, natural disasters, and so on. If we take them in order, there are no accidents on Ar-Z," I explained. "On Earth most accidents are travel accidents; the Ar-Zians do not travel. There are no cars, planes, boats, or trains — no modes of transportation at all. The word 'travel,' as in the Travelers, is a misnomer. They used that term so I will know what they mean. They do not move from point A to point B as we think of moving. They are at A, and then point B…no travel."

I went on, "As you saw in the recording, they traverse short distances by levitating and moving forward very quickly. There are no weapons on either Ar-Z or PW-1, and also there is no such thing as crime. There is nothing poisonous to harm them, as they eat only what NID provides. There are no animals, so you can't be mauled by a bear or killed by a venomous spider or snake. Nothing on the planet is flammable, so there are no fires."

Continuing, I said: "Secondly, illness ...there isn't any. Through thousands of years of genetic engineering, cloning, and DNA manipulation, they have become immune to all disease. The Travelers' health is closely monitored on the ships, so as not to bring any foreign bacteria or viruses to another world, or back with them. NID and Life Center also monitor everyone's health condition on a constant basis.

"There is no such thing as death by natural causes; their bodies never wear out. When they are born, they age as we do but much slower. What we would consider adulthood, eighteen to twenty-one, would actually be about hundred for them. At that point the aging process stops. They look exactly the same, about twenty in Earth years, from then until they die.

"Murder is unheard of — they don't even have a word for it. That is why Zo-L was taken aback when I joked that I would have killed myself if I had forgotten the gemstones they had given me. They truly love each other as though they were one big family. In fact they consider everyone on both planets family.

"As for Natural Disasters, the Ar-Zians completely control their planets, including the weather. The temperature is nearly constant throughout the day and night, never varying more than a couple of degrees throughout the entire year. The Ar-Zians themselves are perfectly comfortable in temperatures ranging from minus twenty degrees to 140 degrees Fahrenheit. Because of the thicker atmosphere and lower gravity, rain falls at a much slower rate, and the drops are huge compared to rain on Earth. There are no floods, tornados, landslides, fires, hurricanes, or earthquakes. Even lightning does not hit the ground; electrocution is an unknown phenomenon. Everything that requires electrical power uses the energy available in the atmosphere. That's why there are no switches or outlets in their homes.

"While exploring the galaxy the Ar-Zians have come up with a thirteen-category scale of planetary identification, which you see displayed on the monitor, including six classes of humanoid populated planets. They are as follows:

Ar-ZIAN PLANET CLASSIFICATION

1. No life, useful elements, water, or atmosphere.
2. Microbial life, some useful elements, water, and atmosphere.
3. Uni-cell or multi-cell plant life — mold, slime, algae, etc.
4. Fungi and primitive plant forms.
5. Plant life — root and leaf structures.
6. Primitive animal life — insects, worms, jellyfish.
7. Vertebrate animal life — fish, frogs, birds.
8. Class 1: Humanoid intelligent life — primitive societies.
9. Class 2: Structured societies, governments, commerce.
10. Class 3: Electricity, flight.
11. Class 4: Controlled environment on planet — weather, solar, geothermal.
12. Class 5: Planetary travel, gathers energy from space, stars, and asteroid mining.

13. Class 6: Travel galaxy, control matter at an atomic level. Able to create energy from anything.

"By contrast, we are a 'Category 10 Class 3' civilization, which derives its energy mainly from fossil fuels (oil and coal). At our present rate of technological advancement we might expect to reach 'Class 4' in about 200 to 400 years, 'Class 5' in a few thousand years, and 'Class 6' status in one hundred thousand to five hundred thousand years. These time schedules seem lengthy but are small when compared to the age of the universe itself.

"Ar-Z is a 'Category 13 Class 6' civilization, which explains how they are able to do such amazing things. Somehow they have engineered all plants so that when a leaf or branch becomes disconnected from the main plant, it disintegrates before it hits the ground. The entire planet is completely spotless of any kind of debris. Amazingly, there are no bad odors anywhere on the planet. There is no excrement, gasses, rotting debris, or anything that would produce a foul smell."

Joyce broke in, "If they are not exposed to anything that would kill them, why do they die after 7,216 years?"

"Good question," I stated. "Actually, they have the ability to live forever. Because they believe in the same God we do, they know that when they die they will all go to heaven because of the way they live. They have made a conscious decision to have a determinate lifespan. As far as *why* they die, I'm not exactly sure. Think of it as buying a new car; it's filled with gas, and you drive it off the lot. Sometime later, it runs out of gas and dies; it's still new, but it ceases to function."

"How old are Zo-L and Ra-L?" Joyce asked.

"They were both born on the same day, and are 3,127 years old."

"Tell me more about their bodies and how they differ from ours."

"Their bodies are extremely durable; their skin is almost indestructible. Even if they fell a long distance without stopping themselves through levitation, they would not be hurt. Their one-piece cartilage skeleton, lower gravity, and thicker atmosphere keep them from being injured. Their skull is very flexible and actually comes in contact with the brain; this prevents them from getting concussions when they stop suddenly. Their very large eyes take in a much larger field of vision than ours, and their brains can magnify that image thousands of times. The human eye sees less than one percent of the total light spectrum; the Ar-Zians see nearly everything, which they can filter mentally by wavelength. They have two eyelids, a clear one for underwater vision, and a completely opaque one for resting or sleeping. Their sense of smell is very acute, probably similar to a dog, and they can also adjust their hearing from zero percent to five hundred percent. They are fully aware of their surroundings, even without seeing it; we refer to this as a sixth sense. Ar-Zians also have the ability to remote-view."

"I'm not familiar with that term. What is it?" Joyce asked.

"During the cold war, both the U.S. and Russia were experimenting with using only the power of the mind to view things remotely, both near and far away. Although never proven reliable, it has been said that some of the results were impressive."

"They have eliminated all bad traits; you're familiar with the 'seven deadly sins,' right?"

Joyce answered, "Yes, but please review them for our viewers."

"First there is pride, then covetousness, envy, gluttony, anger, sloth, and finally, lust.... They have none of these. This is another improvement brought about by gene manipulation. They are the kindest, most benevolent beings you could possibly imagine."

"Since we are talking about behavior, you mentioned earlier that they believe in the same God we do. Did He give them any rules to follow such as our Ten Commandments?"

"The Ar-Zians live near an asteroid belt, as do we. Their civilization was virtually wiped out by an asteroid nearly 805,000 years ago," I explained. "During their desperate struggle to rebuild, they went in search of things they could use toward that end. As they were doing so, a vessel was found that contained a written statement of ten commandments that are identical to ours. This incident is very similar to our discovery of the Dead Sea Scrolls."

"What was their civilization like before the asteroid impact?" Joyce asked.

"No one really knows for sure," I said. "It was so long ago, and all records had been destroyed. The impact knocked their planet slightly out of orbit, which became more elliptical than circular, stretching further and further every year. Winters became colder and longer each year, while the summers were cooler and shorter. They knew if they did not remedy the situation, their planet would eventually break free of the suns gravitational field and fly off into space causing certain extinction. They calculated they only had 893 years to accomplish this mammoth task. There are rumors they were assisted by another civilization, but no one knows for sure how they eventually solved the problem."

"Tell me about their language, Ral," Joyce queried.

"It is very simple; because they can send mental images to each other, there is no need to have detailed descriptions of — or names for — everything. For instance, they have one word for plants that is 'Na.' This includes everything from algae to trees. If they want to tell someone about a particular plant, they would say 'Na,' and show them a mental picture of the plant in question. Their language has no negative words whatsoever."

"What do you mean, exactly?"

"Things that would be hurtful to others like ugly, fat, lazy, etcetera. They say only positive things about everything.... It's really quite wonderful."

Joyce said, "I have always heard that we use only ten percent of our brain; however, a recent documentary I watched put that number at thirty-five percent. Do you know how much brain usage you started with and by what percentage the Researchers increased your ability?"

"First of all," I said, "I saw that documentary as well. As I recall they used thermal imaging and brain scans to show areas of the brain that were being used while doing several mental and physical tasks. While thirty-five percent of the brain showed activity, there is a big difference between using something, and using it to its full potential. Imagine you are driving down a freeway at night, you look to your right and see the sports stadium all lit up. In your mind you're imagining there is a big game going on with fifty thousand screaming fans in their seats, players all over the field, thousands of conversations, and a flurry of other activities. The next day you read in the paper that the electrician was just testing the lights for an upcoming game."

"The Researchers informed me that I was using about 8.3 percent of my brain's potential, and I think I'm a pretty average guy. After they 'broadened my horizons,' so to speak, it jumped to 23 percent. They, on the other hand, use the full one hundred percent. If you think about the things they do mentally, we also possess some of those capabilities. There are people with photographic memories, people able to do the most incredible mathematical calculations in their head, and so on . . . we call these people 'savants.' I think all of us have experienced a *déjà vu* moment, where you think a situation has happened before, and we might even know what will happen next. Another common experience is feeling as though you are being watched."

"Why were the Ar-Zians unable to rescue the Travelers; they must have known where they were?"

"Yes," I responded. "They knew the Travelers were in our solar system and probably on Earth. Normally if a ship is in distress, an Orb is automatically sent back to the Spaceport to alert them of the situation. Each ship carries several of these

Orbs for just such an emergency; however, they were rendered inoperative by the power failure."

"Why didn't the base send ships to locate them?"

"They did." I replied. "A whole armada of them, plus hundreds of Probes. The ships had no idea where to look, and with the invisibility cloak still marginally functioning, they weren't able to locate them. The Probes had the same problem."

"I thought they could communicate mentally over the entire planet. Was that not tried?"

"The atmosphere on Earth is quite different than their planets; they can only communicate over very short distances here."

"Can you show me what you are able to do with your new abilities?"

"I'd be happy to," I said. I placed the glass of water the crew had given me on the table between Joyce and me, and said, "I will make this glass of water vanish. I raised my arm to a vertical position with my elbow still resting on the table. Then as I extended my index and middle fingers, I moved my arm forward toward the glass until I was pointing at it, and the glass of water disappeared."

"Oh my goodness!" Joyce exclaimed. "That was amazing! Where did it go?"

"Actually, it's still right there," I said. "Just in a different dimension."

"Can you bring it back?"

I moved my arm in the same manner as before, and the glass reappeared.

"Wow!" was her response.

"I can also disintegrate items, and they will be gone for good."

"Please do," she said. I obliged, using the same hand gestures, and the glass and water vaporized instantly.

"How is that possible?" Joyce wondered.

"With the increased mental capacity I was given, my brain waves can interfere with the shared electrons that hold atoms together, and they simply disperse."

"Can you demonstrate something else?" she asked eagerly.

Using my mind, I moved her still-full glass of water more toward the center of the table. I then pointed my two fingers at it and raised the water about one foot above the glass. Joyce's eyes opened widely in amazement, as I directed her, "Stick your finger in the center of the water, and make small circular motions." As she did the water began to form a circle. I asked her to retract her finger, and we watched the circle of water expand into a ring about a foot in diameter and about one-half-inch thick. I raised the still-expanding ring of water up higher. When it was about three feet in diameter, and less than one-quarter-inch thick, I asked her to place the glass at an angle and enter it into the spinning ring of water. As she did the glass refilled. She was blown away!

"Can you make large objects like a car disappear?"

"Yes and no," I replied. "I would have to concentrate on each individual part, to either send it to another dimension or disintegrate it. With the glass and water it is easy, because there are only two items. With a car there are thousands; the door alone contains hundreds of individual pieces, and so it would probably take many hours to make the whole car disappear."

"You mentioned both Orbs and Probes.... What is the difference?"

"Well, Joyce, Orbs are small devices anywhere from two inches to six inches in diameter and are used mostly for communication and basic recording. Probes are usually twelve inches to twenty-four inches and contain a great deal of sophisticated scientific equipment, similar to the Probes we send into space only significantly more sophisticated."

"Can you lift heavy objects as you did the water?"

"In that case, size doesn't matter; I have lifted cars before."

"Can you lift this table?" she asked.

I did as she requested, saying, "I figured if I did something like this, the viewers would just think it was a trick.... That's why I went with levitating the water; that can't be faked. It's funny, when someone asks me to lift something extremely heavy, they are more impressed when I use my arms and legs rather than just use my mind."

Joyce was really taken with my abilities and eagerly asked, "What else?"

I held up a phone book I had borrowed from the hotel and said, "I memorized everything in this book last night."

"You're kidding!" she said. I handed it across the table to her and said, "Give me a page number and a location on that page, and I will tell you the name."

"Okay," she responded "Page 495, the seventeenth entry down."

"That would be Agnes Sedwick, 487 East 45th Street, Queens, phone number 718-555-8790. Give me another one."

"Page 934, the last entry on the page."

"Arlene Smithson, 782 West Maple Street, Apartment 6B, Queens, 347-555-0267."

"That is so amazing, Ral," she said. "Anything else?"

"I am able to control bodily functions, I can stop pain and itching, even hunger."

"Isn't that dangerous? I thought pain was a warning."

"It is," I said, "but I can tell the difference between something simple like a sore muscle or headache, as apposed to appendicitis. I also have very heightened reflexes." I pulled a dollar bill out of my wallet and asked Joyce to hold the short side of the bill between her thumb and index finger. Facing her I placed my thumb and index finger in the center of the bill, not touching it. "Whenever you are ready, release the bill by moving your thumb back slightly, so I cannot tell you have let it go. I will attempt to catch it with my fingers before it slips through."

We did this several times, and I was able to catch it each time; Joyce was not able to do it at all. "Let's make it more interesting," she said. Reaching into her purse she removed a quarter. "I'll bet you can't snag this," she said.

"You're on, lady," I replied jokingly. I had never tried this before, but I managed to catch it consistently. "I'm going to try to catch it with my eyes closed."

"How can you possibly do that?" Joyce asked.

"The Ar-Zians have given me a heightened sixth sense; I can't read minds as they do, but I can deduce when something is going to happen." I held my left hand over my eyes and with my right hand I put my thumb and index finger on either side of the coin. "Anytime you're ready, Joyce."

She waited several seconds to try to catch me off guard, but I was able to catch it anyway. "That is absolutely astonishing," she said. "What else can you do?"

"While my physical abilities are fun to show off, my favorite thing is being able to go to sleep at will. I am a hopeless insomniac and have been as long as I can remember. Now I lie down, tell myself to go to sleep, and I do so instantly. I can also speed my brain up dramatically, which turns out to be something that happens to most people automatically during stressful situations such as a car accident. I'm sure you have heard people say after a traumatic situation, 'It seemed as if everything was happening in slow motion.' That is because their brain has sped up. This is really handy when I am trying to remember something, or to think of a clever response while speaking to someone; it also helps me play the guitar much faster. With my brain speed and reflexes increased, I can actually catch flies using just my fingers."

"Any new abilities that you have just recently discovered?" Joyce asked.

"Yes, I can disappear." Having said that, I vanished right before her eyes, then reappeared.

"Where did you go?" she asked. "Into another dimension, just as when I make anything else disappear. I always thought I might be able to do it, but I was afraid to try. One day while I was out shopping near my home, a large Rottweiler broke free from his owner and decided he might like to try a little Italian cuisine. He was charging me at a furious rate, barking loudly, and slobbering all over the place. I decided now might be a good time to find out if I was able to actually disappear. You should have seen the look on the dog owner's face...priceless. The dog was totally confused and kept going around in circles trying to figure out what just happened.

"What's it like in another dimension?"

"I can see everything, but it all looks colorless and translucent.... It's spooky, and I really don't like to do it. In my mind, I'm afraid I won't be able to get back."

Joyce laughingly asked, "Have you ever fought crime now that you have superpowers?"

"Funny you should ask that. One morning around eight-thirty, I went to the bank located in the Spruce Valley Lake Town Center to get money from the ATM. The bank opens at 9:00 a.m. and the Town Center opens at 10:00 a.m., so I wasn't expecting to see anyone. As I approached the ATM, I noticed the bank power was out. I could hear noise coming from inside the bank and figured it was the bank employees preparing to open. Then the voices sounded very stressed, and there was a lot of yelling. I used my ability to enter another dimension and walked into the bank.

"I could hear a woman trying to explain to the gunman standing in front of her that she could not open the vault because lightening had knocked out the power. I got a little closer, and I could see four more employees on the floor, their hands and feet bound with duct tape. I heard the gunman say, 'I'll give you one more chance to open that vault or I'm going to kill you.'

"The woman was shaking and her voice was quivering as she again tried to explain the situation to him. He pointed the gun, and fired directly at her head! She fell to the ground just as I entered back into the first dimension. I screamed at him to drop the gun, or I would shoot him; of course, I didn't have a gun but hoped he would stop before he killed the other four people.

"I then used my ability to speed up my brain so I would have more time to think of what I needed to do to end the situation without anyone else getting hurt — including me. The gunman spun around very slowly, and I noticed he had a gun in each hand. When he was about halfway turned around, he began firing. I used my mind to force his arms down, as he continued to pull the triggers. One shot shattered the glass front door about four feet to my left; another struck the floor just in front of me and to the side. I then forced his wrists to bend toward himself to avoid my getting shot by a ricochet off the floor.

"He was so incensed; he continued to pull both triggers in an effort to shoot me, while he was actually shooting himself. Both guns emptied, and he was still pulling on the triggers. He fell straight down to the ground, having shattered nearly every bone in both legs with the twelve bullets that entered them. I ran to the assistance of the bank employees and was delighted to find the bank manager had not been shot after all. She fainted just as he pulled the trigger, and the bullet left a perfect hole in her hair just above her scalp. I freed the others as the manager called the police department, which is only three doors down from the bank.

"I went over to the gunman to see if I could help him by trying to stop the bleeding. As I walked toward him he tried to sit up. He screamed obscenities at me, and then he cocked his arm back and threw one of his guns at me. I stopped it in mid-air with my mind and hurled it back in his direction, focusing on his head. It was a perfect strike, landing with such force it made a loud crack, and he was knocked unconscious. The police arrived within a matter of seconds, and the ambulance shortly thereafter. We were all asked to walk down to the police department to give our statements; the bank remained closed for repairs the rest of the day.

"Two days later the police chief, Eugene Scarpelli, called and informed me that the gunman was wanted in three states on a number of charges, and there was a $200,000 reward for his capture.

'We have applied for the reward in your name,' Chief Scarpelli said.

'I would prefer you give it to the five bank employees,' I replied."

Joyce was leaning back in her chair, and said, "Wow! I wasn't expecting that, Ral. Tell me the difference between Ar-Z and PW-1."

"At one point," I began, "There was only the one planet...Ar-Z. As their population began to grow, they decided to look for another planet to colonize. They were sure that the thousands of Probes they have mapping the galaxy would provide them with many suitable prospects. While mainly concentrating on planets already part of an existing solar system, they were pleasantly surprised when a Probe discovered a 'rogue planet' wandering through the galaxy. It was frozen solid but looked very promising. Travelers were dispatched for a closer look. It was slightly larger that Ar-Z, had oceans, a large land mass — everything they were looking for. They were able to capture the planet and move it into an orbit around their sun, just opposite Ar-Z. They also moved two gas giant planets into orbit outside the Ar-Z and PW-1 orbits; this provided safety and stabilized the orbit of Ar-Z. Gas giants act like vacuum cleaners pulling in space debris with their gravity, and hopefully preventing another catastrophe such as the asteroid impact of the past. Jupiter provides that protection for us on Earth. It took hundreds of years for the new planet to thaw and become inhabitable. I don't know exactly what else was required, but when the planet was ready, they moved hundreds of MID's there and programmed them to replicate. Their goal was to relocate one million Ar-Zians to the new planet for colonization, with plans to populate many more in the future. They named it PW-1, meaning *Perfect World One*."

I explained, "That was the reason for the creation of Ki, which can move five hundred thousand people at one time. Ten years after the initial transfer, there were enough volunteers to raise the population of PW-1 to over two billion; it continues to grow. There is a system of automated shuttles that anyone can summon to take you back and forth between planets to visit family and friends, etcetera."

"What would a typical day in the life of Zo-L and Ra-L be like?" she asked.

"Let me start in the evening," I said. "There is no preparation involved before going to bed. Their skin is kept perfectly clean by MID; they are not wearing any clothes, there are no teeth to brush and no hair to comb....They are essentially good to go. Sex is a very big part of Ar-Zian life, and there is no stigma attached to it as there is here. No jokes, snickers, or embarrassment at all connected with lovemaking. It is considered to be a precious gift from God to be enjoyed, and it's quite common to see people engaging in sex wherever you go.

"After having sex they embrace each other and essentially put themselves into a standby mode. They close their eyes and immediately fall asleep. They never get up during the night unless they are raising a child . . . even then it would be very rare. When morning comes, they both wake at the same time and make love again. As they traverse the wall into the main room, MID immediately cleans them as they walk over to NID. They both take their bowls of food and decide where they would like to sit and discuss what they will do that day. Each day is a blank slate. No appointments are ever made; everything is spur of the moment. There are no jobs to go to, no shopping to do, nothing to maintain. . . . The day is yours to do with as you see fit."

I continued, "While eating, they might discuss having MID create a game, a pool, or perhaps a patio cover outside. Nothing created by MID is ever kept; it is disintegrated immediately after use. This way there is no maintenance, and besides, it is considered prideful to have material things lying around. Also, with MID, anyone can have anything they want, so there is no reason to show off. After eating they might decide to go out for a while. If it is more than a few miles away, they would usually have MID make them clothing to wear. The uniforms contain a mini-MID, which can produce a limited number of things, such as clothes, umbrellas, snacks, toys for kids, etcetera. It is also capable of illuminating the area around the person, anywhere from a few feet to a few hundred feet. There are millions of incredibly beautiful places to visit on Ar-Z, and PW-1, and while there, they would probably make love again."

"You mentioned children," Joyce said. "Do Ar-Zians marry? How does family life come about?"

"They mate for life," I began. "There is no such thing as divorce. Everyone is almost exactly the same; there are no cultural or religious differences, and everyone speaks the same language. Since they all live 7,216 years, give or take a week or two, the only marriage criterion is age. When children reach adulthood, about hundred Earth years, they can stay at home until married, move out, or get married...pretty much the same as here. When either a male or female decides to marry, they let it be known through Life Center by entering their name and date of birth. They are then matched by birth date to all available members of the opposite sex. You select a person, and more or less go on a date. Ninety-five percent of all marriages are to the person you first select. The courtship period is usually very short, just a matter of days. Remember, they are basically all the same, so there is no real reason to shop around."

"When a child is born, rearing is actually very easy. Life Center monitors the pregnancy through the entire gestation period. The woman simply stands in front each day, and Life Center scans for any abnormalities.... There are never any. NID prepares extra-fortified morsels to be eaten during this pregnancy. When the child arrives, Life Center, NID, and MID all work together to feed, watch over, and teach the child. Since Ar-Zian children have no elimination functions, there is no need for diapers, powder, wipes, and etcetera. They almost never cry, as the mother can sense when the baby is hungry. They breastfeed till about age three in human years, then NID takes over. Toys and learning devices are integrated each morning for the baby and disintegrated in the evening by MID, which also is aware of the baby's whereabouts at all times. There is virtually nothing in the home that could cause the baby harm. MID prevents the child from going outside by making the lower part of the dome wall impenetrable; however, there is nothing harmful outside either. Even if the parents are not home, they can actually communicate with the baby mentally and can sense exactly what he or she is doing.

"As the child gets a little older, Life Center begins the learning process. All children are taught exactly the same thing at exactly the same time during their childhood. This goes on for many years, probably achieving the equivalent of a PhD. After that, they can choose what they wish to learn."

"Getting back to marriage, is there an engagement period?" Joyce asked.

"No," I said. "They decide to get married almost immediately. Before they do, they travel around the planet and select a place to live; this typically takes a day or two. Using the mini-MID inside their uniform, they produce a large red circle the size of a dome on the ground; this shows their intention to create a home and live there. The dot will remain for one day, then disappears, thus relinquishing their hold on the location. No one owns land, or anything else for that matter; it is all considered to be provided by God and to be shared by all.

"Next, they would typically go to the parents' home of the bride-to-be and introduce them to her soon-to-be husband. As with everything else on Ar-Z, this takes only a short time; then they all go to the parent's home of the groom-to-be. After a short get-to-know-you time, they are ready to be married. The groom's father instructs MID to create another MID to be given to the newlyweds. Replicating themselves is also how MIDs are used to create large structures or objects; one MID creates another, those two create four, and so on. Multiple MIDs would then work in unison to create something large.

"While the newlywed's MID is being created, the group will hold hands, and bowing their heads in reverence, one by one gives a short speech of how happy they are to welcome the newest members to their families. This completes the marriage ceremony. As soon as the new MID is created, they encircle it, hold hands, and transport themselves and MID to the new couple's selected home site. MID then creates a dome for the newlyweds, which includes NID, Life Center, the table and chairs, and a bed. Exactly the same as every other dome on the planet. MID then assumes its position in the dome and everyone goes inside.

"The newlyweds stand in front of Life Center and place their headsets on. The four parents symbolically place one hand on the newlyweds and command Life Center to start instruction; this would include sex education and puberty. Of course on Earth, puberty starts automatically, but the Ar-Zians have changed it into a learning experience. For that reason there are no children born out of wedlock. When couples decide to have a child, it has to be a mutual decision. The males produce no sperm, and the women no eggs until each of them makes a commitment to parenthood. Because of that, there are no unplanned pregnancies. Sex education and puberty download in a matter of seconds, and after a brief group hug, the parents leave, and the newlyweds begin what we would call the honeymoon. Lust is tied to love for your spouse, so they mate for life and feel no sexual attraction whatsoever for anyone else.... What a perfect union."

"What happens if the newlyweds don't like the place they have chosen to live?" Joyce asked.

"Since no one owns anything including land, they are free to move at any time. They would first select another site and mark it as before, then go back home and have MID disintegrate everything, return with MID to the new site, and create another dome. They can do all that in a matter of minutes. Ar-Zians move quite often as they discover new and exciting places to explore on their planet."

"What about death?" she wondered.

"As I mentioned earlier they select a mate based upon their age; that way when death comes, the remaining spouse will not be alone for very long. As they approach their 7,216th birthday, they know they don't have much time left, so they do as much with their family as possible. At the end, they don't feel ill; they just seem to loose their energy and have to lie or sit down frequently. Amazingly, they still look exactly as they did when they first reached adulthood. When they die, they disintegrate, just as everything else does when it dies."

"How do the spouse and family react to this tragedy?"

"Surprisingly well," I said. "They have a big celebration including all family and friends."

"You mean like a celebration of life, as we have here?" she asked.

"No," I said, "an actual celebration of death."

"That seems odd," she responded.

"Not really, Joyce; they know every Ar-Zian will go to heaven, so they celebrate that fact. Look at it this way," I continued. "If your parents worked hard all their lives, retired, and were going to take a leisurely trip around the world that is expected to take a number of years, you would be happy and excited for them — wouldn't you? You know you will be seeing them in the not-too-distant future, and you would celebrate their departure."

"Did anything funny or unusual happen while you were there?"

"Well actually, yes," I responded, "although it might not be part of this show. Your director told me there wouldn't be enough time for all the recordings to be included; so I will tell you the story. Just as Zo-L and Ra-L were ready to show me around the planet, I sneezed. They were horrified! They had never seen anyone do that before. As they looked at me with eyes wide open in amazement, they asked, 'Are you all right?' I couldn't answer, as another sneeze was coming on. I raised my forearm with my index finger extended, as if to say, wait a minute ...then I sneezed again.

"They were panic-stricken; and both grabbed me by my arms and immediately flew me over in front of Life Center for a quick exam. The sudden acceleration and abrupt stop gave me a slight concussion, and I was temporarily unable to speak. On Life Center, I could see all sorts of strange symbols lighting up and heard a number of bizarre warning sounds, as I was not a normal body being examined. All my extra body parts sent Life Center into a full-tilt mode. I soon regained full control of my faculties and explained to them what a sneeze was. . . . We all laughed uncontrollably."

"Why don't UFOs make themselves known to us?" Joyce said. "I've heard it said many times, 'Why don't they just land on the White House lawn?'"

"Well," I explained, "suppose you and I were in a helicopter flying over an uncharted jungle somewhere. Suddenly, we spot a large clearing with dozens of people walking around. . . . Would you want to land?"

"You make a good point," she responded.

"I watched a documentary on UFO's once," I said, "and they stated that the military of several governments were under orders to shoot down any UFO they encountered."

"Why," she asked.

"For technology," I answered.

"The Bible tells us that God created the Earth and the heavens, then Adam and Eve some six thousand years ago. How then is it that there are other much-older, more-advanced civilizations out there? Did God create them first?" Joyce asked.

"Those are excellent questions, Joyce. Unfortunately, I don't have the answers."

"One last question," she said, "Where are Ar-Z and PW-1 located?"

"They are in the same little slice of the galaxy as us, but 812 light years away," I answered.

Joyce said, "Absolutely fascinating, Ral," as she reached across the table to shake my hand. "Thank you very much for sharing your incredible story with us."

"It was a pleasure, Joyce."

She concluded by saying, "This is Joyce Aims for *Hard Facts* wishing you a pleasant evening, and thank you for watching."

Peter yelled, "That's a wrap, people!" Everyone in the studio burst into a thunderous round of applause.

"Please stick around people!" Carol shouted. One by one everyone came up to me, shook my hand, and told me what a great job I had done. For a shy guy like me, all the attention was a bit overwhelming.

The studio doors flew open, and two waiters from the break room wheeled in carts of champagne, glasses, and hors d'oeuvres. Carol asked for everyone's attention, and said, "I want to thank you all for your professionalism, dedication, hard work, and just plain doing a damn good job. We have made history here today, and I am extremely proud of all of you. I have reserved a banquet room at the Chaparral Lounge for tonight at 8:00 p.m. After we do some well-deserved celebrating here, I want everyone to go home and get some rest, then grab your spouse and take a cab to the Chaparral." As everyone was shouting in approval, Carol loudly announced, "And...everyone has tomorrow off!" Now the shouting got even louder, and champagne corks began to fly.

As everyone else was having a good time, Carol asked to talk to me for a moment. "You know, I can't believe we were able to pull this off in only three days." Looking down at her watch, she said, "Actually, two hours *short* of three days. You were amazing! We had to re-tape more of Joyce's mistakes than yours....That's funny."

Carol looked around sheepishly, hoping Joyce wasn't within earshot; she turned back toward me and said, "I have a bit of work to do tomorrow morning, then I will pick you and Tina up around noon, and we will go somewhere fun — how does that sound?"

"Fantastic," I replied.

"Then Friday morning," she continued, "I will pick you guys up again. We'll go to the office and get your money, then spend the rest of the day out on the town. I want to take you to a Broadway play tomorrow — interested?"

"I'm up for it...and I know Tina would love that."

"It's settled then. What kind of play would you guys like to see?"

"Anything but a musical," I responded.

She said, "I'll see what I can do."

The celebrating ended around the usual quitting time, and Carol and I walked down to the lobby to meet Meg and Tina. As usual, the girls had another great day on the town. They hugged each other and Meg said, "I'll see you guys tonight at the Chaparral." I could tell the girls were really getting close. We got back to the hotel around 6:00 p.m. I fixed a little "Jack and Seven" for Tina and me, and we sat down to relax.

I asked Tina, "Do you believe this? We're sitting in a suite in a ritzy hotel, looking out over Central Park, holding a 'Jack and Seven.' At home we wouldn't be doing jack diddly!"

We both shared a laugh, and she replied, "I could get used to this."

"Don't!" I begged.

We took a shower and got ready for the wrap party. We hailed a cab and I said to the driver, "Chaparral Lounge, please." I felt like a real New Yorker. The cabbie was very friendly, and told us a few things about the restaurant.

"They claim," he said, "to be able to make you any American, Italian, or French dish you want; it doesn't even have to be on the menu. If they fail, you can order whatever else you want from the menu, and it's on the house. It has been reported they also boast the largest selection of wine and liquor in the tri-state area."

We pulled up in front about 7:50 p.m., right on time. The cabbie opened the door; I gave him a generous tip from the WAM and thanked him. As we entered the restaurant, we were met by the maitre d' and told him we were with the *Hard Facts* group.

"Very good, sir," he said. "Please follow me to the Long Horn Room."

The Chaparral Lounge is mainly a steak and lobster restaurant that also has barbecue, Italian food, and French cuisine thrown in for good measure. The place was beautiful! It is decorated in a western theme and very tastefully done. Someone put a lot of money into this place.

As we entered the Long Horn Room, there was a band playing, a full bar, and an hors d'oeuvres buffet that was to die for. Also included were three dessert carts and another one filled with liqueurs. We were overwhelmed and actually didn't know what to do first. It was a large room usually reserved for parties of a hundred or more. There was only going to be Tina and me, Carol and Meg, the crew and their spouses ... about twenty-four of us. *This is going to be a special night*, I thought.

Carol spotted us and started walking over, drink in hand. She was wearing a designer dress with her long black hair down. She had on makeup that made her emerald green eyes sparkle. . . . She looked absolutely stunning. I would guess her to be in her late thirties to very early forties. When she reached us she said, "Look behind you." We turned around, and over the entrance door was a large banner that read, "THANKS RAL" on it.

I shook my head in disbelief and said, "You guys are something else....Thank you."

Carol said, "C'mon, let's fill those hands," as she led us to the bar.

Tina and I mingled for a while, danced, and had some of the fabulous food The Chaparral is famous for. We ended up at a table near the back of the room with Carol and Meg. Tina and I got a kick out of Meg's use of the English language, which was mostly punctuated with texting acronyms. I couldn't understand much of what she was saying, so I asked her to explain some of them.

"Well," she said, "AFC is away from computer, OMG is oh my god, BDN is big damn number, HUD is how you doin', and JAM is just a minute."

"Okay," I said. "I think I have it; let me give it a try. OMG! The MPG on my JEEP is CRAP.... How's that?" I got a good laugh from everyone, and I excused myself and went to the restroom. When I returned, Tina, Carol, and Meg were in a huddle and whispering. I thought it would be funny to come up behind them, lean in, and say in a soft voice say, "What are we all whispering about?"

As I leaned in, I heard Carol telling the girls about how her hemorrhoids were itching and driving her crazy. I tried to back away quickly, but it was too late. Carol looked back at me and said, "I am so embarrassed."

"No need to be," I said. "I have the same problem myself." I reached into my pocket and pulled out a small tube of hemorrhoid cream, handed it to her, and said, "I'll tell you an embarrassing story. Mine were also driving me crazy one day as I was cutting up some jalapeno peppers to use in the salsa I was making. I finished as quickly as I could and made a dash to the bathroom. I grabbed my usual large tube of cream and slathered on a goodly amount. I stood and started to pull up my shorts, when all of a sudden there was a fire down below. The jalapeno juice on my finger had set the old sphincter ablaze; the more I tried to wash it off, the worse it got." Carol got up, laughing loudly, and headed off to the ladies room, tube in hand. If we hadn't all been half in the bag, I would never have said anything like that.

When Carol sat back down, I said, "I have only seen you with your hair in a bun and wearing a business suit and high heels, but now ... Wow! You look absolutely stunning."

"He's right," Tina chimed in.

Carol replied, "You're not so bad yourself, Ral. I've seen both you and Zo-L naked on the recordings, and I have to say, you represented the human male species very well."

Tina smiled, nodded in approval, and said, "You know everything about Ral and I ... especially Ral; tell us about yourself."

"Let's see," Carol said, "I started out as a weather girl at a small station in New Jersey. From there I became a news reporter at a larger station in upstate New York, then an anchor. From there I moved into this job."

"Is there a Mister Avery?" Tina asked.

"There was, but we got divorced many years ago. We tried very hard to make things work, but with him being a doctor and me with my job, we almost never saw each other. We did, however, have two beautiful children together. They are both grown with kids of their own."

I turned around to ask Meg her background, but she was having a blast on the dance floor, so I asked

Carol. "Meg came to work for me straight out of college; she was highly recommended by a friend of mine. I wouldn't want to do this job without her; she is absolutely amazing. She has a memory like the Ar-Zians gave you, Ral....She never forgets anything."

"I don't want to appear rude," Tina said, "but don't all the OMGs and ROFLs get to you sometimes?"

"It did a little at first," Carol replied, "but I thought back to my college days, and we had a language of our own too.... I think all kids do."

Tina said, "OMG! You're right."

We started talking about how the band was absolutely amazing; they played every song anyone requested: rock, country — you name it. My wife mentioned that I used to have a band in my high school and college days and played professionally for many years. As Tina and I were dancing, Carol got up on stage and asked for everyone's attention. She called me up on stage and made a very short speech about the importance of my story and how much everyone loves being a part of it. She then presented me with a commemorative bottle of Jack Daniels, my favorite. This was the best party Tina and I had ever been to; it must have cost a fortune.

Carol continued, "As it turns out, Ral plays guitar himself, and I'll bet with a little encouragement, we can get him to play us a tune." Since everyone was blitzed, the encouragement was a thunderous round of applause and whistles. As I handed my bottle of Jack to Tina, the lead guitarist handed me his second guitar, which was on a stand just behind him. I played the old Lonnie Mack hit "Memphis." It sounded pretty good if I do say so myself. They kept yelling for

110

more, and I obliged, playing and singing some Chuck Berry tunes and a little Creedence Clearwater Revival.

The party lasted until the wee hours of the morning; I don't think a single person went home early. We slept in late, and then went down for breakfast. Neither one of us could believe how much fun we were having. Before the Medical Researchers cured all my ailments, we did very little. Carol called us at about 1:00 p.m. and asked, "You guys ready for a great afternoon? Pick you up at 3:00."

We made the 4:00 p.m. performance of a Broadway play called *The Older You Get*, which was a parody on aging, and it was really funny. Afterwards, Carol asked where we wanted to go for dinner. "You know, we have been treated like gold since we got here, always getting to choose what we would like to do, and where we would you like to go. You choose somewhere Carol."

"Do you guys like pizza?" she asked. Being full-blooded Italian, I answered, *"Ma Shu,"* which is a colloquialism for "why sure." She took us to a little place way off the beaten path whose pizza made the pizza in California taste like catsup on stale bread in comparison. After that she took us to an exclusive place called Club 359, which sits high above Manhattan. The rooftop dance floor is open to all, but the downstairs lounge is invitation only. We sat in the garden area of the rooftop at a little table in the corner, and I asked Carol why they call it Club 359.

She said, "Stand up and look around."

"Wow," I said. You can see the entire city from here."

"Not quite," she said. "See that flag pole over there?"

"Uh huh," I answered. "That's why they don't call it Club 360."

"That is pretty clever," Tina remarked as she was laughing.

Unexpectedly, a very well-dressed man approached us; he spoke to Carol and invited us to follow him down to the exclusive lounge. It was gorgeous; all done in ultra-modern furnishings, with lights everywhere.... It was breathtaking. The entire bar was made of lucite with chairs to match. Colored lighting in the floor traveled up through them and made everything glow ... absolutely beautiful. The lounge featured two bands, one rock and the other country. Carol wouldn't let Tina see the drink list, and we found out later there was a $525 bottle service. I had to ask someone afterwards what bottle service was. Drinks are so expensive at these clubs; it can be cheaper to buy the entire bottle of liquor rather than paying for it by the shot. There were celebrities everywhere; we were totally blown away when several of them came up to Carol and began conversations. She introduced us to all of them, and we were on top of the world.

I turned to Carol and said, "Thank you so much, we have never met a celebrity before. . . . That was amazing! I can hardly wait to tell all our family and friends about this."

She replied, "Don't you realize that when *Hard Facts* airs, they will be bragging to their family and friends about having met you?" I was stunned. "Also, while researching the Food Formula story, several financial analysts we spoke with put your estimated net worth in the tens of millions within a year, and a billion within ten years."

I responded, "If Meg was here she would say I'm going to need a BAPB."

"What's that?" Carol asked.

"A big-ass piggybank," I replied. As the realization of all this newfound wealth sunk in, I slumped back in my chair and just said, "Wow!"

We left in the wee hours of the morning again, and Carol said, "Why don't you guys sleep in tomorrow; I have a meeting first thing, then I will see about your money. I'll call you late morning and send a car for you, Ral, and we will go from there...Okay?"

"Sleeping in sounds good to me," Tina said.

"Me too" I agreed.

Carol called around 11:00 a.m. and sent the limo shortly thereafter. Meg escorted me up to her office, and Carol introduced me to the vice president of marketing for JK Sterling Corp, Mr. Adamston Ling. We shook hands and he said, "Please call me Adam; may I call you Ral?"

"Please do," I answered.

"Adam has gone over the tapes of the show, and says there would be no problem transferring them to DVD. He is very interested in seeing the disk if you wouldn't mind, Ral."

Adam got very close to me, as he had seen on the tapes the disk was kept in my neck; I humored him by removing it slowly. "Could you play me a small section, please?"

"Anything in particular?" I asked.

"When you first arrived at the Spaceport; that is my favorite part."

"Yes, sir," I answered. When I played that portion of the recording, he was absolutely mesmerized to actually be immersed in the recording itself.

"I have never even heard of anyone suggesting that this kind of thing was possible, and we have a pretty talented group of future product engineers."

Mr. Ling was a very distinguished older Asian gentleman and asked Carol if he could speak to her privately for just a moment. The two of them stepped outside her office for a moment, then came right back in. Carol explained to me that Mr. Ling did not think it would be proper for him to ask me to do something without going through her first.

I turned to him and said, "Thank you very much for your kindness; but you can ask me anything you like." He wanted me to go with him to the JK Sterling research lab to show the disk to his engineers. He thought they might be able to come up with a better way to record the disk contents to DVD. "It would be my pleasure," I said.

He replied, "As your alien friend would say, 'I promise to have you back here in under four hours.'" We all laughed, as Mr. Ling and I walked out. I handed Carol the voided blank check she had requested so she could have the money they were paying me transferred into my account.

JK Sterling headquarters was only about a twenty minute drive away. Mr. Ling was a very interesting man to talk to, so it seemed like we arrived in no time at all. He personally escorted me to a very high security area, which made the security measures at

SBS look like that of entering a local nightclub. As we walked down a long hallway, red lights on the ceiling came on and began to blink and rotate. They were spaced about five feet apart and accompanied by a loud voice that said "Visitor on the floor," over and over again. This is their way of telling everyone working on any sensitive projects to put them away until after I left. I had been to two other planets, but I felt more uncomfortable here than I did there. Mr. Ling sensed that I was a little uneasy and repeatedly apologized for the strict security measures.

I was taken into a large empty room and introduced to several engineers, scientists, and physicists, ten in all. I thought to myself, *You guys think you have something here that requires flashing light and intimidating voice recordings. I have something that will blow your socks off.* I retrieved the disk from my neck and held it in the palm of my hand so everyone could have a good look. Mr. Ling had already cautioned them that they could not touch it. I set it on a table and activated it. *All socks, completely blown off,* I thought to myself. They walked around the table completely amazed, checking it out very carefully.

"What does it do?" they asked. I looked at Mr. Ling, who had a big smile on his face; he nodded toward me, as if to say, "Okay, show them." I searched for the Spaceport section of the recording, as I knew Mr. Ling would enjoy seeing it again.

As the recording filled the room, there were audible gasps from everyone. Mr. Ling had told me that JK Sterling was working on a new form of recording medium, but I knew it couldn't compare to this. I showed them only a few minutes of the recording, and then shut it off. Mr. Ling then asked them what they thought.

No one really knew what to say. He then asked, "How can we transfer this to DVD without missing a great deal of content?" No one had a ready answer, and they were much more interested in the disk itself than answering Mr. Ling's question. All ten of them were bent over the table looking at the disk very closely. I cautioned them again myself not to touch it, but one of them just had to try to pick it up. He immediately collapsed to the floor, and everyone rushed to his assistance. To my great relief, he recovered quickly, and I placed the disk back where it belongs.

They all seemed hell-bent on being able to reproduce the disk. Completely ignoring Mr. Ling, they asked me if I was told how it worked and did I think it could be reproduced here on Earth. I said, "The information given to me was that it would run forever and needed no power source. I was the only person in the entire universe that can operate it. The disk cannot be taken apart without destroying it, and it cannot be duplicated on our planet, as we lack the necessary elements.

"I don't want to appear rude," I said, "but I thought I was here to see if there was a more efficient way to transfer the contents of the disk to DVD — something better than the *Hard Facts* taping." I immediately regretted what I said; after all, if someone showed me something created by an advanced civilization, I would want to know all there was to know about it. I think that was actually the reason I was here, and it had nothing to do with DVDs. As they talked amongst themselves, I sat at a table a few feet away. All I wanted to do was get back to SBS, get paid, and go back to the hotel and crash. All this partying was catching up to me; after all I'm sixty-eight years old. After a few more minutes, I got my wish.

Mr. Ling said, "Thank you so much for your kindness, Ral. I will have a car take you back to SBS."

"It was a pleasure having met you, sir," I said. As he opened the door for me, those annoying lights began flashing, and that same recording began....I couldn't wait to get out of there.

I arrived back at Carol's office about 2:15 p.m. She asked me to come over to her computer and check my bank account online. I sat down, entered the web site and my password, and there it was...a total balance of $4,221,024.56 Until now this had all been a kind of fantasy, talking about such large numbers; but there it was. I got up, hugged Carol tightly, and thanked her. She then asked, "Well, what would you guys like to do on your last night in New York?"

I said, "Stay at the hotel, have an early dinner, and go to bed."

She put her hand on my shoulder and said, "Oh, thank God! I'm exhausted!"

"Please sit down for just a minute," she said. "I want to fill you in on what happens next. First of all, have a great evening; also, I don't know how to thank you for all you have done for me."

"The feeling is very mutual," I interrupted.

"The limo will be taking you back to the hotel shortly, and I will call you in the morning and let you know exactly what time the corporate jet will be taking you home. I will have the limo take you to the airport, and another limo will pick you up at your local airport and take you home. *Hard Facts* will air two weeks from today, so it is very important that you not discuss the contents of the show with anyone.

"Please don't think I'm talking down to you," Carol continued, "but I cannot impress upon you how important the 'non-disclosure clause' is. Let me tell you a story. There was a very well-known doctor working here in New York at a prestigious hospital. There were instances of incompetence that resulted in the deaths of three patients. The hospital covered up the entire thing for fear of being sued. The doctor came to us and wanted to expose the whole ugly affair. We taped the interview without him ever appearing on camera, and we also disguised his voice; he was so dedicated to his mission, he wouldn't even accept money for the interview. The show was to air in two weeks when he received a phone call from an old Army buddy he hadn't seen in fifteen years. They met at a bar they used to frequent in the old days before they both became medics in the Army. They had several drinks, and the doctor began telling his buddy about the problems at the hospital.

"Long story short: his buddy was a drug addict who sold the story to a tabloid. The doctor violated the non-disclosure agreement and ended up losing his job; he was considered a pariah and no one would hire him. He ended up moving to Costa Rica and now works for a clinic in a small town; he literally lost everything! In your case, if the story got out ahead of the taping, you would forfeit your payment and probably be sued as well."

I said, "Point taken, but you know my entire family and a few close friends know everything."

"Yes," Carol said. "That's fine; just please don't discuss anything about the show, and urge your family to remain silent until after the airing."

CHAPTER 6

RETURN HOME

The trip home was uneventful; everyone treated Tina and me wonderfully, and the limo was at Lakeview Airport right on time to take us home. We got in the door at 6:30 p.m. California time, and we were absolutely beat. Our internal clocks were still set to New York time, which was three hours later. We sat down and watched TV for a couple of hours, and then went to bed. The next morning, my neighbor, Arthur Isles, saw Tina and me returning home from church.

He came over about an hour later and asked how the trip to New York had gone. I grabbed a couple beers from the refrigerator, and we went out back and sat in the gazebo since it was such a beautiful day. I told him I had signed a non-disclosure form and was not able to talk about the show at all until it aired in two weeks. I added that they told me to ask everyone else to do the same. Arthur completely understood privacy rules, as he used to be a NASA engineer.... In fact, that is how I met him.

When I graduated from college with an AA degree in electronics in the late '60s, I looked for a job all summer long. Two of my college buddies found jobs almost immediately and moved into a small apartment near the ocean in downtown Long Beach. They were constantly bugging me to move in with them, but I told them not until I find a job. I was open to just about anything in the field of electronics except aerospace. My father had worked for just about every aerospace company there was — over a nineteen-year period. Everything would go along great for a year or two, then the government contract would run out, and he would be laid off. I had told him before that I would never go to work for an aerospace firm. By summer's end my attitude had changed. Pop asked me to sit down with him and told me that Alvo Aeronautics, which is where he worked, was hiring. He said, "I know that's not your cup of tea, but you can work there until you find something better." I had to agree that anything was better than going out looking for a job every day as I had been doing all summer.

The next day when Pop got home from work, he said, "I have set you up with an interview tomorrow morning at 9:00 a.m. with Mister Abrams, the human resources manager. He is a friend of mine and has offered to see you first thing." He drew me a map of how to get to the correct building, as it is a very large complex. "Don't be late," Pop said.

"Am I ever?" I asked.

The next morning as I entered the human resources building, Pop was right there waiting for me. He took me to Mr. Abram's office, introduced us, and then left. After a short chat and filling out a few forms, he said, "The only thing I have available is an electrical assembler position."

"I'll take it," I said.

"Don't you want to know what it is?" he asked.

"Forgive me," I said, "but I have been looking for a job every day since I graduated from college four months ago, so I am thrilled to have anything offered to me." I was hired on the spot. He got on the phone and called the department where I would be working, and they sent someone over to show me around.

The job entailed fabricating wire harnesses to be used in the Apollo program. I was introduced around to about twenty other people whom I would be working along side. There was a long row of benches with plywood jigs standing lengthwise on top of them. Each sheet of plywood had a pattern printed on it where various wires were to be run. My job would be to take pieces of numbered wires from a spool and run them through a series of pegs that separated each wire bundle from the next until it reached its destination, then cut it off. When all wires had been run according to the blueprint, I would either crimp terminals on the wire ends or solder them into pins, which would be then inserted in special gold-plated connectors. After all the wires were run correctly, I would tie them together with a special flat-waxed string. All harnesses would have to pass both company and NASA inspection at each stage of completion. It was really an entry-level job, and my peers were mostly wives and grandmothers. I didn't care.... It was a job!

I spent the first week going to a NASA crimping and soldering school, third shift, where I passed and received a NASA certificate. It was only a level two job, and I was hoping to be promoted to something higher eventually, but for now I had an income. There was a NASA engineer named Arthur Isles who would come by periodically to put his inspection stamp on our work. I think he took a liking to me and saw some potential as well. We began having lunch together and quickly became friends. One day there was a problem in the potting lab. He asked me to come with him and have a look.

The potting lab was where they fill electrical component assemblies with foam or silicone-rubber compounds to firmly lock them in place. When a Saturn Five rocket blasts off, the vibrations and heat can destroy and tear components apart. The potting, as it's called, remedies that problem. The trouble they were having was trying to get the silicone rubber from a large plastic syringe to go into a place that was four inches down and three inches to the left inside a small metal box. They called for a NASA engineer to help solve the problem.

Arthur looked at me and asked, "What would you do, Ral?" I looked around the room and spotted a spool of plastic tubing about one-quarter inch in diameter. I took out my pocketknife, cut off an eight-inch piece, and slipped it over the end of the silicone rubber-filled syringe. I guided the tube into the area to be filled and pressed the plunger. Arthur was very impressed, patted me on the back, and said, "Good job, Ral."

One day my boss called me into his office and said, "It seems you have friends in high places. NASA has requested you to work for them as an assistant to assembly engineer Arthur Isles." I couldn't believe it; I was thrilled and accepted immediately. Arthur is the one who got me interested in UFOs in the first place.

He would tell me stories that some of the astronauts had told him about strange objects they had seen while in orbit. I asked if he had ever seen a UFO himself.

"No," he said, "but my brother did. He lives in the upper desert about hundred miles outside of Las Vegas, and every evening he goes for a five-mile walk. It's a steady incline of about two-point-four miles, and then it crests on a small hill. He sits for a while admiring the view, and then walks back.

"One night as he reached the top of the hill, he saw a UFO on the ground not two hundred feet in front of him. He immediately lay on the ground to keep from being spotted. It wasn't the usual disk shape you always hear about; it was pyramid in shape, about thirty feet at the bottom and about twenty-five feet tall. There were six beings in long white robes walking around outside. He said he watched for about thirty minutes, then the beings stepped inside, and the thing just seemed to vanish."

I knew Arthur was telling me the truth; otherwise, he would have said he had seen it himself. I worked with him until he retired and moved up to Spruce Valley Lake. We kept in touch, and we even visited each other on occasion. After several years had passed, Tina and I had both retired and decided we might like to live near our dear friends, Arthur and Pam Isles. It's a beautiful area, and we both wanted to get out of the crowded city and live on a few acres somewhere. Tina had always loved horses, and this would allow her to have one. I called Arthur, who was thrilled at the possibility of us becoming neighbors.

He practically shouted, "The ranch right across the street from me is for sale! The house is nothing to brag about, but you can live in it while you build something more suitable, and it sits on forty acres. It has been for sale for quite some time now, and I think you can pick it up very reasonably. I know two contractors who can build you and Tina anything you want."

"Let me talk to Tina, and I'll call you back," I said. After what had to be the shortest conversation my wife and I had ever had, I called Arthur back.

He answered, saying, "I'm on the computer right now, and there is a flight leaving tomorrow morning at 7:00 a.m. It will put the two of you in Sacramento at 8:15; should I press purchase?"

"Yes," I said.

"Ral, I'll email you the information, and call the realtor to set up a showing for tomorrow." This was all happening so fast — Tina and I were very excited. Needless to say, we purchased the property and have been living there ever since.

Now back to the gazebo . . . Other than my family, Arthur was the only one who knew all about the Food Formula and my experience with the Ar-Zians. We spoke until dark, and then Arthur went home. Tina and I just relaxed all day Monday trying to readjust to the time difference and get used to not having every minute planned out for us. Early Tuesday morning, Arthur called and said, "Did you catch the *Allen Sorrento* show last night?"

"No, I don't really like that guy," I answered.

"I can't stand him either," Arthur said. "But I was having trouble sleeping and decided to do some channel surfing when I heard your name mentioned. I listened, and he was talking about some nut that was claiming to have been abducted by small creatures and taken to their planet. I turned on the recorder as quickly as I could.... You have to come see this," he insisted.

I immediately went over and watched what he was able to record, and I was horrified! This idiot was mentioning my name over and over, calling me all sorts of names, and I was getting pissed! My cell phone began ringing; it was Carol.

"Have you heard about the *Allen Sorrento* show that aired last night?"

She asked. "I'm watching it as we speak," I answered. "I'm so sorry." she said, "We've got a leak somewhere."

"Who do you think it is?" I asked.

"It had to be one of the extra people we brought in during the taping," she replied.

"How did the information get to Allen so quickly?" I asked.

"Actually, the *Allen Sorrento* show is taped two floors down from *Hard Facts*," Carol lamented.

"Wonderful," I said, facetiously. "What do we do now?"

"Let's just hope that's the end of it. Maybe he will pick on someone else tonight; fortunately, no one I know watches that sleaze ball."

The *Allen Sorrento* show is one of those late-night cable talk shows. He amazingly has a pretty large following and manages to get some pretty impressive guests. I watched a couple of times but found it very distasteful. If Allen likes you, you're golden; if he dislikes you, you're in deep trouble. He has a unique style of interviewing. He leans way back in his chair, almost as if it was a recliner, then he bursts forward very quickly and screams at you. That's how he got the nickname of "The Yo-Yo." He is known for having "eye candy," or pretty girls, on his show — some of them former porn stars.

I recorded the Tuesday night airing, and it was worse than Monday night. This time he called me an idiot and a moron. I was getting furious with this guy! I called Carol to see what we could do, and she said they were still working on it.

"Even if we do find the snitch, other than firing him or her there's nothing we can do.... The cat is out of the bag." She continued, "I don't think it is someone directly connected with our show, as Allen seems to have only a few facts, as if he overheard someone talking about the show. We are trying to figure out a way to use this to our advantage."

"How?" I asked.

"By possibly leaking some bad information to him, so he will look foolish when *Hard Facts* airs. As they say, even bad publicity is still publicity. I'm really sorry, Ral. I'll keep working on this and get back to you. Try not to let it bother you."

Arthur came over later the next morning and asked how I was doing. "You saw last night's show, I imagine," he said.

"I sure did. I want to punch that bastard." Being Italian, I have often joked about having a relative in the mob named Uncle Nunzio, who doesn't really exist.

"What are you going to do?" Arthur asked. "I think I'm going to call Uncle Nunzio and have him break Allen's leg. Actually, he is having a holiday special: two broken limbs for the price of one....You can even mix and match.... It's really a very good deal."

Arthur laughed and said, "I'll pay half."

Wednesday's show was the worst of all; he continued calling me names and now was even making fun of my wife. That was it! I called Carol and demanded to be a guest on his show.

Carol said, "Do you really think that's wise? He will tear you apart! It's only another week before *Hard Facts* airs. Why don't you just hold off?"

"I'm sorry, Carol, but my mind is made up."

"I'll see if I can get you on," she said. Carol called back about 10:00 a.m. and said, "It's all set; you are scheduled to appear on tomorrow night's show. Are you really sure you want to do this, Ral?"

"You're damn right," I said. "I'll have the corporate jet in the air within an hour; call you with the details."

Tina and I arrived at Lakeview Airport later that day and were on our way to New York; we were feeling like jet setters. We arrived in the early morning, having gotten a couple hours of sleep on the plane. Carol had set us up at the same hotel and sent a car to pick us up around 9:00 a.m. Tina and I arrived at Carol's office about thirty minutes later. After the usual greetings, Carol and I got down to business.

"I have to tell you, Ral; I think you are making a big mistake."

"Let me tell you what happened after we spoke yesterday," I said. "I got a call from my daughter, who informed me our ten-year-old granddaughter was being made fun of at school for having a stupid grandfather. She was teased all day long because of Allen Sorrento. Yes, I want a piece of him."

"You know, the non-disclosure clause is going to keep you from saying much of anything."

"I know that but can I use my abilities?" I asked her. "Allen has already said he heard I was given special powers by space aliens. That has nothing to do with the Food Formula. He can't even connect me to that ... right?"

Carol replied, "I'll have to check with legal on that. Boy, this is really cutting it close; taping begins in a couple hours."

Carol, Tina and I went down to the *Allen Sorrento* show studio and were escorted to the guest room. We sat down, and Carol kept trying to get though to the legal department to find out what I was and was not allowed to say or do. For some reason she was not having much luck. A couple more guests arrived, of the eye candy variety, and one musical guest. Shortly afterward Allen came into the room to welcome all of his guests. He made the rounds, shaking hands, and when he reached me, I was greeted very politely. He said how happy he was that I could make the show and looked forward to asking me a few questions.

"Please, everyone, make yourselves comfortable," Allen said. "There is a cart over there with alcohol and other beverages and a snack tray is on its way; thank you all again for coming."

When he left, I turned to Carol and said, "He doesn't seem so bad."

Carol countered, "He is like a snake; he will just lie there all friendly for a while, then bite the hell out of you. Don't get a false sense of security."

As time went by, all the other guests had been called out, and I was next. Carol still had not heard back from legal despite having left seven messages.

"Ral," she said. "Let's just call this off, I'll make some excuse, and you sneak out the back and go up to my office. There is four million dollars at stake if you screw up!"

"I can't do that," I insisted. "It's personal now."

"Okay," she said, "just don't make him angry. He hates being called Al, and he is sensitive about being overweight, short, and bald. Also, when he gets flustered he turns bright red; if that happens ... run like hell. You can talk about UFOs in general but try to be as vague as possible; we want to save all the good stuff for the *Hard Facts* airing. Whatever you do — don't mention *Hard Facts* or the Food Formula! Please!"

A page peeked in the room and said, "You're on next, Mister Diamond."

Carol said, "I'll be in the front row; if I hear anything from legal, I will signal you. You just want to know if you can use your abilities — right?"

"That's right," I responded. Allen introduced me and I was as nervous as could be. I walked across the stage, waved hello to the audience, shook hands with him, and took my seat opposite his desk. He wasted no time, leaning back fully in his chair, and I knew he was preparing to strike.

He suddenly lunged forward at me and said, "So UFOs, huh? I understand you claim to have been abducted by aliens, taken to another planet, treated like royalty, and given super human powers — is that right?"

"Well, not exactly," I said. "I was not abducted. I went willingly."

This brought a slight chuckle from the audience, as Allen leaned back again and said, "What are these special powers you have?"

"They gave me the ability to do difficult mathematical calculations in my head."

He leaned forward and said, "There are a lot of people that can do that; I have had a number of them right here on my show." He leaned back again and asked, "What else ya got?"

I was looking for help from Carol, who was just sitting there; she gave me sort of a shoulder shrug.

"I'm waiting," he said loudly.

"I can remember everything. They gave me a photographic memory," I asserted.

He flew at me even faster, and in an even louder voice, said: "There are people that can do that too, you jackass." The audience seemed to be on Allen's side, and I was being laughed at. He leaned back again, preparing to strike once more, and said in a slow mocking voice, "What super-human powers do you have that no one else has?"

"I was given the power of telekinesis," I said. "Wooo. Big word for such a dip stick!" he growled. I looked over at Carol, who was on the phone; she nodded "yes," hung up the phone, and mouthed the words: *Take...him...down.*

"Explain to our audience what telekinesis means," Allen said.

"Why, don't you know, Al?" The audience reaction was mixed, some laughter and some "ooohs." "It's mind over matter. I can control things with my mind. I can move things or make them disappear."

Trying to regain his superiority, he lunged at me so fast he was only inches from my face and screamed, "Show me something, and I don't mean pulling a quarter out of my ear or bending a spoon!"

I cocked my hand up as usual and said, "How about if I make your clothes disappear?!" I moved my arm forward, and he was completely naked. Before he had a chance to react, I said, "How about if I move your desk over to the band area, Al!" I pointed to his desk, raised it about one foot off the stage and quickly moved it about thirty feet to the band area. He covered his crotch with his hands and tried to scoot off stage, but I had made his chair immobile. The audience was going crazy! Allen was turning as red as a fire engine, and the two eye-candy girls were laughing hysterically with their hands over their mouths; the audience was on its feet. This felt great! I milked the situation for a while and just as the audience was quieting down, I raised my arms up and said, "Slow down, folks." Then I pointed toward Allen and said, "There's a red light ahead." They loved it.

Allen was screaming at the top of his lungs, using every curse word he could think of. I completely ignored him and slowly leaned forward to get the coffee cup of water they had given me. As I looked at Carol she was standing, laughing, and applauding furiously. . . . I winked at her. As Allen kept on screaming, I turned toward the girls and started a conversation. In a desperate effort to regain control, I heard Allen ask, "Can I please have my clothes back?"

I turned to him and said, "I thought the whole purpose of your show was to entertain and make people laugh. Look at the audience, Al, they seem to be very entertained and are laughing their asses off." I leaned in toward him and said, "You are a very funny guy, Allen Sorrento!" He asked for his clothes again and I said, "As we Italians say, I'm going to make you an offer you can't refuse. I'll give you a chance to apologize for all the embarrassment and ridicule you have caused my family and me. If it's believable, I will let you keep your chair."

"You're no Italian, you lying bastard! He screamed. "What kind of Italian name is Diamond?"

In a very calm voice I explained, "My grandfather wanted a more American-sounding name when he came to this country from Sicily during the thirties at age fifteen. He shortened our last name to Diamond; my original name is DiAmando."

I reached into my pocket and retrieved a sheet of paper, unfolded it, and said, "You have always made a big thing of being Italian yourself, when according to my research, you are only one-fourth Italian, the rest being Russian, English, and Polish. The audience actually began to boo; this had never happened to Allen before. I have never seen a person so angry in my entire life. If he weren't totally naked, I actually think he would have physically attacked me.

Just then, the bandleader put his guitar down, removed his jacket, and began to walk toward Allen to give it to him so he could cover up. I cocked the old arm and made his jacket disappear. Pointing at him, I raised him about a foot off the floor, shook my head "no," and set him back down. He backed away with the palms of his hands together and bowed toward me. The audience was totally on my side now, and it felt great.

Allen made a halfhearted apology, and I looked at the audience and said, "What do you think, guys?" There was a mix of every possible response. I turned to Allen and said, "I know you're not smart enough to have come up with all those nasty remarks by yourself, so if you will point out your writers, I would like to have a word with them as well."

I stood up because I knew exactly where they were seated. I cocked my arm up, and you should have seen them run. One of them fell twice as he slipped trying to get away. It took about two minutes for the audience to settle down, and Allen asked once again for his clothes. I said, "Tell ya what I'm gonna do. I'll give you back your desk to hide behind like the coward you are." I pointed at the desk and brought it forward so fast it startled Allen, and he fell backward and was sprawled out onto the floor, stark-ass naked, and in a spread-eagle position. I had released his chair from the floor just beforehand. Needless to say the audience was in the palm of my hand.

Allen looked like he was going to have a heart attack and was begging for his clothes. "Okay, tomato face," I said. "I'll give you back your clothes." I pointed to the top of his desk and a huge pair of red thong underwear appeared. I picked them up, stretched them out to show the audience, and handed them to him.... He was the only one in the studio who was not amused. I pointed again, and a very large matching bra appeared — again, not funny according to Allen...but the audience thought so. Then I made his pants appear, but as he grabbed them, I changed the color to yellow. I gave him all the rest of his clothing back but made them all different hideous colors.

I stood up, turned to Allen, and said, "It's been a pleasure, Al. I'd shake your hand but I've seen where it's been." I waved goodbye to the audience, and started walking off stage; I reached out my left hand into the air and retrieved the bandleader's jacket. I walked over to him, shook his hand with my right hand, and draped his jacket over his left arm. "No hard feelings, I hope," I said, and I walked back to the guest room.

Tina was waiting for me with open arms, as the old saying goes. She had a smile I hadn't seen since our first child was born. "I am so proud of you," she said, and then gave me a great big kiss.

A moment later Carol burst into the room practically screaming, threw herself at me, and said, "Come here, Ralph DiAmando, you magnificent bastard; you really showed that son of a bitch!" She wrapped her arms around my neck, lifted both her feet off the floor, and planted a big kiss right on my lips. After a much longer kiss than I expected, she let go, looked at Tina, and said, "Sorry hon."

My wife said, "That's okay. I had the same reaction, except the language I used when referring to Allen was much more colorful." Just then we heard a very loud bang! Carol peeked out the door and began to laugh under her breath. She beckoned with her finger for Tina and I to come and have a look. We were amazed to see that Allen's dressing room door was broken in two and hanging by only one hinge. Carol closed the door, and we all broke out laughing. "Let's go up to my office," she said.

Tina and I sat down, and Carol reached into the drawer where she kept the scotch. As she brought it out, she said, "You know, this 'special occasion' bottle has been in that drawer for six years without being opened. Since I met you guys, we have drunk from it twice in one week; thankfully, I bought another one in anticipation." Carol poured herself and me a small glass, and holding up the bottle, looked at Tina, and said, "Tina?"

"Oh, what the hell," Tina said. "This certainly is a special occasion." We all clinked glasses, and Carol and I chugged it right down. She grabbed the bottle and began to pour herself and me another shot, while Tina was still staring at hers; after all she's a wine drinker. Tina suddenly gulped the whole thing down saying, "OMG!" in a barely audible voice. Carol, still holding the bottle and with a big smile on her face, said, "I guess you won't be having another?"

Tina slammed the glass down on the table and said, "Hit me!"

Carol looked at me and asked, "What would you have done if legal would have said no?"

"The same thing," I answered. "I prayed about it and asked that everything go as I had planned. If so, I would donate the four million dollars to my church and other charities; if not I would have lost it anyway, so it didn't really matter what legal said. Besides, Tina and I are still living off the two hundred fifty thousand dollar signing bonus from Able Chemical; add that to the royalties that will soon be coming in, and it's really not a big deal."

"How did you create that gigantic underwear for Allen," she asked.

"I didn't. Tina and I stopped at a plus-size clothing store on the way to the airport. I moved them into another dimension and put them in my pocket. When the appropriate time came, I placed them on Allen's desk and brought them back to this dimension."

As we continued to drink, Carol said, "I can't begin to tell you, Ral, how much what you did tonight means to me. Let me start at the beginning. There was a show many years ago called *So, I Bet You Can't Sleep*, a cutesy title based on the fact the show aired so late at night. The host was Nigel Cromwell, an English fellow who tried very hard, but the show was falling in the ratings. SBS began looking around for a new show and a new host. Nigel knew that his show would soon be cancelled and accepted the inevitable. There was a new and upcoming comedian named Allen Sorrento, who had been in a few low-budget movies, did standup, and had appeared on numerous sitcoms. SBS offered him his own show to replace Nigel's. He agreed to do the show if it was named after him, and he wanted his own studio which would remain his as long as he did the show.

"The newly constructed SBS building is twenty-one stories, and we were only occupying the first ten, so that was not a problem. The contracts were signed, and the deal was set in stone. SBS built Allen a state-of-the-art studio on the nineteenth floor, as construction was only completed to that level. That decision was all driven by Allen's ego; he wanted to be as high as possible. I was hired to produce the show, and that is when my hell began. Allen started to sexually harass me from the very beginning. He would grope me, make all sorts of sexual innuendos, and tried to kiss me on several occasions. I didn't want to lose my job, so I put up with it for months; I really hated that SOB."

Carol continued, "The show started out slowly, but gained momentum, and Allen was able to get a better group of guests as time went on. His show peaked around the third year, and then started to backslide. That was when he decided to go in a new direction, becoming more aggressive. For some insane reason it seemed to work for him; the ratings started back up again. SBS hated the new direction and was looking for a reason to get rid of him. Allen made enough money doing other things to eventually buy his show from the network. With his ironclad contract, as long as the show was making money, the network would leave it alone. He would practically have to kill someone to be fired. Allen eventually alienated everyone who used to be his friend. After tonight's profanity-laced tirade, SBS may get its wish and be able to get rid of him once and for all. So as you can see, Ral, I am absolutely thrilled. I hope you and Tina are going to stick around for another day; I've got a night on the town to plan that will be fantastic."

Neither Tina nor I were in a big hurry to go home, so we agreed. We went back to the hotel for some much-needed rest. The next morning Carol called and asked if we would join her for lunch. She took us to another out-of-the way Italian restaurant. The food was exceptional, reminding me of my mother and grandmother's cooking. She informed us that the decision had been made to cancel the *Allen Sorrento Show* shortly after we left last night.

Carol was ecstatic! "I did a phone interview with our entertainment show this morning, and intentionally let it slip that we might be at Club 359 tonight. You, Ral, are the talk of the town. I am betting every celebrity in the area will be there tonight to meet you. I hope you don't mind. Most of them have grown to very much dislike Allen over the years, as he loves to put celebrities down every chance he gets. You are the only person that has ever put him in his place. I am bringing one of our photographers to document the whole thing, so you guys will have some incredible memories to take home. When *Hard Facts* airs and it becomes known that you are behind the Food Formula as well, your picture will be on every newspaper and magazine around the world.

"Oh, before I forget — Misty may contact you and want to do another interview. It's up to you, but it will give you an opportunity to plug the *Hard Facts* interview, which is good for all of us."

After lunch Tina and I went back to the hotel to rest, as we knew it would probably be a very long night. Carol picked us up at 8:00 p.m. with Meg and a photographer, and we headed off to Club 359. The club does not allow pictures to be taken inside to protect the celebrities' privacy; however, the owner made an exception in our case thanks to Carol plugging the club on the air and the owners' dislike of Allen Sorrento. We were asked to get the permission of each celebrity who was to be filmed so as not to upset anyone. I received a hero's welcome at the club and was personally greeted by the club's owner, Mr. Paul Arnoff. It seems his dislike for Allen stems from an incident that happened two years ago. Allen wanted special treatment at the club, believing he was such a huge celebrity, and the owner refused to give it to him. Allen made a big scene and then started dissing the club on his show, which infuriated the owner and celebrities alike.

Mr. Arnoff seated us at the best table in the club, and with a thick accent said, "Mister DiAmando, I cannot tell you how happy you have made me. Please order anything you want; you and your friends are my guests tonight." Behind him, celebrities were lining up to meet me; I was flabbergasted! We must have met twenty-five or more very famous people, each with their own "I hate Allen Sorrento" story to tell. I have to admit I had never heard of several of them....It was an amazing evening. We got to the hotel at 3:00 a.m. and slept till 10:00 a.m. when Carol called. She had been deluged with calls wanting to interview me, but I was just too beat. All I wanted to do was go back home and vegetate for a while.

We arrived back in Spruce Valley Lake around 2:30 p.m. local time where a cab was waiting for us; we arrived home around 3:00 p.m. There was a line of news vans and reporters all along our fence ...dozens of them, including Misty. I told the cab driver to let me out and take Tina up to the house. I leaned over and whispered to Misty, telling her to stick around after the others had gone. I kind of felt sorry for them; after all, they are only trying to do their job, and I imagine many of them had been waiting for hours. I spoke to as many as I could individually, giving short interviews then one statement to all of them.

I asked them to respect our privacy and not continue to try to contact us. After they had all gone, Misty and I — along with her cameraman — went up to the house. I was filmed in silhouette and my voice would be disguised as before, since my identity had not yet been revealed. She asked about the Food Formula, which would be airing soon on *Hard Facts*. Misty filled me in on her meteoric rise to news anchor, and how she and Jane had moved out of the small apartment and purchased a house together. She then had to rush back to the studio to prepare the interview for airing.

Tina and I got some much-needed rest the next few days, and then *Hard Facts* aired. I didn't think the phone would ever stop ringing; we finally just pulled the plug out of the wall. Carol called the next morning to the cell phone she had given us and said, "Homeland Security wants to stop production on the Food Formula, because they feared it might be contaminated somehow by the aliens in a plot to kill us all and take over our planet. The President is expected to make a statement as soon as he has reviewed all the facts. I hate to tell you this since you just got home, but I think he wants to meet with you."

"I guess I had better plug the phone back in then," I said.

"Our news division is trying to reach President James, and we will give him this number if that is okay with you."

"Of course, that's fine," I said. It wasn't long thereafter that two secret service agents came to our house. They informed me that the President Clayton James had requested my presence at the White House, and a military jet was waiting to take Tina and me to Washington. *Damn*, I thought, *we usually never go anywhere. We haven't taken a vacation in years; now we are flying around the country every few days but not as vacationers.*

We arrived at the White House, where we were greeted by the President and First Lady and made to feel very welcome. The President wasted no time ushering me into the Oval Office, while the First Lady gave Tina a tour of the premises. The President shared with me his concerns about the possible sinister purpose of the Food Formula and asked my opinion.

"I have been eating produce grown with the Food Formula for some time now," I said, "and I feel perfectly fine."

Then the President asked if I would submit to a blood sample being taken for analysis.

I said, "Certainly, sir."

He called in the White House physician, who promptly took the sample and left. "They will rush that through, and we will have the results shortly."

"Mister President, consider the advantages of the Food Formula; besides food, it can be used for energy production. We can grow vast amounts of corn, sugar cane, switch grass, and other plants that we can use to produce fuel. We can completely end our dependency on foreign oil imports and create hundreds of thousands of jobs and new industries."

"That is all well and good," he said, "but what about the other side of the coin? What is going to happen when the drug cartels get a hold of this formula? Tell me, Mister Diamond, why is it you think there is nothing to be worried about?"

"I expressed that very concern when I was given the formula. I was told there were certain families of plants on which the formula will not work. Cocaine, for example, is made from a family of plants called the erythroxylum genus, which contain approximately 200 species, of which seventeen will produce cocaine. Heroin is made from poppies in the opiate, or papaveraceae family, and marijuana is the cannabis genus of plants. All these plants and many others contain certain chemicals that when mixed with the Food Formula produces a poison that will destroy the seed and prevent germination."

"I'm impressed with your knowledge Mister Diamond," the President said. "Please don't take this personally, but I owe it to the people of the United States, and in fact the entire world, to confirm this to be true."

"I wouldn't have it any other way, Mister President; what do you propose?"

"NASA has a lab not too far away that has been experimenting with growing plants for the space program. If anyone can determine the facts about what will and will not grow, it would be them." The President then called one of his assistants into the room and instructed him to contact NASA immediately.

"Sit down, Mister Diamond," he said, "This shouldn't take long....How about a drink?"

I was quite surprised by his offer and said, "I wouldn't say no to a little Jack, sir." He walked over to a beautiful black walnut credenza and pressed a hidden button on the side. The top opened, and a well-stocked bar including glasses and ice rose up out of it. He poured a generous amount for each of us, and sat down across the table from me.

"NASA on line two, Mister President," came over the communication system in front of him.

"Hello, Bob," he said. "Thanks for the quick response. I'm going to put you on speaker; I have Mister Ralph Diamond here with me." The President explained his concerns and asked if NASA would be able to confirm what I had told him about the Food Formula.

"Certainly, Mister President, I'll get right on it."

"This is a rush, Bob; please get back to me ASAP."

"Yes, sir, Mister President," said Bob.

The commander-in-chief raised his glass toward me and said, "I pray for all of us that they will have good news when they call back; this is far too important to the entire world."

I raised my glass in kind and said, "I could not agree more, sir."

"Did you see the airing of *Hard Facts* last night, sir?" I asked.

"No, but I was briefed on it this morning."

"Mister President, the Ar-Zians have no desire to harm us; in their eyes I have done them a great service, and they would never do anything to hurt me or our people. They would have absolutely nothing to gain by eliminating us. They have perfect lives, they can create anything they desire and have learned to live in complete peace with everyone. Their world is absolutely pollution-free, and they would never adapt to our world with its different atmosphere and increased gravity. They have already created a new planet PW-1 and have no need to take ours. They have given us precious gifts that will save millions of lives; what will they think of us if we don't even use them?

"Also, sir, think of the money our country will save by not having to provide food to starving nations around the world. We can simply send them a few barrels of the Food Formula accompanied by bags of various seeds, and they can provide for themselves for years to come. Who knows? There may be more gifts in store for us in the future."

I showed him a few recordings from the disk, including my return trip to convince him how non-threatening the Ar-Zians are. "Mister President, if you stop production of the Food Formula, the whole world will hate the United States. We are in a truly unique position to help starving nations and end world hunger forever. I would like to see us deliver the formula free of charge to all Third World countries and build a lasting peace with everyone. If you like, you and I could go together to these impoverished countries and deliver the formula in person. Imagine what great publicity that would be for you and the United States."

The White House doctor soon returned to the Oval Office and handed the president the results. "Everything is normal, Mister President," he said.

"Thank you, John; that will be all." The President called one of his aides to entertain me while he met with his advisors. After a couple of hours, I was summoned back to the Oval Office to hear the president's decision: "NASA has informed me that initial tests show the classes of plants I was concerned about will in fact *not* grow in the Food Formula. Please forgive my hesitance at accepting your word, but there is a lot at stake here, and I have to be very careful before proceeding with this. I've decided that things should go ahead as planned. I have informed Homeland Security to contact Able Chemical and tell them that they can resume production."

"Thank you, Mister President, I promise you won't regret this." Tina and I were invited to stay the night at the White House and to join the President and First Lady for dinner. We were ushered to an extremely elegant room to rest and freshen up before joining our hosts for dinner. Tina and I are very humble people, and all this attention was very overwhelming.

We were flown home the next morning, and Tina and I hoped things would soon get back to normal. Carol called later that day, and she said that DVD orders were through the roof, over a million so far. "This might be a good time to tell you something," I said. "I made a deal with JK Sterling for you to get a one percent royalty on every DVD sold. I know that doesn't sound like much, but millions of pennies add up. Hopefully, you will make enough money off this and the next DVD to retire and have the social life you have been missing out on." There was complete silence on the other end of the phone, and then I heard her sobbing.

She said, "You are without a doubt the nicest man I have ever met." I thanked her and told her how much I appreciated her as well, and that she definitely deserved everything she was getting.

The news people were leaving Tina and me alone as we requested, but the tabloid paparazzi were relentless. Even after giving them several interviews and posing for a number of pictures, they still kept on coming. I would meet them outside our gate, and being mindful of the fact that they have a job to do, I tried to be very accommodating. Nothing was ever enough for them; they kept showing up unannounced, yelling at the house, and generally pissing me off. Since technically they were not on our property, the military guards at the gate couldn't do anything about them. I finally had to hire two security people to keep them away. Now, finally things were returning somewhat to normal. I had enough information to do a second interview, but I wanted to hold off for a while. I hadn't let Carol or anyone connected with *Hard Facts* know any details about my return trip to PW-1 and Ar-Z or the new gifts they had given me.

CHAPTER 7

THE RETURN TRIP AND INTERVIEW #2

It has been about a month since *Hard Facts* aired, and things were back to normal. I wanted to do a second interview before the FSS (Fire Suppression Sphere) hit the market, so everyone would know what it was, and where it came from. I phoned Carol, who had been anxiously waiting to hear from me. I informed her I was ready to do a second interview, and she was *thrilled*. She made the usual arrangements, and soon Tina and I were in a corporate jet on our way back to New York. Carol and Meg met us at the airport, and we were soon on our way to the hotel. Carol informed me that the Food Formula was to hit the market tomorrow; I was thrilled, knowing this was going to help so many people.

DVD sales of the first interview had topped one hundred million, and there were orders for another one hundred fifty million; things couldn't be better. Royalty checks are paid quarterly, so we were both in for a very nice payday.

Usually, Carol is ninety percent business, but this time she was almost giddy; it was wonderful to see her so happy. I knew that when all this was over, she would be able to retire and become more involved with her family. She had confided in Tina earlier that she felt she had put her career ahead of her family and had regretted it ever since.

Tina and I had so much going on at home now that we didn't want to stay in New York any longer than we had too. We were going to start the taping the next morning, but there were three days of recordings to go through rather than the four hours previously. Since I am the only one who can operate the disk, I knew Peter and I would be spending a lot of time going over all of them and selecting the ones he wanted to air. We settled in at the hotel, had a nice dinner, and went to bed. We arrived at the studio early, around 7:30 a.m. the next morning, and met with the usual folks. Peter informed me they had worked out a few bugs, and this taping should go more smoothly than the last.

We got started almost immediately after I previewed part of the recording for Peter. Joyce gave the usual audience greeting and program identification, then introduced me and started with the interview.

"First of all, Ral — welcome back."

"Thank you, Joyce; it's wonderful to see you again."

"I understand the Ar-Zians have made you their guest again; please tell us all about it."

I reminded Joyce and the viewers that the Ar-Zians had told me last time they would send me an Orb with all the pertinent information about my return trip. "I wanted to capture that Orb on tape, so I set up a camera in the hallway of our home. One morning as I was walking to the kitchen to get some coffee, the Orb appeared. It was bluish in color and about the size of a grapefruit; 'Greetings, Ralph Diamond,' a voice said. I knew if I answered, the message would start playing immediately, and I would miss capturing the beginning. I quickly turned around and started the video camera then walked in the direction of the kitchen again. 'Greetings, Ralph Diamond,' came the message again. I knew it was Overseer's voice, so I said 'Greetings to you as well, Overseer.'"

Joyce said, "Can we please roll that tape?"

Joyce and I watched the monitors, as both Overseer and Zo-L appeared in my living room. They were so life-like that you would swear they were real and not just recordings. Overseer said, "All preparations for the 'Ralph Diamond Jubilee' have been completed, and all that is necessary is your presence."

Zo-L asked if my wife and I would be available to be escorted to PW-1 in five Earth days from now, at this very time. It was currently 7:35 a.m. Thursday. He explained that he and the original Travelers would take us to PW-1, where we could stay as long as we wanted.

"Please feel free to bring whatever you would like to make your stay as comfortable as possible. The actual celebration will take place on day two of your visit."

The recording froze, and I knew this is where I was to respond. Since I didn't have anything important planned, such as rearranging my sock drawer, I said, "That time would be great." I thanked them both very much and said how excited I was to be coming back to see them, especially since I could share the experience with my wife.

The camera then returned to Joyce, who asked, "What did you and your wife do next?"

"Tina and I were trying to think of what we needed to take with us; how do you pack for a trip to another world? I didn't know this was going to be an open-ended invitation; now we not only don't know what to pack, but we don't know how much of it to pack either."

"What *did* you decide to take?"

"We figured, since they don't use electricity as we know it, hair dryers, curler sets, electric toothbrushes, etcetera, would be useless. They don't even have running water; in fact they don't use water for anything except recreation, so we probably should bring a case of that. I wasn't there long enough the first time to ask for anything to drink or need to use the bathroom. The Ar-Zians don't do either! I'm not even sure they know we have bathroom needs. This could be a very embarrassing trip; maybe we should pack adult diapers. We ended up taking our personal things such as grooming items, clothes, water, a bottle of Jack Daniels, and a twelve pack of Seven Up. Since they cured me of all my ailments, there was no need for me to take any of my medication. We wouldn't have to bathe, so no need for all that stuff; we actually took very little."

"What happened next, Ral?"

"Well," I said, "Tina and I were awake most of the night in anticipation of our trip. We got out of bed around 6:00 a.m. and started going over what we had packed. It's not like we can stop at Wal-Mart on the way if we forgot something. The most important things were our cameras; we had our usual ones and we purchased two more with four extra memory cards and battery packs. This was not just a once-in-a-lifetime experience; it was a once-in-an-eternity experience!"

"Did they arrive on time?"

"Exactly on time, and just as before, they recorded the entire trip for me." I reached into my neck and retrieved the disk, set it on the table, and turned it on.

Joyce had reminded me earlier that there would be new viewers watching this time, and I might have to explain things because they hadn't seen the first show. I told our new viewers how the disk worked, saying, "Let me set this up for you. Tina and I are sitting down watching TV, when all of a sudden Zo-L and Ra-L appeared right between us and the TV; I will start the playback there." I reached out and touched the outer ring and the recording began to play:

Tina was visibly startled as we both got up to greet them; she, of course, had never met either one. They both levitated and came toward us, arms spread in a welcoming posture. They wrapped around us, and it was a beautiful moment. I had almost forgotten that feeling of love that accompanied those hugs. We separated, and both Zo-L and Ra-L began looking around our house. Ra-L, especially, was flabbergasted by all the stuff in our home.

Now we're not hoarders — we have the same stuff as everyone else; but, remember, Ar-Zian domes only contain seven to ten permanent items, and that's it. I have at least ten items in the pockets of my pants alone. I didn't dare tell them about storage units people rent for all the excess items.

Both of them were familiar with Earth houses from Probe recordings, but neither of them had seen the inside of a house before. They first noticed the two acoustic guitars I keep next to the recliner where I was sitting. "What are these?" Zo-L asked.

I explained they were musical instruments and showed him how striking the strings caused them to vibrate producing music. He asked me to demonstrate how it worked. I played an old '60s instrumental called "Mr. Moto," and they were fascinated. They asked me to play another, so I played and sang my version of "Life in the Fast Lane" by the Eagles. They were intrigued, as they do not have music on their planets. They asked if I would please bring the guitar with me. I got the impression I was going to be exposed to a whole new audience. This was great because if I make a mistake, they won't know the difference.

Still looking around, Ra-L asked, "How many people live here?"

"Just Tina and me," I answered. "Why do you ask?"

"I see there are so many places to sit."

"Yes." I said "From time to time we have family or company come over for dinner or just to visit."

"Speaking of food," Ra-L said, "what do your people eat?"

They followed me into the kitchen, and I opened the pantry door and said. "This is where we keep canned food and non perishable items, which will last for years if unopened." Next I opened the refrigerator door. "This is where we keep the perishable items, things that will go bad if not kept cold; they will last a week or more." I then opened the freezer section and said, "This is where we freeze food, and things kept in here will last for months." The look of amazement and confusion on their faces was priceless.

"What is this large box for?" she asked.

"That is an oven," Tina replied. "That is where we cook some of our food; it is used for large items that require an hour or more to cook."

"Why are there two?"

Tina answered, "That allows us to cook another item at a different temperature or something that might require a different amount of cooking time."

Zo-L pointed at the range top and asked what it was used for. I turned on one of the burners, and they were both startled when the gas ignited into a flame. I grabbed a frying pan from the cupboard and placed it over the flame. I added a little olive oil and broke an egg into the pan. They both just stared at the pan as the egg cooked; they were fascinated.

"Is that the only thing you would eat for a meal?" Ra-L asked.

I opened the freezer and pulled out a package of bacon and told her we would probably fry a few pieces of this to have with our eggs. Then I put a piece of bread into the toaster and pushed the lever down. I pointed to the silverware in the drawer, the butter in the refrigerator, and the jam on the counter. I further explained that when everything finishes cooking, we would take the bread, spread some butter or jam on it, put all the items onto a plate, grab a fork and knife, and sit down and start eating.

"Why don't you just eat things as they are? Why do you have to cook them?" Zo-L asked.

155

"Some things are not safe to eat raw; you have to cook them thoroughly to prevent becoming ill," I explained.

"What are these items made from?" he asked.

"The egg is from a bird called a chicken, the bacon is from an animal called a pig, and the bread is made from grains grown in the ground." Ra-L noticed several pictures on the wall behind us of our beloved dog Pudd. She was a longhaired Chihuahua who recently passed away — We had her for sixteen years.

"Is this one of the animals you eat?" she asked. Tina had to turn her head to hide the look of horror on her face. I explained how some animals are used for food and other animals people keep as pets, and they are considered part of the family. Tina began to cry, missing Pudd terribly. Not having any animals on their planet, they didn't really grasp the whole concept. They had seen several animals in some of the recordings taken by the Probes they had sent to investigate our civilization, but they had no idea what they were used for.

I then showed them the microwave and toaster ovens; they were now completely confused. I opened the freezer and removed a container of ice cream, I grabbed four bowls and spoons, and we all sat down at the breakfast table. I dished each of us all up a little bit, handed them a bowl and spoon, and said: "Try it." They watched Tina and me and did as we did. They have never had anything cold in their mouths and weren't sure what to expect.

I said, "Just let it melt in your mouth, and you will taste the flavors." They both had smiles on their faces and really seemed to enjoy the experience. Tina handed *each of them a Reese's Peanut Butter Cup, saying, "You're going to love these." They both asked if we could bring some with us to eat, and also to have the Research Center see if they could replicate the flavor. . . . We were happy to oblige.*

"Where do you get all these items?" Ra-L asked.

Tina answered, "There are large buildings called supermarkets where we go about once a week to buy the items we want, and then bring them home." They both wanted to know what we did with the bowl and spoon when we were finished.

I pointed to the dishwasher and said, "We put all the dirty dishes, cooking pans, and whatever else needs to be cleaned in there, and the machine washes them all at one time. When they have been cleaned, we remove them and put them away." They looked at each other in disbelief at how much effort went into such a simple thing as eating.

"Let me see if I understand what you are telling us," Ra-L said. "First you go to a supermarket building, get the items you want to eat, take them home, store them, later select items, figure out where and how to cook them, put them on plates, eat them, wash the items used to cook and eat them, and then put them away?"

"Yes," Tina said with a frustrated look on her face. The whole thing sounded pretty ridiculous, hearing it from someone else. They wanted to see everything, as this was a new experience for the two of them. They noticed all the different types of lighting and asked why we needed more than one type of light.

I didn't have a real good answer, but said, "Most of the lights are for aesthetic purposes. They all put out light: some a little, some a lot . . . mood lighting if you will."

"Do you have to turn on each light individually?"

"Yes," Tina answered.

"The globes or tubes that put out the light — do they last forever?" Ra-L asked.

"No," I said. "You have to replace them after a thousand hours or so."

"So you have to keep extra bulbs and tubes of each type on hand?"

"Yes," I said. I got the feeling we were not coming across as being very intelligent. I sure hope they understand that everyone does this not just us.

"Why all the plants inside the house? Aren't there enough outside?"

"They are not real," Tina said. Now Zo-L and Ra-L were totally confused; Tina and I just smiled and moved on to the bedroom. On PW-1 there is only a mattress on the floor and nothing else in the entire room. As we entered our bedroom, they were surprised by all the other stuff in the room including another TV. . . . This is the fourth one. By now they had so many questions, I think they both thought we were just crazy. When Tina opened her closet door that was the last straw.

"What is all that?!" Ra-L exclaimed.

"Those are some of my clothes," Tina replied.

"Why so many?"

"Different occasions require different attire."

"What do you do with them after you wear them — do you throw them away?"

Tina replied, "I put them into the washing machine to clean them for the next time I will wear them."

"Is that the same machine you put the dishes in?"

"No," Tina said. "There is a separate machine for that — in fact two machines, one to wash the clothes and one to dry them. Some clothes require what is known as dry cleaning; we have to take it to a special place to have that done."

Picking up one of Tina's shoes, Ra-L asked, "What are these for?"

"We wear them on our feet for protection and style," Tina replied.

"Why so many and what is style?" Ra-L asked Tina.

I thought to myself, I have been wondering that for years now. . . . This should be good. Tina began to tell her how everything should complement each other in color and style. Ra-L pointed to a purse and asked what that was for. Tina said, "We use that to carry our makeup, lipstick, a wallet, and anything else we wish to have with us when we go out."

Again, came my favorite Ra-L question: "Why so many?" I love this woman!

Zo-L asked, "How long do these things last?"

Tina answered, "A few years, but they can go out of style before then, and I would throw them away or give them to charity."

"With all these things in your house, does anything require maintenance?"

"Practically everything," I answered. "This floor covering will last about fifteen years, the walls need to be painted every ten years, and the towels, sheets, and blankets need to be cleaned and eventually replaced on a regular basis. All the appliances also need to be maintained or repaired periodically. The cars, electrical,

plumbing, and just about everything require maintenance and that doesn't even take into consideration
cleaning everything."

"With such short days, how do you manage to take
care of everything?"

"It can be a challenge; thankfully, now we are both
retired," Tina replied.

"What does that mean — retired?"

I answered, "The people that work at your Research
Center are just a very small percentage of the total
people on your two planets, less than one- millionth of
one percent. On Earth nearly everyone works for about
one-half their lifetime, then they retire, which means
they no longer have to go to work. Tina used to be a
teacher, and I repaired copy and duplicating machines."

Ra-L asked Tina, "What would a typical day be
like before you retired?"

"First, I get out of bed, have some toast and coffee,
and get ready to go to work. That would involve
washing my face, brushing my teeth, putting on my
makeup, curling my hair, selecting something to wear,
getting into the car, and going to work. After eight
hours, I would return home, get into something more
comfortable to wear, and begin to make dinner.
Usually, there are chores to do such as vacuuming the
floor, doing the dishes, washing and ironing clothes,
making a grocery list of things to buy, and any number
of other things."

"When do you have time for fun?" Ra-L asked.

"Usually on the weekends. We work five days and
have two days off.... Those are fun days, although not
if there is maintenance to do or things to shop for,"

Tina replied. Both Zo-L and Ra-L were dumbfounded at what complicated and busy lives we lead.

"You mentioned 'car'. What is that?" Ra-L asked.

"Come into the garage, and I will show you."

I pointed to one of our two cars, and we all got inside. "This is how we move from one place to another when it's too far away to walk."

"How fast do you go in this?"

"About fifty miles per hour on average," I said. I thought to myself, "I am explaining how we get around at fifty miles per hour to people who can travel the universe instantly. They move around their planet without the assistance of any form of transportation; if they don't start laughing I will be very impressed at their restraint."

We walked outside, and they saw a plane go overhead. I explained what that was, and how it worked. ...I don't think they were terribly impressed. I figured since we were already on the subject of travel, I would be bold and ask them how they managed to move so freely on their planets without the aid of any vehicles whatsoever. Zo-L began explaining the whole process to me, and I didn't understand a single thing. The physics involved were so far ahead of anything we could even dream of.

When he finished I said, "Got it."

We all laughed and Ra-L said, "Good one."

I took them into the game room and showed them around; they were particularly interested in the pool table. They asked me to show them how it was played, as they do play games on PW-1. I racked up the balls, and Tina and I played a shortened game of eight ball, explaining the rules as we went along. I asked if they *would like to try playing a game; they agreed and I racked up the balls again.*

Zo-L and Ra-L looked at the rack, selected the balls they each wanted, and using their minds moved them immediately into the pockets; it took about one second. He looked at me and said, "Gee, that was fun!" If they think this is a simple game, I wonder how they would feel about golf.

I told Zo-L I had something I wanted to give to Overseer, and to him and Ra-L. I wasn't sure what the proper etiquette would be, and I didn't want to embarrass myself. I showed him two identical boxes, which contained the same items. Holding up one of two DVDs, I said, "This contains recordings of something we call the encyclopedia; it will explain a great deal about our civilization. This other DVD is all about the animals on Earth; you can watch these on this device called a portable DVD player. This last item is the Holy Bible," I said. I gave them the New Testament only, thinking the Old Testament is pretty violent, and I imagine they consider us barbarians already.

He explained there was no such thing as proper etiquette in their society, nor jealousy, envy, or having your feelings hurt by someone else. He said, "The first thing Overseer will do is make the recordings available to everyone."

I handed him one of the boxes and said, "Please accept this as a small token of our appreciation and respect for both you and Ra-L." We all hugged, and they said how much they appreciated it. Tina and I were very relieved, as we had been racking our brains for days, trying to think of something to bring the Ar-Zians.

Now there was the matter of a personal situation that Tina and I were very concerned about. I took Zo-L into my bathroom and hoped he would know what I was about to show him was used for. Thankfully, as I pointed at the toilet, he said, "Not to worry, we have set up something for you and your wife to use." He told me after they brought me back to Earth that they sent several Probes and Orbs here to learn as much as possible about our culture, so we would feel at home during our visit. . . . I should have known as much.

The time had come for us to depart and instantly the four of us plus our luggage were onboard; the crew seemed very happy to see Tina and me. Zo-L gestured toward my wife and said, "This is Ralph Diamond's wife, Tina Diamond." I thought I recognized the crew members from the last trip, but since they all look nearly exactly alike, I wasn't sure it was them.

Sensing my unease, Zo-L said, "You probably remember the other Travelers, but I don't think you were ever properly introduced." They each stepped forward one by one and stated their names, then gave both Tina and me a hug. Their names are so unusual that I knew Tina might not be able to remember them; I figured with the brain enhancements they gave me, I would. I asked them if they would give Tina a group hug, so she could feel that love sensation that increases with additional people. They did, and Tina became very emotional.

This ship was much larger than the one I had been on board the first time. Tina's eyes were open wider than I had ever seen before, trying to take in the wonder of it all. As before, the ship went from transparent to opaque then back again, and we were on PW-1, just outside a second dome right next to Zo-L and Ra-L's. I warned Tina about the gravity and atmospheric differences, so she wouldn't panic when she had difficulty breathing. They let the outside air in slowly so we could more easily adapt. We exited the ship, and Zo-L noticed a group of people off in the distance, too far for Tina to see. He seemed to be in communication with them mentally, and he turned and asked me if it was okay for them to meet us. Tina and I immediately said, "We would love to meet them, and they suddenly appeared before us." It was great! There were about twenty-five of them, and I could tell they were very curious about us, particularly our hair, height, and dress . . . all the usual stuff. As always, they do everything so quickly it was over in a flash.

Zo-L handed me a small spherical container and said, "They have each brought you some of those rocks your people seem to be so fond of."

I turned to Tina and said, "He is speaking of gemstones." Tina said, "Tell them thank you very much for us — would you please, Zo-L?"

He pointed toward the new dome. "This is for you and Tina. We have made some changes, and I hope you will find them acceptable. You needn't worry about your clothes or other accessories disappearing this time. The belongings you brought with you are already inside. Please enter and get settled, then come over to our dome whenever you are ready."

As we walked toward the dome, Tina asked, "Where's the door?"

"There isn't one." I answered. "Just follow me." I walked through the outer skin of the dome, and Tina followed. The instant MID sensed someone had entered,

Tina's makeup, lipstick, and hair spray disappeared. She had not noticed it, as we were both flabbergasted by what we were looking at. Our entire house was sitting right in the center of the dome.

"Oh my gosh!" Tina exclaimed. "I don't believe it!" There were no doors or windows, as it was a house within a house. We walked inside, and everything was exactly the same as our house on Earth. It was completely illuminated with the same lighting that filled the dome...not a shadow anywhere. Out of force of habit, I reached for a light switch and tried to flip it on. ... It wouldn't move. I went into the kitchen and tried to open the refrigerator, but it was a facade as well. Since there is no electricity, as we know it, they would not have worked anyway.

"How did they do this?" Tina asked.

"I have no idea; I think they are able to do absolutely anything." Tina looked into the mirror in the hallway and let out a sigh; I knew she had discovered her new look. Trying to get a chuckle out of her, I turned to MID, shook my finger at it, and said: "Bad boy!" I think the darned thing was trying to understand me, as it made a few peculiar noises.

I felt so badly for Tina; she had her hair done the night before and was being very careful not to mess it up. I was still holding the container Zo-L had given me as I sat down at the dining room table. "Come here," I beckoned. "This will cheer you up." She sat down beside me, and I showed her the sphere-like container, which was about three inches in diameter.

"How do you open it?" she asked.

"I haven't got a clue," I answered. I looked everywhere for a cap or door or anything that might indicate how to open it. ...There was nothing. I set it on the table, and with one finger touched the top of the sphere. A small hole appeared at the top, which opened rapidly until it just reached the top of the gemstones inside, and then it stopped. The sphere was filled with diamonds, rubies, emeralds, sapphires, and gemstones we had never seen before.

"Touch it again," Tina said. I did and it closed back up. ...We were fascinated. "Let me try," Tina said. She rolled it around on the table, and then touched it as I had done, but it would not open. After several tries, she handed it back to me, and I was able to open it each time I tried.

"This must be like the disk," I said. "It's tuned only to me." It didn't seem to matter what position it was in — it always opened at the top. We played with it for quite a while, like two little kids playing with a ball for the first time. We poured the contents out on the table. ...They were striking.

Tina had worked in her parents' jewelry store for many years before we met, and she was very familiar with gems, both precious and semi-precious. She separated several unusual ones and said, "Look at these, Ral. We have nothing like these on Earth. I have never even seen colors like these before; they must be worth a fortune!"

"No doubt," I replied.

As with the last group of gemstones I was given, the sphere that holds them is made of some type of extremely lightweight indestructible material; this would be very useful on Earth. "What do we do now?" she asked.

"Well, there is no sense in redoing your hair and makeup, so let's open the bottle of Jack we brought and have a drink to toast our new ... well, everything!" I went to the kitchen to try to retrieve a couple glasses. Our cupboard doors have glass inserts so I could see all our glasses inside. The door however wouldn't open, and the glasses weren't real anyway. Fortunately, Tina had thought to bring some plastic cups. There is no such thing as ice on PW-1, so we had to drink the Jack and Seven at room temperature. We walked out of the house and into the dome to enjoy the view outside. I tried to summon the two chairs with my mind, but couldn't. I was, however, able to grab them and pull them over near the edge of the dome. Tina was very apprehensive about trying to get into a chair that was far too small, and floating in mid-air. ... I wasn't too crazy about the idea either.

"Well," I said, "I'll try it first; if I get hurt I'm sure the Ar-Zians can fix me." I handed my drink to Tina and held the side of the chair and slid into it. Just as before, the chair expanded and hugged every curve of my body. "Your turn," I said.

Tina was still a little apprehensive, and after all, the chair has no legs. She handed me our drinks, and she was able to sit down as well. "That is absolutely amazing, how can it do that?" she asked.

"Like almost everything else here, I haven't got a clue," I said. It was so beautiful outside; we were mesmerized.

Tina said, "Look how clean everything is; there's no graffiti, no litter — there isn't so much as a dead leaf on the ground.

"A far cry from our planet, huh?" I remarked.

Tina said she needed to use the bathroom, and asked what she should do. I told her that Zo-L said it was taken care of. We got off the chairs and walked back into our house toward her bathroom. The toilet looked exactly like the one at home, except there was no water in the bowl and no toilet paper. "What should I do?" she asked.

"Just go, and I will try to find something you can use for toilet paper." I looked around our house for something, but everything was just a facade. The rolls of toilet paper on the shelf in the utility room were just shells. As I continued looking, Tina came out of the bathroom and said, "You're not going to believe this, but everything just disappeared before it even hit the bowl, and afterwards I was perfectly clean. ...We have got to get one of those!"

Peter yelled, "Cut! That's it for today people." Everyone was very disappointed, even though we hadn't had a break in hours. As everyone left, Peter and Carol came over to me, and he seemed very frustrated.

"What's the matter, Peter?" I asked.

He said, "I have to figure out how to take three twenty-four-hour recordings and turn them into one two-hour special. Everything you have shown so far has been incredibly interesting, I wouldn't cut a thing!"

"There are places that are pretty mundane," I said, "but on the bright side, the DVDs will have to be a box set this time."

Peter said, "You realize that I have to watch the entire recording — don't you?"

"I do," I replied, "but I don't have to be awake during the entire process."

"What do you mean?" Peter asked.

"I have to be present, since I am the only one that can operate the disk — right? I was thinking, after dinner why don't you and your crew come over to my hotel room. I will start the recording for you, and I can rest while you guys take shifts watching."

"That's brilliant!" he exclaimed. "You are a genius!"

"No," I said, "I just don't want this to take any longer than you do."

Peter left, and Carol and I went back to her office where she broke out the old bottle of Scotch, and we toasted another day of shooting. Carol said that Tina and Meg would be late as they were engrossed in shopping, and asked if I would join her for dinner. Neither of us felt like going out anywhere, so we decided to just have dinner in the break room; the food there is excellent! We had a really nice talk, and she informed me that her ex-husband Parker had recently contacted her. They had spoken by phone on several occasions, and he indicated he would be coming to New York next month and wanted to get together.

"Are you going to?" I asked.

"I think so. I never did stop loving him; we just had no time for each other. He told me he was retiring, and wanted to buy a place in New York. I don't know if he would be interested in getting back together or not."

"Are you?" I asked.

"I would like that very much," she said. "Maybe when this is all over in a few months, I'll have enough money to retire, and we'll see what happens."

After dinner I went back to the hotel to wait for Peter, James, and Arnold. When they arrived, I started the recordings and pointed out several areas where there was nothing of real interest, and he would probably want to skip over them. I then laid down on the couch and listened to some music I had recorded on the new device given to me by Mr. Ling. Tina, Meg, and Carol were out for a night on the town, and I think Carol had much to celebrate. Peter nudged me awake a few hours later; he told me they were going to take shifts as I had suggested. He asked if I would start the next recording. I skipped over the boring stuff I had shown him earlier and found an interesting recording, started it, and went back to sleep. This progressed throughout the night, and we had accomplished quite a bit. When we all arrived at the studio the next morning, Peter knew exactly what he could skip, and what he wanted to capture. He was a happy camper, as the old saying goes.

DAY 2 OF TAPING

Joyce asked me to please continue with the recording.

Tina and I decided we were probably being rude to our guests and should go over and see Zo-L and Ra-L. We walked through our dome and into theirs. Before we could even say hello, Zo-L looked at Tina and apologized profusely. "I had not thought about the items you put on your skin and hair; I am so sorry."

"I told MID he was a bad boy, but I'm not really sure he understood me," I said.

Zo-L replied, "Good one," as he left to go have a talk with MID. Ra-L hugged us both and had their MID create two more chairs and arranged them in a small circle so we could chat. Tina was dumbfounded as two more chairs were rapidly being formed in mid-air and then flew across the room into a circle. Our two chairs increased in size as they drew near to us. When Zo-L returned, he informed us that the MID problem in our dome had been remedied. He also told us that NID was now set for our physiology and hoped we would enjoy the new experience. If you require more than NID serves you, just think or say, "Snacks. That is how you pronounce it — isn't it?"

I nodded in agreement, and he continued to say, "There are four containers of water on the shelf next to NID that MID will replace as they are used." He sat down with us, and we began to chat. After a few minutes, Tina and I looked at each other and burst out laughing. We both realized at the same time how incredibly ridiculous it was to be sitting in a dome on another planet, talking to two aliens as if we were at home talking with the neighbors. Usually, conversations are about things you have in common. . . . This was just the opposite.

Ra-L asked if it would be okay for a few family members to join us. "They are very anxious to meet the wife of the man who had saved the Travelers and to see Ralph Diamond again."

"We would be honored," Tina, replied. In less than five seconds, there were about forty people in the dome with us including children, all doing the happy dance.

It was so cool! One by one they hugged us, and thanked me in Ar-Zian for what I had done. I couldn't tell if this was the same group as I met last time or not. I also was wondering if Tina was concerned that she did not look as she had intended when meeting our newfound friends.

Everyone was particularly interested in Tina, as they had never seen such a tall woman. My wife is very attractive, and the fact she had no makeup on really didn't matter; no one knew the difference anyway. They were fascinated with the fact that she had hair, and that it went down to the middle of her back. She could tell everyone wanted to touch it by the way they were looking at her, but they were too respectful to ask. Tina pulled it around in front of her and gestured for them to feel it; they were really fascinated.

Zo-L whispered to me and asked, "Would you play a song for them on your guitar?"

"Sure," I answered, "let me go get it." In a split second, it was right in front of me; I almost forgot they could summon anything they wanted. All eyes were on me as I opened the case and removed the guitar. I was having trouble tuning it, as their atmosphere made the strings vibrate differently. When I finished tuning, they all did the whooping noise and the happy dance....They thought I was finished. Since I can now speak Ar-Zian, I told them that was not the performance, just the preparation.

I then played a few songs for them, and they were genuinely spellbound. They had never seen an instrument nor heard any music. As I finished each song, they went crazy; Tina got such a kick out of their appreciation. I ended up playing a half hour or so, and they loved it. I have been playing for over forty years, and I have never had a more attentive or appreciative audience. As usual, they disappeared almost as quickly as they arrived; Tina and I were kind of disappointed as we were having such a great time. After they left, Zo-L brought us an even larger spherical container filled with gems.

Tina said to him, "I don't think you understand how much these mean to us. They are worth a fortune on Earth, and with the money we get for them, we'll be able to help a lot of needy people." She was crying as she leaned over and embraced them both.

When they separated, Ra-L said, "I don't think you understand what a pain in the feet these things are. I have stepped on them many times, and they can really hurt. The fewer of them there are around, the better!" We all laughed. It really is amazing to think of the worth we assign to something as silly as a pretty rock!

Because the Ar-Zians learned a great deal about us from the Probes they sent to Earth in preparation for our visit, we actually felt right at home, as strange as that sounds. Tina and I were getting a little hungry and as usual our guests sensed it. Before we had a chance to say anything, they asked if we would like something to eat. "That would be wonderful," Tina said.

Zo-L told us that their NID was also set up to handle our nutritional needs. We walked over to NID, and I told Tina to insert her finger in the hole and remove it. As she did, it was fascinating to watch a small bowl being created right before our eyes. In just a few seconds it was filled with all sorts of small interesting morsels of various shapes and colors. As I was preparing to take my turn, I noticed something *outside. There was a beautiful canopy and four chairs being integrated just in front of the dome and nothing touched the ground.*

"I thought you might enjoy eating outside," Ra-L said.

As soon as everyone's meal was ready, less than a minute total, we walked outside. There was now also a table with two containers of water for Tina and me. Everything was just suspended in mid-air. . . . It was wonderful. Ra-L pointed to a grouping of plants about a hundred feet away and said, "This is the time of day they bloom."

As we continued to watch, the most beautiful flowers began to slowly open. They were huge, about three feet in diameter, and the fragrance they gave off was heavenly. Each flower was completely different from the others, even though they were on the same plant. They each had patches of color that changed continually.

"Those are the most beautiful plants I have ever seen," Tina said. We continued to sit, eat, and very much enjoy the company of our hosts. It was eerily quiet, which seemed very unnatural. There were no animal noises, no construction sounds, no traffic . . . nothing at all!

"These morsels are absolutely delicious," Tina remarked.

"I am so glad you are enjoying them," Ra-L said. "Just leave the ones you don't like in the bowl and NID will not serve you that flavor again."

Tina said, "This sure beats the heck out of the way we do it. Since you have no chores, nothing to shop for, and no maintenance to perform, what do you do all day?"

"Anything we want," Zo-L said. "When we finish eating, we will show you around PW-1 so you can get an idea of all the things there are to see here."

Tina has a real fear of heights, and if they were going to show us around the way they did me last time, locking arms and ascending some five hundred feet in the air, she is going to be scared to death. "Tina is afraid of heights," I said. Ra-L moved her chair over closer to Tina, extended her arm, and touched Tina's head with two fingers.

"Not anymore," she said.

"How do you feel, Tina?" I asked.

She said, "I really do think it's gone."

"Something like that would take months of therapy on Earth," I remarked.

We finished eating and Zo-L said, "Let's go in the house and get some traveling clothes on the both of you." We walked into the dome, and were asked to stand with our feet slightly apart, and our arms slightly away from our bodies. We were instantly nude, and then clothes began to take form on our bodies. Tina was a little embarrassed by the form-fitting nature of the clothing but was a good sport about it.

We all locked arms, with Tina and me in the center, and Zo-L and Ra-L on either end. We were instantly high in the air with the most incredible view of the neighborhood where they live. There is no air pollution on PW-1, and you can see forever. We could see trees with colors that resembled the fall in New England. Some trees had hundreds of different colors and others

175

only one. We traveled around the planet, stopping at a number of incredible sights including a few islands.

The Ar-Zians have imported thousands of exotic plants from numerous planets they have encountered through their "Mapping the Galaxy Program." There were beautiful meadows full of colorful plants and grasses, areas of gigantic trees hundreds of feet tall, and amazing waterfalls that descended slowly as the raindrops did. There were multicolored plants clinging to the surface behind them, and at night they glowed the most brilliant and amazing colors that danced through the waterfall. One island had trees with black trunks and limbs, with purple octagonal leaves about the size of your hand. The trees grow about fifty feet high, then the limbs stretch out and arch down to the ground, where they root and create another tree. Eventually, they form a never-ending series of tunnels.

On another island, there were plants and trees that were lighter than the atmosphere with only one thin root acting as a tether to the ground. They swayed back and fourth, undulating with the slightest breeze. . . . It was all so unreal.

We arrived back at the dome, and I told our guests that Tina and I might have to take a break and nap for a while. We thanked them several times for being such wonderful hosts and went back to our house to lie down.

Peter yelled, "Cut! That's good for today, guys. Great job. Thanks, everyone." He turned to me and said, "It's 5:30 p.m. now; we'll see you around 7:00 p.m. at the hotel — okay?"

"That will be fine," I said.

Carol walked me down to the lobby to meet Tina and Meg. "Are you up for another girls' night out?" Carol asked.

"Sure," Tina replied. "The boys are going to be working at the hotel anyway, so I might as well go out and have some fun."

Carol, Tina, and I went to dinner at yet another one of the hotel's fabulous eight restaurants. This one was Japanese; everyone there was dressed in traditional Japanese clothing, and the restaurant was masterfully authentic in every sense. Naturally, the food was to die for, and we all had more sake than was required. The girls took off, and I went back upstairs to await Peter and the others. I wasn't really looking forward to another evening stuck in my hotel room, but after all, I was being paid an absolute fortune for this interview. Besides, Peter and the other two, James and Arnold, were probably not even getting paid overtime. I felt badly that I was being such a baby about the whole thing, so when they showed up I greeted them graciously and pointed to a ton of goodies I had ordered from room service, and we got down to work.

DAY 3 OF TAPING

The next morning, the SBS building was all abuzz about the Food Formula beginning in distribution. It was all over the news, and my picture was on every TV we happened to see. The New York Stock Exchange had not yet opened, but it was expected to be a record day. The whole world seemed to be in a good mood, as one reporter put it. Carol asked me if I would mind doing a short interview with their news department.

"I would be happy to," I said. "After all, I had been waiting for this moment to arrive for a long time now."

Carol escorted me down five floors to the SBS News headquarters office and introduced me to Angela Bingham, the morning news anchor.

Angela introduced me, and then asked the usual questions you might expect. After all, everyone was very familiar with the Food Formula by now; it had been on the news nearly every day for months. She asked, "Is there anything new with the Food Formula you can tell us about?"

"Actually, yes," I said. "We are working on a dry formula that can be used to coat seeds, which would then be encased in a gel cap or some other water soluble envelope. This would allow us to drop them into burn areas to begin growing the next rainy season. This could be used for reforestation or simply to cover burned hillsides, thus preventing mudslides. Tests so far have been promising."

"Wow," she said. "Anything else?"

"We have been trying to come up with a way to replant areas that have been deforested due to the need for firewood or to bare the ground for agricultural usage. As you are aware, deforestation is a major problem in many parts of the world. We are experimenting with biodegradable cones that would be filled with water. Coated seeds indigenous to the region to be reforested would be placed over a thin membrane suspended above the water. This would all be wrapped in a very thin biodegradable covering, so that thousands of these cones could then be dropped from a plane or helicopter. The idea is that when they hit the ground, the cone would bury itself a few inches into the soil, the membrane will break, and the seed will fall into the water and begin to germinate."

"That sounds like a very ambitious plan — do you think it will work?"

"Yes, I do. I think it is just a matter of finding the right materials."

"Aren't you kind of letting the cat out of the bag? Now that others know what you are trying to accomplish, aren't you afraid others will try to steal your idea?"

"I hope someone does," I said. "This is not about making money; it's about helping mankind."

"I know you have to run," Angela said. "Thank you very much Mister Diamond for taking the time to talk with us."

Carol and I went back upstairs. We entered the studio, where everyone had been watching the interview while getting ready for today's taping. Joyce introduced me, and we began where we had left off:

Tina and I awakened from our naps a couple of hours later and went back to Zo-L and Ra-L's. We sat down and began discussing the Galaxy Mapping Program. He asked if Tina and I would like to see some recordings of what they had discovered so far. We were very excited, as this would be something no human being had ever seen before.

We were all sitting in the center of the dome when Zo-L instructed Life Center to begin with a trip around the galaxy. We were completely surrounded by stars in every direction, as if we were just suspended in space. It was a very uncomfortable feeling at first; we thought we would fall into oblivion.

We began to rise up at a phenomenal speed to where we could see our entire galaxy. The Milky Way has seven distinct arms, a fact no one on Earth is aware of. We began to circumnavigate the galaxy, flying completely around it in a matter of about ten minutes. Zo-L explained that the Probe taking the recordings traveled one light year, took a series of recordings, then another light year and so on. It took 218 days to complete the journey. We ended up where we started, directly over our little place in the galaxy.

"Earth is sixty-nine percent of the way out from the center on arm number four," he explained, "and Ar-Z and PW-1 are a bit closer. The total size across the galaxy is 118,409 light years from tip to tip of the longest arms. To put that in perspective, one light year is 5,865,696,000,000 miles."

He pointed out the narrow slice of the galaxy they had mapped so far. It amounts to approximately .386 percent of the entire galaxy. Using the information we have gathered in that slice, we can surmise there to be about 387,468,321,889 stars and 895,776,274,064 planets. He began to take us through that mapped slice and show us what they have discovered so far.

We saw recordings of a tiny frozen planet, which orbited a large blue star. The hottest stars in the galaxy are blue, because they are larger than red or white stars. To be a blue star it must be at least three times larger than our own sun. Even if it were hundred times the size of our sun, it would still appear blue. The planet has an extremely large orbit, putting it very far away from its sun, and that's why it is frozen. Beneath ten miles of frozen water, the Probe discovered a vast ocean covering nearly the entire planet. Using a special application Probe, they were able to enter the ocean underneath, where they discovered forms of life previously unknown.

They were very small translucent animals that lived together as a colony. They emit their own light, and each colony appeared to be a different color and shape. When they detect danger, they break apart into millions of individual segments, and their luminescence extinguishes. There were larger animals, which vaguely resembled fish, but without eyes or fins. They had a ridge on top and bottom of their long thin body that undulated to achieve motion.

Zo-L pointed out twelve planets that had civilizations on them, but we never got close enough to any of them to see what they were like. I know that they must have visited those planets, as that is the whole purpose of the mapping process. I could sense he did not want to divulge that information, although I'm not sure why, so I didn't ask.

He showed us several planets from which they had taken vegetation samples for use on PW-1 and Ar-Z. He switched to a recording of a particularly interesting planet taken by one of the mapping Probes. There were no humanoid-type life forms, but there were many strange animals. "The gravity is 3.78 times that of your Earth," he said. "That is why the animals are so strange looking." Nearly all of them were built low to the ground and had really stout legs, kind of like an elephant but much shorter and with a smaller body. They all seemed to be herbivorous with plenty of vegetation around to eat. The planet was tropical in appearance, but the plants were far different than Earth or even PW-1 and Ar-Z. They were like the animals, low to the ground with large trunks or stems, and low-hanging branches and leaves. There were lots of rivers and ponds around — really quite beautiful in its own way.

Zo-L turned off the recording and asked if I would like to see if I was able to operate Life Center. He thought with my mental enhancements it might be possible. We walked over in front of it and he said, "You will have to communicate in Ar-Zian, just think Ku, which means On, and see if it works."

Since I was given the ability to speak Ar-Zian as one of my enhancements, I was thrilled at the possibility of operating such an amazing machine. I repeated over and over "Ku" in my head, but nothing happened.

Zo-L handed me the headset and said, "You might need to actually make a physical connection with Life Center." I reached out and touched the shelf in front of it, and it illuminated. I was so excited. "Tell it to show you recordings of the mapping process," Zo-L said. As I did amazing images began to flood my brain with information; it was similar to when Ra-L had given me information about the Ar-Zians. Although thousands of images per second were bombarding my brain, I was able to make sense of it all.

One particular recording caught my eye; as I focused on it, I was looking at Zo-L. He could see the recording as well, but I again sensed a reluctance to share that information. I asked him anyway if it would be okay for us to view, and he agreed. We all sat down, and since physical contact had been broken between Life Center and myself, Zo-L had to start the recording.

It began with pictures taken by a Probe of a planet whose surface was frozen over. Information attained by the Probe indicated that there were buildings on the surface, as if it was inhabited at one time. The Probe circled the planet, recording everything in its path. It was discovered that the planet was gradually moving further away from its sun, and the surface had become too cold to inhabit. That was all the information they could retrieve at the time, so they moved on.

Many years later the Ar-Zians had developed a device that made it possible to look into and through objects to reveal what was beneath the surface. They called it an Electron Motion Impede, or EMI. It works similar to a strobe light — you know — the kind you see on dance floors that make people look as if they are frozen in time.

The principle is that if a light flashes quickly enough, it will appear to freeze the electrons orbiting the nucleuses of atoms, and they will appear to be invisible. Atoms are actually much different than I was taught in school. The pictures I remember seeing were of nuclei about the size of a ping-pong ball with the electrons orbiting about one inch above it. In actuality, if the nucleus were the size of a tennis ball, the electrons would be orbiting in a sphere five miles in diameter. An atom is actually 99.99999 percent nothing . . . unbelievable. Just imagine — everything in the universe is made up almost entirely of nothing. They seem solid because the electrons are traveling so fast, they appear to be an object. It is sort of like seeing the propeller of an airplane; at rest you can see all around it, but when the engine starts, it appears to be somewhat of a solid circle. Now if that propeller were spinning at millions of miles per second, it would appear to be a solid circular object.

The Ar-Zians also have a device that can reduce the electrons orbits closer to the nucleus, thus collapsing objects to a fraction of their original size and making them much more dense. They use this device to compress the ground, creating lakes and tunnels. They are able to depress an area on the surface of the planet as deep and wide as they want. Then, from the bottom of the depression, they can shoot a beam to the ocean or other water source, widening it into a tunnel of very dense material. This acts like a pipe, filling the lake; all this is done in a matter of minutes.

With the EMI onboard, the Travelers paid another visit to the frozen planet. They were now able to peer beneath the surface and began to see signs of more recent activity. The deeper they observed, the more recent the signs. At a depth of 350 feet beneath a frozen lake, they discovered what was left of the civilization that once lived on the surface. The inhabitants had to go deeper and deeper underground as the planet continued to move further away from its sun, becoming colder and colder. The Ar- Zians were able to return the planet to its original orbit and have monitored their progress over the years.

It took many years for the surface to thaw enough to become inhabitable again, and there is a huge celebration each year commemorating the first day they were able to once again set foot on the surface. They still have no idea how this miracle came about, so they attribute their salvation to God. I asked Zo-L why he was reluctant to share that information with Tina and me through the recording. He said, "Such acts of *kindness lose their significance if they are shown to others; it is like boasting. An act of kindness is its own reward."*

Zo-L turned off Life Center, and we all began to talk. I asked Zo-L and Ra-L about celebrations, such as the one tomorrow. "Are there others?"

"We used to have a celebration nearly every day; it got to be overwhelming. Our civilization has been around a long time, and there were celebrations for everything. We finally decided to eliminate them all; anyone wishing to know more about a particular event can find all the information on Life Center. The Jubilee tomorrow is a very special celebration, as it is the first in over 169,907 years. ... You have done a very special thing for us my friend."

"Will I be expected to make a speech?" I asked.

"Guests are just that...guests; nothing except your presence is requested. You are free to do what ever you like; after all, this day is all about you."

Overseer said, "We are planning to have this celebration every year, and we hope you will always be our guest of honor."

"Are you talking about an Ar-Zian year or an Earth year?" I asked.

"An Ar-Zian year...why?"

"That would be ten Earth years; we would probably only be able to make the next two celebrations," I said. Zo-L and Ra-L looked perplexed. "We only live about ninety-one years for a man and ninety-six for a woman; we are both sixty-eight years old now."

They looked at each other and became very sad. "We had no idea you lived such short lives," Ra-L said.

185

Zo-L went outside for a few minutes, and Ra-L composed herself and asked, "Do you die as we do?"

"No, we usually become weak and infirmed as we get older, or our organs begin to fail; it can take quite some time," Tina answered.

This was more than Ra-L could stand; she began to weep uncontrollably. Tina and I hugged her and said, "It's okay; that's just the way it is for us. Everyone hopes to die in their sleep; that's the best way to go." That was sure the wrong thing to say. Ra-L was almost hysterical now.

Zo-L came back into the room and immediately knew what the problem was. He comforted Ra-L and said, "I have great news! I have just communicated with Overseer, and he said, according to the Researchers who helped with Ral's health problems, they can extend your lifetimes by about a thousand years. How does that sound?"

Tina and I looked at each other with astonishment; we were absolutely speechless. "You don't have to make up your minds right now," he said. "Just think about it while you are here."

"Cut!" came the familiar cry from Peter; and we were done for the day. We did the usual after-taping routine. Carol and I had dinner together. Peter, Arnold and James came to the hotel room, and we previewed the recordings. These were some very long days for those guys, and I felt really badly for them. I spoke to Carol the next morning about the matter, and she said there would be some serious bonuses in the offing for everyone. ....That made me feel better.

CHAPTER 8

THE DAY OF JUBILEE

DAY 4 OF TAPING

Excitement was high as everyone couldn't wait to see what would happen next. Following the usual countdown, Joyce proceeded with the welcome and introduction. "Ral," she said, "you must be very excited to see that the stock market was up 548 points yesterday thanks to the Food Formula."

"Yes, that was a wonderful surprise. I had no idea it would go that high."

"It's your second day on PW-1 now," she continued. "Please show us what is in store for you and Tina." I reached over and started the recording:

It was early morning on PW-1, and Tina and I went outside to enjoy the sunrise. Because their atmosphere is made up of different gases than Earth, the colors are very different. Sunrise usually produces beautiful greens and blues throughout the entire sky, while sunsets are more in the purple, aqua, and yellow spectrum — Every day is totally different. I reminded Tina that the days here are thirty-two hours long, and that the jet lag we felt going from California to New York and back was nothing compared to what we were in store for here. We sat there for about half an hour, and then we got up and had NID fix us something to eat. We decided to go out for a walk while we enjoyed our breakfast.

As we walked around outside the dome, we happened to see Zo-L and Ra-L doing the same thing. We spoke briefly, and Zo-L asked if we would like to go on a sight seeing trip through the mapped portion of the galaxy. We noticed he had summoned a ship, which was sitting on the other side of their dome. We said a very enthusiastic, "Yes, please."

We hurriedly finished breakfast and went onboard the ship. I was very pleased to see the original crewmembers there, as they would be escorting us to Ar-Z for the Jubilee later that day. We all sat down, and instantly we were above the galaxy just as before while watching the Life Center recording in their dome. This, however, was the real thing, and we were absolutely thrilled. I want to show you something that is both interesting and upsetting; the name of the planet is La-Gon. We were immediately over a planet many light years away, and the ship became transparent as we descended through some clouds.

We could see there were many interesting structures coming into view. They were all pyramid-shaped but varied in height and width. They seemed to be made of a glass-like material but not nearly as reflective. They also varied in color from shades of blue and green to a smoked glass appearance. We were still quite high above everything as we continued to move over the surface of the planet. We spotted several large areas that looked like crop fields, but only a very small portion had greenery, while the rest appeared dead.

As we began to descend, we could see everything was in a state of chaos. Although the buildings looked new, the surroundings were filled with trash and dead vegetation with no people around. "What happened here?" I asked. "It looks as if it was a beautiful place at one time." Just then we saw a few people run quickly from one building to another.

Zo-L said, "This planet was very much like PW-1 in the not-too-distant past; they were a very spiritual and very blessed people. Everybody loved one another and life was good; then a terrible plague ravaged the entire planet killing nearly thirty-two percent of the total population. No one knows how it happened but everyone blamed God, since they had never had any catastrophes in the past. The people were grieving terribly and asked their spiritual leaders how God could let such a terrible thing happen to them; but there was no answer forthcoming.

"Grief quickly turned to anger and the people turned against their leaders, each other, and God. It was everyone for themselves, neighbor turned against neighbor, and family member against family member. They would steal what ever they needed to survive. . . . No one shared anything. They were now on a downhill slide from which there would be no recovery."

"Couldn't something have been done?" Tina asked.

"They could have overcome their situation early on, but they lost their faith. . . . Once you turn your back on God, he does the same to you. As the older people died off, the younger generations were not raised in a spiritual environment. They did not believe they would be held accountable for anything they did. There was no God to judge their sins, no afterlife, and no Hell. They did what ever they wanted to. . . . It was utter anarchy. No one had children, as that would take away from what meager food and possessions they had," Zo-L said. "This will be most likely be the last generation this planet will see."

"What will happen after that?" I asked.

"The structures will survive for many thousands of years, and I suspect eventually another species will re-colonize here."

"Wow," Tina said. "That is so sad!" As we continued to tour the planet we were all an emotional wreck. This reminded Tina and me of the apocalypse from the Book of Revelations in the Bible.

"On a happier note," Zo-L said, "I want to show you a planet I'm sure you will enjoy. We have named it R-T Diamond, representing Ralph and Tina Diamond." Tina and I looked at each other in wonder.

He continued, "Six-point-seven-six billion years ago, two smaller planets collided at a low impact speed, creating immense heat and pressure. Huge chunks of both planets exploded apart and eventually, over millions of years, gravity caused them to coalesce and cool into a single planet. Both planets were mostly carbon based, and now the new planet is comprised entirely of Zilians, better known to you as Diamonds."

That being said, we were suddenly over a large rocky planet consisting of extremely reflective multicolored surfaces made of solid diamond. Tina and I had our mouths completely open, as we tried to take it all in.

We flew lower over the planet, and there were diamonds of every imaginable shape and color laying everywhere like rocks and pebbles in a quarry. They *ranged in size from a grain of sand to gigantic boulders and everything in between. Zo-L explained that upon impact, the various minerals in the original planets mixed with the carbon producing diamonds in an incredible array of colors. There were entire mountain ranges that were one solid multicolored diamond ... unbelievable! I thought back to the $3,500 I paid for Tina's engagement ring, and tried to imagine an entire planet made of the same material; I don't think we have a number other than infinity to express what the value of this planet would be. Tina and I were literally spellbound!*

He took us to another part of the mapped portion of the galaxy, more toward the inside. We stopped near a cluster of small stars just a few hundred to a few thousand miles across. Zo-L said, "Look closely at the smallest one over there." As we did it got smaller and smaller and also whiter in color; then it exploded violently. We were expecting all the debris might hit the ship, as we seemed to be fairly close.

As the debris field expanded, it slowed down rapidly, stopped, and then fell back toward the star. Just then another one did the same thing. There were hundreds of these stars all exploding and reforming in a matter of minutes. Tina said, "This must be the popcorn cluster." We all laughed.

Zo-L explained that the gravity of these collapsed stars is so great, and compresses matter so quickly, that the immense heat and pressure generated causes them to explode. Then gravity brings it all back, and the process is repeated over and over again. I expressed my concern that some of the debris might hit the ship.

"The ship is protected by a disintegration beam, similar to the one used in the MID." This was all so cool; we were seeing things that no one on Earth had ever imagined. I could hardly wait to see how the scientific community would react to seeing all the wonders we were privy to.

Next we were over another planet that looked quite ordinary. There were oceans, lakes, mountains, and all the typical stuff you would expect to see. It seemed to be revolving at a very fast pace, so I asked Zo-L about that. He said, "The days are six hours long, and a year is sixty-seven days." As we went closer to the planet we could see things speeding around so fast you could not tell what they were. We went closer still, and we could see primitive buildings — huts, really. Tina and I were baffled.

"What are those things moving around?" Tina asked.

"Believe it or not, those are people," Zo-L said. "Time on their planet is greatly accelerated, although the sunlit portion of the day is only three-point-four hours long; to them it seems much longer."

I thought to myself, if I remember correctly, Einstein considered time to be the fourth dimension, but I don't remember him saying anything about it being capable of changing speed. We know that time slows down as you approach the speed of light, but this was something entirely different.

"Are there planets where time is slower?" I asked.

"We haven't discovered any as yet, but based upon this planet, we think there must be."

Our next stop was a planet that was stationary with two stars, or suns, orbiting around it. Zo-L said,

"The surface temperature here is 279 degrees and slowly rising because it is in constant daylight; surprisingly, there are primitive life forms here. The animal life lives underground and sleeps most of the time. They only come out occasionally to feed."

There was lots of vegetation on the surface, resembling a tropical jungle, only everything was steaming. "Life forms here are mostly reptilian and rodent," he continued. They didn't resemble anything Tina and I were used to seeing. The ones we did see were very light in color, probably to reflect the sun's rays.

Zo-L continued, "Most of them are herbivores; the rest are omnivores. They move very slowly due to the extreme heat, and as you can see there are no visible signs of standing water on the surface; it's all underground. Some of the reptiles are metallic looking, and the sun's rays will reflect off of them like a mirror. The rodents, on the other hand, have very thick fur for insulation, and the reptiles have thick octagon-shaped scales to help dissipate the heat." It was a very unusual place indeed.

We left that planet and entered into an area that was nearly totally void of stars. We approached an object from behind that looked like a small black hole; it was barely visible except for a faint circular outline. We started to move around it, so we could see what was on the other side. From the side it looked like a parabolic dish with a very faint stream of blue light emitting from it.

"It is called a Blue Ray Emitter; the stream of blue light you see are sub-atomic particles traveling at nearly the speed of light. When they come in contact with matter, they excite the electrons orbiting the nucleus of atoms and heat them up slowly. It is a perfect device to defrost frozen planets, comets, and etcetera. It can also be used to heat up an asteroid to the point that material will explode off of it, changing its direction — very useful if it is headed toward an inhabited planet. I wish we had known about these when we moved PW-1 into place; it would have saved a great deal of time bringing the planet to an optimal temperature."

"How are they formed?" I asked.

"They are a type of partially collapsed star; this is the only one we have discovered so far. I hope you have enjoyed your journey," Zo-L said. "We should head home now, so you and Tina can rest before the big Jubilee tonight."

"That sounds like a great idea," Tina said. We landed just outside our dome and we all went inside. Tina and I thanked Zo-L and the Travelers several times. . . . What an unbelievable experience! The Travelers were very anxious to see our house, so we gave them the grand tour. We couldn't really show them what everything was for, since nothing worked, but they got the general idea. We had NID make us all something to eat and sat down to discuss the upcoming Jubilee. I had a number of questions I wanted to ask Zo-L, but he beat me to the punch.

"We are supposed to arrive on Ar-Z just before dusk," Zo-L said. "I really don't know much more than that, but I'm sure Overseer has something really special planned, and I am really looking forward to it. As you know both Ar-Z and PW-1 are synchronized, so it is the same time on each planet."

Peter yelled, "Cut! Take lunch people." As everyone broke for lunch, Peter came over and sat next to me. "As I recall," Peter said, "nothing much happens at this point until you all leave for the Jubilee, is that correct?"

"Yes," I said. "Tina and I crashed for a few hours, and then walked around outside. We walked quite a distance and wondered why we didn't see anyone. It was so quiet and beautiful; we lay down under a tree and could smell so many different fragrances coming from the various flowers around us. We were so relaxed we actually fell asleep again. I don't think you want to include any of that."

Peter agreed. After lunch we resumed taping, and I started the next recording:

Tina picked up the present we had for Overseer, and we were on our way to Ar-Z. We were totally in awe of the situation and had to remind ourselves that this was for real. We were transported high over an unpopulated open area of Ar-Z, and up ahead we saw what looked like the largest tornado anyone had ever seen. It was several miles across at the bottom and rose and expanded many miles into the atmosphere.

Tina and I were very startled and asked, "What is that?"

"That is your welcoming committee," Zo-L said. "The entire population of both planets; 5,378,902,569 people are all here to see you."

I was totally astounded. The ship turned completely transparent, and we slowly descended through the center of the circle of people. They were lined up in rows one behind and slightly above the other, similar to the first time I saw the people at the Space Base. They were all doing the happy dance, and we were just amazed.

"How did they get all the people from PW-1 here?" I asked.

"We built a fleet of Ki, the people mover, as you call it."

"That must have taken forever," I said.

"It took several days to build the fleet and housing for everyone, and several more days to get everyone moved. Overseer gave the people of PW-1 the option to come here or to simply watch the recordings on Life Center. ...Everyone wanted to be here."

"This is absolutely the most remarkable thing I have ever seen," Tina said. I agreed.

We continued to descend until we were on the ground in the center of all those billions of people; it was mind numbing. Because the Ar-Zians have magnifying eyesight and amazing hearing, they were able to see and hear us as if they were right in front of us. As we all exited the ship, there was a thunderous roar, as they all leaned their heads back and yelled in approval. If they were facing us while they did that, the cumulative sound waves would have destroyed the ship and us.

Overseer came over and greeted us all individually. When it was my turn, I handed him the box and thanked him for such a glorious greeting. He made his way down the line, and the crowd reacted as he hugged each of us. Overseer turned toward the crowd and said, "It is with great pleasure I welcome you all here today, especially our good friend, Ralph Diamond."

He then played the now-famous recording of my helping the Travelers to a thunderous reaction from the crowd. He came over to me and whispered, asking me if I would like to say something. I nodded yes, and in Ar-Zian I said, "I am completely humbled by this incredible outpouring of love. I did nothing special to receive such a response. I pray that when the people on my planet see these recordings of events that Overseer has given me, they will see how wonderful life can be when people all get along. I can't begin to tell you the importance of the gifts your people have given to mine. They will save millions of lives on Earth; I am so indebted to all of you. . . . Thank you so much!"

Zo-L and the other Travelers all made short speeches expressing their sincere thanks for my help. The wives of the Travelers spoke next, starting with Ra-L. They all gave very emotional speeches that had the entire crowd crying. Since no one has died accidentally in over 125,000 years, we can understand why they were so appreciative. That is one heck of a safety record! Tina was originally going to say a few words, but she was too emotional to do so.

Overseer pointed to a small dome where a long line of hundreds of children exited; each was carrying a large hundred foot long colored flag. They immediately took flight in a large spiral upward in the center of the audience. They performed many synchronized maneuvers, creating numerous patterns with the flags changing colors in mid air. It was spectacular. They finished by creating a giant full color picture of me hundreds of feet off the ground and received an incredible ovation; it was very touching. Overseer then played a recording of me playing the guitar for Zo-L's family, and the crowd went crazy. I loved it! It was dark now, and Overseer had something really special for everyone.

He instructed the people to separate and lie on the ground facing the ocean. As they did several lights converged on a spot many miles off shore. A huge column of water dozens of miles wide rose out of the ocean and headed skyward. As the column rose, it began to atomize into a mist and continued to rise. As it reached up several miles, the mist began to freeze. Being backlit by the sun, it produced millions of tiny rainbows, which merged with other ones, producing larger rainbows and so on. ...It was so striking. The ice crystals began to fall very slowly until they melted back into a mist. The tiny droplets began to form into larger and larger ones producing prismatic colors covering the entire sky. I don't know how they do the things they do, but the smaller water drops began to fall faster than the larger ones. It looked like a giant multicolored waterfall coming down from the sky.

When the water had fallen back into the ocean, we could see four very large comets fly by very close to the planet, stopping just before they went out of sight. On the other side of the sky, four more comets came into view and stopped. One comet from the left and one from the right began to accelerate heading toward each other. When they were directly overhead, they collided. The explosion was breathtaking; the heat generated vaporized the ice and all other components of the comet into a gigantic steam cloud rapidly expanding in all directions. Illuminated by the sun, it was gorgeous. Two more comets began speeding toward each other. The make up of these two comets was different from the *previous ones and produced a wider variety of colors. Large chunks of them flew off into space and disappeared from sight. The third and fourth pairs were even more spectacular. The coupe de grâce was when two large asteroids came into view, one on each side of the sky.*

Zo-L said to Tina and me, "You are going to like this."

"I don't think we could be any more spellbound than we are already," I said.

Both asteroids headed on a collision course but much faster than the comets. When they hit, the resulting explosion was epic — it filled the entire sky. Gigantic pieces of glowing red-hot and white-hot fragments jetted out in every direction, many of them heading directly down toward us. Tina and I looked at each other, thinking something had gone terribly wrong. Just before the debris entered the atmosphere, Zo-L said, "There are ships with MIDs onboard that will reduce the size of those huge fragments to ones the size of your hand, and they will burn up in the atmosphere."

Just as he said that, the entire sky as far as the eye could see erupted into every imaginable color. The rare minerals and metals that comprised the asteroids produced the most beautiful fireworks show anyone had ever seen...including the Ar-Zians.

Everyone rose to their feet and gave Overseer a well-deserved ovation; it was almost deafening and lasted for several minutes. It is a good thing they were all able to adjust their hearing to lessen the volume; Tina had to cover her ears.

Overseer had one last ace up his sleeve, as he pointed to an area in the center of everyone. A huge

199

sculpture hundreds of feet high of the Travelers, their ship, the Oxygen tank and salt pellets, and myself suddenly appeared. It was made of one solid diamond from the planet they named after Tina and me. This particular diamond is comprised not only of carbon but a multitude of rare metals and minerals not found anywhere else. It is one thousand times harder than the diamonds found on Earth and is comprised of billions of small crystals inside, which reflect light off each other, creating millions of colors that seem to flash on their own. It was incredibly impressive. Zo-L whispered to me that they named that particular type of gem, the "Tina Diamond."

Overseer came over to Tina and me and said, "I have something for you and your people." He presented Tina with an animatronic version of our beloved dog Pudd. It was perfect in every way; neither of us could tell it was not her. Tina hugged Pudd and began to cry. He then handed me a small sphere, and said, "Zo-L will explain what this is for; it should help save many lives on Earth."

I couldn't utter a sound; this entire day was all about me, and I just stood there with tears running down my face as the crowd began to do the happy dance. All I could do was hug Overseer and then bow to the crowd."

"Cut! That's if for today. . . . Good job everyone!" Peter, Carol, and I had our usual pow wow; although there wasn't much to discuss, since we were nearly done taping. We went to dinner, and then the three of us went back to my hotel room. Peter had given James and Arnold the night off. There were only a couple

200

hours of recordings left to watch, and we all watched them together. When we were finished, we met up with Tina and Meg, who were a few drinks ahead of us. We were all thrilled that taping was nearly completed and Tina and I would be home soon; this was by far the most grueling interview yet. Tina and I made it back to the hotel around midnight and went right to bed.

DAY 5 OF TAPING

Today was going to be the last day of taping, and we were all very pleased. It should be a short day, followed by an evening of partying, and finally going home tomorrow. We arrived at the SBS building early, as I was scheduled to do another interview with Angela Bingham. The Food Formula had been distributed to several countries in the African continent, and SBS had reporters on the ground. They had been showing video of numerous distribution centers set up by the Peace Corps and the U.S. military a couple days earlier. Angela introduced me and began asking questions.

"Tell me, Ral, how were destinations selected to receive the Food Formula?"

I answered, "As I'm sure you are aware, the African continent has the most starving countries in the world, so logistically it was the best place to start. In countries where we felt it was safe, we delivered the Formula with Peace Corps and military personnel. In other countries we air-dropped barrels of the formula with detailed instructions in several languages."

Angela said, "We have some video that just came in showing the results of the Food Formula in a small village in Northern Africa, where starvation is very high and life expectancy is very low." The video showed people standing around several water barrels with corn and other produce growing out of them. The people were dancing around, cheering and chanting "USA, USA, USA." Many were waving the United States flag. It was very gratifying to know this was going to help so many people.

"What is the grander plan for the Food Formula?" Angela asked.

"We are hoping to distribute it everywhere it's needed, from Afghanistan to Zimbabwe. We are giving away the recipe and preparation instructions to any country that feels capable of reproducing it; otherwise, we will continue to distribute to them free of charge."

"Ral, is there any particular country whose reaction to receiving the Food Formula you are anxious about?"

"Actually yes," I said. "North Korea. As you know tensions are high between the U.S. and North Korea, and I hope the formula will be received in the manner in which it is given — strictly as a humanitarian gesture, and that no one tries to turn it into a political statement."

"What do you hope will be the final outcome of the Food Formula?"

"I hope hunger will soon be a thing of the past forever, and no child or adult will ever have to go to bed hungry again. I also hope that people will be more tolerant of one another, and we will enter into an era of world peace. When people are able to provide food for their families, they feel better about themselves and hopefully will feel better about others. I certainly don't believe this will make everyone love everyone else, but I pray that this will end conflicts between them."

"Thank you very much, Mister Diamond. I think I can speak for all of us when I say we certainly have those thoughts and prayers as well."

Carol and I went up to the studio to finish the last day of taping. After the countdown and introduction, Joyce said, "I'll bet that fireworks display will be the most spectacular thing anyone will ever see. I can only imagine what it must have looked like in person."

"Amazingly, the recording captured it pretty well," I said, "but, yes, we were all totally blown away."

"The planning that went into that must have been intense; do you know how many people were involved, Ral?"

"I don't know the total number, but the entire thing was the brainchild of Overseer. The real time-consuming part was finding comets and asteroids of the right composition to provide the most spectacular visual effects. Planning something on Ar-Z is much different than planning something here. Overseer can contact anyone on the planet instantly, and since he is in charge, the decision-making procedure is much simpler. Here we would have a committee deciding every aspect of the procedure, slowing things down and creating problems. There is an old saying I like that states, 'A camel is a horse designed by a committee'….I think that says it all."

"How in the world did they make that enormous sculpture? Is it really one solid diamond?"

"It is," I answered, "but I have no idea how they managed that; they can truly do anything."

"I have a personal question — I noticed both you and Tina were on the spacecraft and at the Jubilee for quite some time; what did you do when you had to use the bathroom, since there are no such things on either planet?"

"Zo-L added a special application to the mini-MID he carries with him. Tina and I had a secret signal we would use to let Zo-L know when we needed to use the bathroom. He would immediately create a Porta Potty of sorts and lead anyone who inquired to believe it was some sort of atmospheric chamber to aid in our breathing." He edited out all such occurrences to avoid embarrassing us when we showed the recordings here on Earth."

"What's going to happen next?" Joyce asked.

As I started the next segment of the recording, I said, "We will return to our home on PW-1."

Tina and I entered a smaller ship with Zo-L and Ra-L and returned to PW-1. The Travelers and everyone else returned to their homes on Ar-Z, and the fleet of people movers began returning all the residents to PW-1. We landed outside our dome, and almost immediately we could see several of the people movers traveling overhead. It is amazing to think that for a brief period of time, the entire planet was totally void of life. The four of us sat outside for a while, relaxing after what was a very busy day — especially for Tina and me. After a short visit, Tina and I excused ourselves and went into our dome. We each made a drink and just tried to take in all the events of the day. We were both absolutely exhausted, and yet excited at the same time. Thanks to my enhancements, I shouldn't have a problem falling asleep.

"Tomorrow we will be going home to Earth," I said to Tina.

"Isn't that a very weird thing to say?" she asked.

"What do you mean?"

"You said going home to Earth!"

I laughed and said, "I didn't even realize that's what I said ... that is weird!"

The next morning we had breakfast, and I said to Tina, "Let's go next dome and see Zo-L and Ra-L."

"Did you say next dome? Don't you mean next door?" she asked.

"There are no doors here," I said.

"Good one," she replied, and we went over to see our good friends.

As we entered and hugged each other, Zo-L asked, "Have you thought over the thousand-year life extension offer?"

"We have, and I can not tell you how incredibly kind you are to think of us that fondly.... However, we will have to decline."

"May I ask why?" he inquired.

"You remember the television sets I pointed out at our house? We watch different programs on that similar to your watching recordings on Life Center. Many years ago, there was a fictional program called *The Immortal* about a man named Ben Richards. He was a young, handsome test-car driver, whose life was turned into chaos when he donated blood to a worthy cause. Doctors told him that his blood is very unusual and contained antibodies that made him immune to all disease and even old age. His donated blood brought a billionaire back from certain death, but the miracle properties are only temporary."

I continued, "When the recipient learns of how he was given this blood, he offers Ben Richards anything he wants to keep him around for periodic blood donations. Ben agrees, but soon begins to feel like a prisoner. He eventually turns down the offer and must leave his life behind and go on the run to have any kind of normal existence. The billionaire eventually dies, and another wealthy person hires his faithful employee Fletcher, who is handsomely paid to find Ben Richards. Although this is a fictional story, it is exactly what would happen to Tina and me when word got out that we were living far beyond our lifespans. We would be sought after for blood samples, X-rays, and tests of all kinds to find out why we are immortal; our lives would be miserable."

I knew I had to tell Zo-L and Ra-L that we wanted to go home, but I was dreading it. I explained that Tina was having a difficult time adjusting to the thick atmosphere and the reduced gravity. I was doing fine since they had equipped me with the brain enhancements, which had many more applications than I realized. They were both very disappointed but understood completely. I had brought the sphere-shaped gift that Overseer had given me and asked Zo-L what it was for."

"Let's cut here," Peter said, and we all took a break. Joyce, Peter, Carol, and I went to the break room to discuss what the next logical step should be. They decided that Joyce needed to continue on with the interview to break up the recording.

We soon returned to the studio, and Joyce welcomed the viewers back to the show. She turned to me and asked, "What did Zo-L tell you about the new gift?"

I explained, "It's a small sphere able to be manufactured here on Earth that will extinguish any type of fire almost immediately. We are calling it the 'Fire Suppression Sphere' or 'FSS' for short. One two-inch sphere will put out a one-acre fire in a matter of seconds. When it reaches a certain temperature, it rapidly turns to a heavy gas that is drawn to heat, smothering the fire. The gas is non-toxic to all living things and dissipates rather quickly. The spheres can be dropped by plane or shot from a pneumatic cannon onboard a helicopter or fire truck.

"They can also just be placed in fire danger areas and will remain active for decades. I am currently working with Able Chemical to develop smaller ones, which can be placed in the home. The home version will have twelve spheres three-quarters of an inch in diameter, which will be encased in a small attractive cage. They would then be installed, one in each room of the house. The kit also comes with a one-inch drill bit, which allows the homeowner to drill a hole in the wall and pop in the cage. The whole kit can be installed in a matter of minutes and will sell for about twenty-five dollars."

Continuing, I said, "We are hoping that city fire codes will make installation mandatory and that insurance companies will want to pay for the kit themselves. I'm sure all commercial and public buildings will be required to install them as well. As with the Food Formula, I hold the patent and will receive royalties on every one sold. We are also working on versions for cars, airplanes, trains, boats, and trucks. The hope is that any fire caused by a crash will be extinguished almost immediately, saving countless lives and property. Larger spheres with lower activating temperatures can be placed in high fire danger areas to protect structures, wildlife, and, of course, human lives. We are also designing attractive stands with cages on top to be used outdoors as a decorative addition to any setting. You will simply push it into the ground, and your property would be protected. Tina and I are presently opening a charitable foundation called 'Ar-Zian' to distribute all the profits we make from the sale of the FSS; we should be able to help a lot on people."

Joyce then asked me to continue playback of the recording.

After several minutes of tearful goodbyes, Zo-L summoned a ship from Ar-Z to take us home. I wished we could have stayed there for several more days, but I remember the uncomfortable feelings I experienced when I came here the first time, and that was only for a matter of hours. Tina has been feeling that way for days now and only a short time ago mentioned it to me. The ship arrived within seconds, and we said our final goodbyes to Ra-L. Tina and I boarded and were back on our ranch in the blink of an eye. Zo-L teleported the three of us into our home, and we sat down at the kitchen table. I asked Zo-L if we could get him anything.

He responded, "I would love another taste of the ice cream you gave me the last time I was here."

Tina and I smiled at each other; we were thrilled to be able to do even the smallest thing for the man who had done so much for us and the people of Earth. We had truly formed a mutual admiration society.

Zo-L summoned a small Orb, which appeared on the table. "You can use this to contact me whenever you wish." He mentally placed it in another dimension and asked me to summon it. I mentally thought of the Ar-Zian word "Vo," which means "appear," and the Orb was back in sight.

"Once it appears, you can record a verbal message and say my name at the end, and it will come to me," Zo-L said.

Personally, I am still impressed by email, but this was phenomenal! Zo-L said, "I have also returned the items you loaned us; thank you again for your help."

As we shared one last hug, he said, "I will be in touch from time to time, and of course I will see you at the next Jubilee." With that he was gone.

"That's the end," I said. Peter yelled, "Cut!" and we took a short break.

When we returned Joyce continued the interview. "What did you and Tina do next?"

"We looked at each other with very mixed emotions, and we just sat there in silence for several minutes, trying to take in the whole amazing adventure."

TAKE AWAY

"How would you summarize your visits? What did you come away with?" Joyce asked.

"There were many things," I said. "I think one of the most important is that you cannot advance as a civilization until you learn to get along and love one another. We have spent trillions of dollars over time on weapons and war. Imagine if all that money had been used to foster lasting relationships with our enemies. By now we could be working together for the betterment of us all. Think what we could accomplish if we all worked toward a common goal. Secondly, we have nothing to fear from visitations of other civilizations. Anyone intelligent enough to come to Earth has solved their social differences and problems. They would have no ill intensions toward us, so we need not fear them. Presently, there are governments whose militaries have been ordered to shoot down any such visitors so as to reverse-engineer their technology for their own purposes ... usually evil."

I went on, "There have been visitors in the past that we have scared off by firing on them from the ground and scrambling jet aircraft to intercept them. We have always portrayed them in books and movies in a very unflattering light as evil and having come here to do us harm. What possible reason would they have to harm us? If they came here with evil intensions, they know we will fight back, so what would they gain? We have nothing here that isn't out there in the galaxy, free for the taking without opposition on asteroids, other planets, stars, comets, and so on. If we had welcomed them with open arms, there is no telling the advancements we may have had access to. We could all be living in paradise as the Ar-Zians do; instead, we have sabotaged our own advancement.

"With the mental abilities they gave me, I am able to surmise what they are thinking. I cannot read minds as they do, but I can tell what they feel. ... It's kind of a sixth sense. I know they wonder why movie stars and athletes make such ridiculous amounts of money rather than people who cure diseases, promote peace, or make incredible technological advances that help everyone. They also don't understand why we dislike people that are different by color, size, religion, or ethnicity. We are all made by God; if those people are good enough for him, why aren't they good enough for the rest of us? For a civilization to truly advance, you have to get to a point where the people truly care more for others than they do for themselves.

"Once upon a time, I was ashamed of being Italian because of all the terrible things the Mafia has done; now after seeing how the Ar-Zians live, I am ashamed to be a human being. I pray that these visitations I was allowed will make a lasting impression on all of us Earthlings, and we will learn what a wonderful life we could eventually provide generations to come. The last thing I often think of is this. What if on that July day, I had decided not to go with the Travelers to Ar-Z. None of this would have happened. What a blessing!"

Joyce said, "Thank you very much for once again allowing *Hard Facts* to bring your story to our viewers."

"It's been my pleasure, Joyce."

Peter said, "That's a wrap people," and there was a long round of applause from everyone in the room including me.

Carol asked for everyone's attention and said, "I want you all to know how incredibly professional I think you are and what a fantastic job you have all done. I know you have put a great deal of time after hours into this show, and there will be very nice bonuses for everyone." As the place erupted into a joyous mood Carol continued, "That's not all; I want everyone to go home and get some rest. Each of you including your spouses will be picked up by limo for a night on the town. We will first go to the Chaparral room for drinks, dinner, and some surprise entertainment, then on to Club 359 for more entertainment and dancing." Everyone was thrilled with the announcement, especially since it was Friday, and they would have all weekend to recuperate.

I was so thankful that we were done; the whole thing was very exhausting. Carol came over and gave me a great big hug, thanked me over and over for the things I had done for her, and invited me to come to her office. We sat down, and she brought out our old friend "Scotty," as we now referred to the twenty-year-old single malt scotch she kept for special occasions. As I was sipping my drink, Carol called Meg to let her know that taping had wrapped and tell her the plans for the evening. She handed the phone to me, and I spoke briefly to Tina, telling her I would meet her back at the hotel in about an hour.

I looked at Carol and said, "Please don't think I'm being nosey, but I consider you a friend and I was wondering where you and your ex, Parker, stand."

"I am proud to call you a friend as well, and even prouder to say that he has moved to New York, and we have been seeing each other for several weeks now. Thanks to you, I will be able to retire soon from the DVD royalties you set up for me. I do, however, want to see this whole story through to its conclusion before I retire....Is there more to the story?"

"Not right now," I said.

"But Zo-L did say he would be in touch from time to time. Perhaps you could retire with the contingency to come back as a consultant should the situation arise. It's something to consider."

We had another drink, finishing the bottle, and Carol called me a limo. Tina and I arrived almost simultaneously at our room. We were both tired but ready for an evening of fun. She showed me some of the things she had purchased, which included gifts for Carol and Meg.

"That's really sweet," I said. We decided to splurge and go down to the massage room for a little pampering. We both got the works — pedicure, manicure, facials, and a few things neither of us had ever heard of. When it was all over, we felt great! We went back to the room to rest for a couple hours in preparation for our night on the town.

The limo picked us up at 6:00 p.m. sharp, and we arrived at the Chaparral at 6:20 p.m. We were greeted at the door by the maitre d', who personally escorted us to our banquet room, the same one we used last time. A handsome waiter escorted us to our table and was quickly followed by a pretty young lady from the bar. There was a band playing music in the background, and we all sat down and ordered a round of Prairie Dogs. There were less people here this time, as taping went much more smoothly and didn't require additional personnel. The place was decorated beautifully with a large banner over the stage that read, "WRAP PARTY – WE LOVE YOU, RAL."

There were hors d'oeuvres of every kind imaginable: liqueurs, nuts, small desserts, and anything you would care to order. We made the rounds, being introduced to all the spouses, signing autographs, and posing for pictures — We were having a wonderful time.

The band took a break and Carol walked on stage to make an announcement, "I hope everyone is having as good a time as I am," which brought a round of applause from everyone. "We have a special treat in store for you tonight, please give a warm welcome to Stinky Jones." Stinky was a well-established comedian who did routines similar to Carrot Top, using a huge number of props and one-liners....He was hilarious!

Carol took the stage again and introduced the CEO of SBS, Mr. Wilton Remington. He received a standing ovation, not because he was the boss, but because everyone genuinely loved him. When the ovation died down he said, "It is my great pleasure to be here tonight to tell you all what a marvelous job you have done bringing this history-making story to the world. Mister Ralph Diamond, will you please join me on stage?" It was a good thing I had a few drinks in me, as I really don't like to be thrust into the spotlight by surprise.

As I approached Mr. Remington, he extended his arm and we shook hands. He said, "Mister Diamond, you have done more for the image of our company, and have increased our market share more signifycantly than anyone or anything since the company's inception. It is my great honor to present to you the SBS CEO AWARD. This award signifies an extraordinary contribution to the company or mankind. . . . You have done both. I have had the pleasure of presenting this award to only two other people during my thirty years as CEO. Actually, three — I gave one to Stinky a few minutes ago." Wilton Remington is known for his sense of humor, and the audience went crazy.

I accepted the honor with great humility, since I really didn't deserve it. When I got back to the table, everyone wanted to see the award they had heard so much about but had never seen up close. As I passed it around, Carol told me the award is made of platinum, rhodium, and gold, with diamonds set in each corner, and is worth two hundred thousand dollars.

"This award is worth more than my house; I should hang the house on it, not the other way around," I joked. It was time to eat, and the Chaparral lived up to its reputation. Surf and turf was the dish Tina had chosen for the night, featuring a large Maine lobster and a twenty-two ounce steak that was fork-tender and absolutely delicious. We partied until 10:00 p.m., then the limos took us to Club 359. Mr. Remington, who insisted I call him Wilt, joined us. I soon saw why everyone loved him. . . . He is just a regular guy, the kind you would love to have as a neighbor.

Just like last time Carol let it slip to the news media we might be at the club this evening. We sat on the rooftop enjoying the view and a sampler platter of chocolate liquors. Shortly after, the owner came to greet us and escorted us down to a special table in the lounge. There were even more celebrities and notables than last time; Tina was collecting autographs and I was giving them ... very strange. I was approached by a number of giants in the news industry; anchors from nearly every major network wanted to do a one on one interview with me. I explained to them that there was nothing else to tell; *Hard Facts* now knows everything I know. Besides, I wasn't allowed to discuss any details until after the next airing. They could tell I was not interested and politely thanked me for my time; you can't blame them for trying. We all partied till the wee hours in the morning, then Tina and I took the limo back to the hotel.

Carol had arranged for the corporate jet to take us back to California, and we were anxious to leave, very much looking forward to doing nothing for a couple days. We managed to totally relax the first day, but knew we had lots of things that needed attention. Tina began to wade through the mountain of emails and phone messages, while I went to the post office to pick up the mail, as I had stopped delivery while we were gone.

Along with dozens of letters there was a fairly heavy package from Able Chemical. When I got home I opened the package, and it was full of several prototypes of the Fire Suppression Sphere (FSS). They ranged in diameter from three-quarters of an inch to four inches. I was very anxious to try them out, and unfortunately didn't have to wait long. We heard the town siren go off the next morning, and we knew something was wrong. We immediately tuned into the local radio station and learned there was a fire just outside town.

Years earlier for fun I built a "Spud Blaster" from plans on the Internet. It consisted of a four-inch PVC pipe, one foot long with a threaded plug on the end connected by a reducer fitting to a two-inch PVC pipe three feet long. You taper the two-inch end of the pipe so when you cram a potato in it will act as a cutter. With the potato pushed down the barrel about two feet, you unscrew the four-inch plug and spray in a small amount of ether and screw the plug back in place. A barbecue igniter is mounted to the side of the four-inch pipe, and when you press the button the spark ignites the ether, and the potato travels about four hundred feet. I quickly found the Spud Blaster in the garage, grabbed the can of ether and my box of FSSs, and headed toward the fire.

I followed an old logging trail to just above the fire, where I saw fire chief Bob Jennings observing the fire and directing his crew. He asked what I was doing there, as he had concerns for my safety. I told him I had come to test out a new product. The fire was relatively small, only covering about three acres, but was spreading rapidly. I sprayed a shot of ether into the blaster, loaded two one-and-a-half-inch FSSs in the barrel, and pressed the button. They landed at the edge of the fire, expanding quickly into a fog like state, and put out about one-quarter of the fire.

Bob looked at me in utter amazement and said, "What the hell is that?" I noticed the fire was headed straight up the hill about fifty feet to our left. I grabbed the four-inch FSS and ran to a spot right above to the center of the fire. Being a longtime bowler, I gave it my best release, and it headed straight toward the fire.

"Strike," I shouted as the sphere went directly into the center of what was left of the fire. Within seconds the fire was completely out.

Chief Bob was dumfounded; he ran over to me and gave me a giant bear hug, which lifted me off the ground. "Unbelievable!" he shouted.

"I'll take a thousand!" As we looked down at his crew, they were walking around scratching their heads, wondering what the heck just happened.

"What are those things, Ral?"

"Another gift from the Ar-Zians; they are due to hit the market shortly," I answered.

He put his arm on my shoulder and said, "Come on. I want to buy you a drink." Since this is an all-volunteer fire department, the rules are rather lax. He radioed his men to meet us at The Pit, the local restaurant, bar, and grill. Bob called the owner and requested to use the meeting room, and he quickly agreed. I told Bob I couldn't stay long as I had a ton of stuff to catch up on.

"Just have a beer and explain to the boys that they're not going crazy."

When I arrived back home, Tina handed me a list of several people I needed to call; at the top of the list was Able Chemical. They asked me if I had received the samples, and I said, "Boy, do I have a story for you." I was informed that the FSS would be in worldwide distribution in less than two weeks. Like the Food Formula, the government rushed it through approval avoiding a ton of red tape.

The next few weeks were very hectic. The FSS hit the market, the DVDs of the second interview were in distribution, and we were receiving money from everywhere. While dodging interview requests from all over the world, I did make myself available to Misty. Tina and I had grown very close to her and loved seeing her achieve her dream. Things started to settle down a bit and one morning as Tina and I were enjoying our usual coffee on the gazebo, I suddenly remembered what Zo-L had said about returning the items he had borrowed. I mentioned it to Tina, and we both went into the garage to have a look. A bright sparkling object caught our attention.... It was my oxygen tank sitting right next to the acetylene tank on my welding hand truck. I pulled it out into the center of the garage to have a better look. I couldn't believe my eyes. It was one solid diamond, the same type that the Jubilee sculpture on Ar-Z was made of — the one they named the Tina Diamond.

"This has got to be worth an absolute fortune," she said.

"Zo-L said he returned the *items* he borrowed, plural....Let's go check the salt tank." We hurried into the laundry room and lifted the water-softener salt-tank cover. It was filled to the very top with salt-pellet shaped Tina Diamonds as well. Each one was one-half by three-quarters by point four inches. They were oval-shaped, like a horserace track when viewed from above, and football-shaped when viewed from the side. We grabbed a large scoop and began to remove them from the tank. We spread them over our large dining room table and counted 19,608 perfectly shaped diamonds.

"There is nothing like this on Earth," Tina said. "They are priceless!" We sat there in disbelief for quite some time, trying to make sense of it all.

Tina looked at me and said, "What are we going to do with all these diamonds and the oxygen tank?" We contacted our local Spring Valley Lake bank and set up a meeting with Rudy Andrews, the bank president. Rudy and I have been friends since we moved here, and I knew I could trust him completely. We entered a private conference room, exchanged some small talk, then he asked, "What can I do for you, Ral?"

"We have come into possession of something rather valuable, and we need a safe place to keep it."

"What is it?"

I reached into my pocket and pulled out one of the diamonds from the water softener.

Rudy gasped and asked, "Is this one of the Tina Diamonds?"

"It is," I answered."

"This must be worth a fortune — right? We can set you up with a safe deposit box; that should work nicely."

"We have a few more."

He asked, "How many more?"

"19,607 to be exact ... and also this." I slid a photo of the oxygen tank across the table to him, and his mouth almost hit the floor. He leaned back in his chair and was absolutely speechless.

When he regained his composure, he said, "You realize you cannot mention a word of this to anyone — don't you? We're not set up to handle something like this; you need to contact Fort Knox!"

220

Tina and I laughed and he said, "I'm not kidding. If not there, I think they would be safer somewhere on your property. I suggest you protect them the old fashioned way...bury them." I thought he was joking at first, but then I realized that was a great idea. I own a backhoe and could do all the work myself.

"You can be assured. I will not say anything about this to anyone," Rudy pledged. "I would be putting all of our lives in danger. "

When Tina and I got back home we walked around the property to find a suitable spot to bury our treasure. We needed a place where no one could see what we were doing, so we decided to bury it under an old water tank that was sitting on the ground near the center of our property. It was completely surrounded by trees and out of the view of prying eyes. I used my backhoe to tow the tank back about twenty feet. As I was digging the hole, Tina was filling burlap bags with diamonds and searching for a heavy tarp to wrap them in. Everything went amazingly well, and we finished in a couple of hours. With the tank back in its original position, you really couldn't tell the ground had been disturbed at all. We put our arms around each other and felt a huge relief as we walked back toward the house.

Tina said, "I'm going to do a little research and see if I can figure out how much my little namesakes are worth; what would you guess, honey?"

"Probably a few million dollars," I said.

She said, "I'm thinking a lot more than that, having worked at my folks' jewelry store for all those years."

When we got back to the house, Tina went into the computer room, and I grabbed a beer and went out and sat on the gazebo. About half an hour later, she came out and sat down across the table from me. "Well, what did you find out?" I asked.

"First, I called Margaret at Spruce Valley Lake Jewelers and asked what a one carat diamond would be worth these days. She began to tell me all about the four C's: carat, color, clarity, and cut — which all affect the price. Then she began to list a whole bunch of other things that are factored in....I knew all of this but didn't want to interrupt her. I finally was able to get a figure out of her. She said a nice one carat diamond is worth about $9,000 to $10,000."

"Wow! I wonder how many carats we have."

"I figured that out as well; I used our digital postal scale to weigh the one diamond we kept out....It weighs 4.2 ounces. I converted that weight to carats, multiplied that number by $9,000, and that number by the 19,608 diamonds we have."

"So can I buy the new table saw I have been eyeing?" I asked.

"I believe so," she said. The total is $102,561,114,600, and that doesn't even include the oxygen tank or the fact that these diamonds came from another planet....The actual figure could be exponentially higher!"

"What! $102,000,000,000?! You must have hit a few zeros by mistake."

"I checked it four times," she said, as she slid the calculator and figures over to me.

I ran the figures three times myself in disbelief. "You're right! This is absolutely unbelievable! You realize we can never mention this to anyone, not even the kids."

"What do you think we should do?" she asked.

"Let's go find a good hiding place for the one we kept out, and just forget about all this for now. We have more money already than we could possibly spend; we'll worry about them sometime in the future."

"I agree; my head is hurting just thinking about it," she said.

As a couple more weeks passed, the world seemed to actually be changing. For the first time in recorded history there were no conflicts anywhere on Earth; we actually had achieved world peace. Whether or not it will last is another question. It was a phenomenal achievement; every newspaper and news program across the globe was proclaiming this momentous event. Just that fact alone made people want to continue this new way of life. The United Nations wanted to introduce the first-ever world holiday called "Ar-Zian Day," to be held every July 15. Everyone accepted it immediately. In just a few months nearly everyone on Earth was somehow affected by the amazing gifts given to us by our extraterrestrial friends.

CHAPTER 9

INFORMATION ON THE UNIVERSE AND INTERVIEW #3

One morning while waking to the kitchen for a cup of coffee, I heard the familiar "Greetings, Ralph Diamond." We had made many improvements to the house, one of which was a built-in voice and image-activated camera, which initiated operation whenever an Orb arrived.

I answered, "Greetings, my friends." It was Overseer and Zo-L. I was thrilled to see them, even though they weren't actually real; it was still wonderful.

"I hope this visit finds you and Tina Diamond in good health and spirits. We have brought you a few gifts; please place your recording disk on the table."

I did as requested, and when a beam of light contacted it, I knew I had received another recording. Two other objects suddenly appeared before me. Overseer said, "I know you will put these items to good use my dear friend."

Zo-L added, "We have been observing some Probe recordings of recent events on Earth; it is so wonderful to see the changes in social behavior." When they finished speaking, I told them how much the whole world appreciated what they had done for us, and how we had created the first-ever world holiday, Ar-Zian Day.

"It will be held each year on the day that I was invited to visit your planet, July 15." I finished by saying, "Please send my love to your families, and to all the Ar-Zians people." After a quick goodbye, they vanished.

I watched the recording, which contained actual pictures of the universe and a documentary by Overseer and a team of Researchers. This was a phenomenal breakthrough; people on Earth have speculated about the size and shape of the universe forever. I played with the other two gifts they had brought me, and I could hardly wait to do another interview so the world would know what our space brothers had done for us this time. I wanted desperately to keep the goodwill between nations going, and these new gifts will definitely help.

I called Carol's cell phone, and was very pleased that she picked up. She is usually so busy I have to leave a message for her. We both said how nice it was to talk to each other again, and she informed me that she and Parker had gotten remarried. She apologized for not inviting Tina and me, but it was a very small ceremony at her penthouse apartment.

We talked for a while and got caught up, and then I said, "You're not going to believe what just happened. I got a visit via Orb from Overseer and Zo-L, and they brought us a few more gifts. I want to do another interview, and as I promised, you get the first right of refusal. I'm guessing you're retired now since you answered the phone right away."

"Yes, I am. But I have an understanding with SBS that I would have first chance at any future interviews with you."

"It's yours if you want it," I said, "but there is a hitch. I just had surgery, and I am unable to travel at this time. Also, I am really busy here with the charity and everything, so if it's okay, I would like to do the interview here."

"That's even better," she said. "The team loves to go on location. Let me get the ball rolling, and I will get back to you."

"Sounds good," I said. "You know Tina and I would love it if you, Parker, and the team would stay here with us. We have added on to our house considerably and purchased more land around us, so we will have complete privacy."

"That is very kind of you, Ral. I'm sure Parker will say yes. . . . You're his idol. He has watched the interview DVDs probably ten times; I know he would give anything to see the recordings in their original form, and he would love to talk to you about them. He has been a UFO enthusiast since before I first met him, and besides, neither of us has ever been to California."

Ever efficient, Carol called back a short time later. "SBS is totally on board for the interview," she said. "However, Joyce is on maternity leave, so we will have to use someone else. . . . Do you have a preference?"

"You know, Carol, I would love it if we could use Misty Lane; what do you think?"

"You're the boss; with all you have done for SBS you could ask for anything you want. I'm not even going to give them a choice; I'll simply tell them you want Misty to do the interview, and we will go from there. If you would, Ral, please set up a time with Misty. Let me know, and I will make all the other arrangements."

I called Carol the next day and said, "We were all set for this coming Tuesday if that's okay. I was thinking perhaps you and Parker could come out on Saturday and spend a couple days with Tina and me before we get down to business."

"Thank you, Ral . . . that's very kind. Let me finalize everything, and I will get back to you."

Carol and Parker arrived at Lakeview Airport at 9:00 a.m. Saturday morning, and Tina and I picked them up. I was still on crutches from my surgery, but got out of the car to welcome our guests. Parker was a very handsome and distinguished-looking gentleman, and Carol was stunning as always. The two of them made a beautiful couple. Parker remarked how unusual it was to have such a large airport adjacent to such a small town.

"It used to be a military base, which accounts for the long runways; now it's a reserve base that sees very little action," I said. "Occasionally, you will see a large military jet land, but usually it's just small personal aircraft."

We drove back to our house and the two of them remarked several times how beautiful the lake and surrounding areas were. As we pulled into our driveway, they were surprised to see there was a guard shack at the entrance. I waved at Kip, who was on duty at the time, wearing his Air Force dress uniform. He saluted us and opened the gate.

"What was that all about, Ral?" Carol asked.

"The government insists on providing us with full round-the-clock security. We didn't like it at first, but have now grown to appreciate it." I didn't go into any more detail; they seemed to be satisfied with that explanation. As we continued down our winding driveway, our house came into view.

"WOW!" came the loud exclamations from the back seat. "Is that your house?" they both asked. "How many people live here?"

"Just Tina and me. We will explain more when we get inside."

"I'm so sorry I can't help you with your luggage, but I'll make up for it by getting us some drinks while Tina shows you to your room." When I got inside, I climbed into my motorized chair and got to work. "I'll meet you guys on the gazebo," I shouted as I headed outside. Tina and our guests soon joined me and sat down. "I hope Margaritas are okay?" I said.

"Perfect," came the reply from everyone.

"I suppose a good host would have offered you the option of taking a nap first, but I'm just so excited to see you guys I didn't want to waste a minute."

"Parker and I feel the same way about seeing the both you."

I couldn't help but notice that Parker was limping slightly. "Are you okay?" I asked.

"It's an old war injury that he is too modest to talk about," Carol said. "He was shot up pretty good while dragging four injured soldiers out of the line of fire."

"Wow," I said. "It's an honor to be in the company of a real hero."

Parker wanted to get the subject matter off himself, so he asked, "Were you in the service, Ral?"

"Thirty-three years," I answered.

"What branch?"

"Xerox," I said. Parker looked at me with a puzzled expression and I said, "I was a Xerox serviceman for thirty-three years." As he chuckled I said, "Don't laugh; you guys had it easy.... I had to deal with the public, and they didn't give me a gun either." We talked and drank for about two hours while getting to know Parker, and then I ordered some food to be delivered. We really had a wonderful time.

Parker said, "Okay, Ral, tell us about this gigantic mansion you and Tina have, and what is that large dome over there? Is that your Ar-Zian home?"

"To the left is the original house we had built, and where you guys are staying. There are fifteen bedrooms and a few other rooms we added on. Over to the right are quarters for the maid and cook whenever we need them."

"Why so many bedrooms for just two people?" asked Carol.

"We are constantly deluged with requests to see the recordings in person, so Tina and I thought it would be hospitable for us to have them stay here for a night or two. "Follow me to the dome and I will explain more."

As we entered I said, "This is patterned after the Ar-Zian domes, only not quite as large. Behind that wall are fifty motorized chairs ... watch this. Set up three chairs," I said loudly. A wall then moved to the left out of the way and a parade of three motorized recliners entered the center of the dome and spaced themselves in a circular pattern far enough away from each other to swivel without interfering with one another.

"Please sit," I said. "You will notice there is a joystick on each arm; if you press it forward or backward the chair adjusts from upright to a reclined position. Move it left or right and the chair will swivel in that direction. This allows you to focus on any portion of the recording you choose. Up to fifty chairs can be set up in just a couple of minutes."

"That is absolutely amazing," Carol said.

"I hate to be forward, Ral, but can you play just a small portion of one of the recordings?"

"Of course, Parker, I was hoping you would ask." Since we are so close to the actual spot where this whole amazing adventure began, I'll play the very first recording." I inserted my index finger into my neck and retrieved the disk, set it on the tray of my chair and started playback.

After about half an hour, I stopped the recording, and we all got up. I ordered the chairs to "Go home," after which the wall returned to its original position. "What are all those photos and other items on the wall?" asked Carol.

I headed my scooter that way and said, "Those are some of the guests we have had visit us." As we approached the wall both Carol and Parker's eyes popped in amazement.

"Are these photos for real?" they asked.

"Yes," I said.

"There must be over a hundred notable people here," Carol continued.

I had to chuckle as both Carol and Parker pointed and called out the names of presidents, kings, queens, princes, movie stars, scientists, and many others including his holiness, the Pope. After several minutes of gawking over the photos, Parker said, "I see why you added on fifteen bedrooms."

They moved over to another section of the wall and Carol said, "I don't recognize anyone here....Who are these people?"

"This is my favorite section," I said. "These are people with terminal illnesses, many of whom came here from various charities such as the Make a Wish Foundation and other great organizations. Some are just people who have contacted us directly, trying to fulfill their bucket list. The children have been the most inspiring for Tina and me; even though they are dying, the joy on their faces when they watch the recordings is truly gratifying. I use my abilities and put on kind of a magic show for the kids. We have a large building out back that contains every toy, game, clothing item, and anything else a child might want. Before they go we let them have whatever they want. We usually break down into tears after they leave."

INTERVIEW #3

Monday soon arrived, and we went to the airport to pick up Peter, James, and Arnold; it was great to see the old gang again. We wasted no time preparing for the taping the next day; this interview was going to be the easiest by far. The actual recording was very short, only about thirty minutes. The rest would be a one on one between Misty and myself. We had everything totally prepared by 3:00 p.m., and decided to do some partying. Tina had a variety of food delivered from our favorite restaurants and hired a bartender for the evening. It was a beautiful night, and we had a ball reminiscing about our other tapings and swapping embarrassing stories about the past.

Misty arrived around 7:00 a.m. Tuesday morning, and after the usual introductions and hugs, we all assembled in the dome and began taping. Misty started by bringing the audience up to speed on the entire saga. She welcomed me and said, "So, Ral, I understand you have some exciting news."

"Yes, I think the scientific community is going to be amazed at what our space brothers have given us this time." I played the video of the arrival of Overseer and Zo-L, and then I reached into my neck for my recording disk. I explained to Misty that I would like to show the recording they brought me first, and then answer any questions. I would then demonstrate the other two gifts they brought. I informed her that the entire recording was in Ar-Zian, and I would translate.

As I started the playback I said:

The recording takes place on the tarmac at the Space Port on Ar-Z, and is narrated by Overseer. He is explaining that the researchers had been working for thousands of years to answer the questions: How big is the universe? What is its shape? And is it the only universe? There have been thousands of Probes sent into the universe and very few have ever returned. The distances are so great that they are unable to calculate their way back. It is believed the universe is 13.76 billion years old, as we can clearly see 13.76 billion light years back in time in all directions. We cannot see any further because the light beyond that point has not yet had enough time to reach us. The universe may be finite or infinite in size.... No one really knows. We have to assume the universe is much larger, as it is unlikely that we are at the exact center. Today, we are embarking on a new experiment that we hope will answer those questions

As Overseer walks over to a tower of Probes he is saying, "These Probes are the latest technology we have. Each Probe is fully independent but they will work in unison. We have been waiting 1,201 years for galaxies to align themselves such that we will have a clearer path to what we hope will be the edge of the universe. There are fifteen Probes in all, and here is what we hope the mission will accomplish. They will travel as one unit to a distance of two billion light years, at which point they will separate a short distance, while each of them will record their surroundings as a reference point. Probe number one will remain there, and the other fourteen will reassemble and travel another two billion light years.

The separation and recording process will continue until a distance of twenty billion light years has been reached. At this point we hope to be at or near the edge of our universe.

The remaining five Probes will travel one trillion light years further, separate, and record. Probe number eleven will remain there, and the other four will travel an additional one trillion light years in four different directions and record whatever they see.

When this has been accomplished, they will reverse the procedure, linking up one by one and return to Ar-Z. If one or more Probes are lost, each of the remaining Probes should contain all the necessary information to return on its own if necessary." Overseer gestured with his arm, and the Probes disappeared.

Twenty-three days later in Earth time, we observe Overseer standing next to a stack of the thirteen Probes that returned. He explained that it would take some time to examine and enhance the information recorded to see if the mission had been a success. We next find Overseer and three researchers going over the enhanced results. Overseer explains that Probe number ten had not reached the edge of the universe, but had stunning pictures of an additional 7.3 billion light years of universe we were not aware of.

The next pictures are the most spectacular. They show the entire universe, some 20.231 billion light years at its widest part. Finally, the shape of the universe had been discovered....It is slightly egg-shaped because it is traveling through space at a phenomenal 1.674 billion miles an hour.

Only two of the last four Probes returned, but had no results to show for their efforts. It was decided nothing was seen outside our own universe because of the tremendous distances involved. Light simply hadn't had enough time to travel that far. Therefore, the experiment had to be repeated with more Probes and greater distances traveled to see if we were in fact the only universe.

Four months later, Overseer unveiled a new mission with eleven of the original Probes topped off by 1,500 specially designed small Probes, each programmed to travel in all directions over unimagined distances. If they observed nothing, they will continue to travel until they have reached a preset maximum limit, or they have recorded something.

Anticipation was running very high on both planets as a grueling four and a half months passed before the return of the mission. The original thirteen Probes made it back safely, but only 386 small Probes were able to return. It took another four weeks to process and enhance the data before the results were obtained.

Finally, we see Overseer is in a large room with six researchers to reveal their findings. There were thousands of pictures, which showed seventy-four other universes. All of them were much older than our own; the largest was an astounding 1,298,576,000,000 light years in diameter, which is also its age.

The researchers concluded the universes observed were only a tiny portion of what is expected to be out there; in fact information received seem to indicate these universes form a type of galaxy.

Overseer pointed to a diagram that appeared next to him of what the researchers think the entire "Galiverse," as I refer to it, might look like. Now the question becomes, what is its size, and is this the only Galiverse out there? These questions of course will never be answered, because the distances involved are simply too great.

That was the conclusion of the recording, and I turned it off. "Wow," said Misty, "that was truly fascinating. I imagine the scientific community will be overwhelmed by this information."

"Yes," I said. "I imagine we would not be able to ascertain this information on our own for many thousands of years, if ever."

"Cut," Peter said. "That was the easiest taping yet. Take fifteen, people, while Ral and I figure out what's next." As Peter approached he looked at the two objects on the table given me by Overseer. I explained what they were and what he would have to do to properly record the function of each. He had some amazing new equipment that was not even on the market yet.

"Remember Mister Ling, Ral? These are their latest creations from JK Sterling Labs; he asked me to try them out.... How cool is that? If I had this stuff when we did the first two interviews, we could have finished in half the time."

Everyone took their places and Misty welcomed back the audience; she turned to me and asked, "What are the two items in front of you?"

"As you saw earlier, these were left for us by Overseer and Zo-L; both items are quite intriguing."

I grabbed the first item, which was a clear cylindrical container of liquid about the size of a tube of toothpaste. "This is an 'Atomic Bond Integrator' (ABI). Simply put, it acts as a bonding agent at the atomic level. Using this, you can permanently fuse items together regardless of their makeup. I have a prop here that will demonstrate how it works."

I pointed to a clear plastic box on the table, which was approximately the size of a cube of butter. "As you can see, there are white sugar granules in one side and sand in the other separated by a clear plastic divider. These granules represent the individual atoms of two separate items."

I raised the divider and said, "If you look closely, you can see the two different colored granules are mixed at the center where the divider was. Now the two items are bonded at the atomic level, as though they are one."

I poured out a small box containing various items made of different types of material. "Let me show you how the ABI works." I picked up a steel nut and a small glass tube; I placed a small amount of ABI on the end of the glass tube and held it against the nut.... It bonded instantly. I then bonded a small wooden dowel to the glass tube, then a pencil eraser and numerous other items, and handed my creation to Misty. "Try to separate any item from another," I said. She could not.

I placed a piece of steel one inch wide and six inches long flat on the table and placed another piece the same size on its edge on top of and in center of the first piece. I then ran a small amount of the ABI along the seam where they met, and they instantly bonded as well. "This could make welding a thing of the past; this is a cold process that is much stronger than a traditional weld and can be completed approximately a hundred times faster."

I then took out a bundle of precut pieces of wood, each about one-quarter-inch square consisting of different lengths. "Imagine this is a scale model of a house being framed." I bonded all the pieces together in a matter of seconds, handed them to Misty, and said, "Try to break them apart."

As she did, I said, "Imagine how strong houses would be if *all* the individual components were made to be as one, using the ABI. Hurricanes and tornadoes would do far less damage if construction was done this way."

"Will this be available on the market soon?" Misty asked.

"I haven't had a chance to talk to our friends at Able Chemical yet, but I'm sure I'll be hearing from them when this airs."

"Are there any precautions necessary when using this? Will it bond your fingers together if you accidentally get some on you?"

"No, as usual the Ar-Zians have taken every precaution when developing this; it will not work on any living thing including plants."

"Will it be expensive to manufacture?"

"I can't really answer that question; although I know the chemical composition of the formula, I have no idea as to the price of each individual ingredient."

"This appears to be gel-like in nature; does it come in other forms?"

"I'm very glad you asked that question, Misty. As a matter of fact it can be manufactured in any viscosity from water to toothpaste. The more liquid form can be used when bonding large items together such as steel beams, etcetera."

"Are there any draw backs to using the ABI?"

"Yes, you have to be darn sure of what you are doing, as the bond is permanent. If you make a mistake, you will have to cut the bond apart."

"What is the other item they gave you?"

I reached for the handheld "Electron Motion Impede" (EMI). "This is the same technology as the larger EMI, used by the Ar-Zians to peer beneath the surface of planets as was discussed in a previous interview. As you can see it is roughly the size of a soda can. This is actually a child's toy."

"How does it work?"

"As you can see there are three small depressions on the top and one on the bottom. When I move my thumb over the bottom detent, the unit will became energized." A viewing area about eight inches by twelve inches became visible projecting from the end facing me. "I will place my index finger into the first small detent on the top and keep my other fingers just outside the remaining detents. In this configuration the unit is set for very short distances."

I held the unit about six inches above my hand and asked the cameraman to focus on the viewing area. As I slowly moved the unit closer and further away from my hand, you could see the entire structure of the hand. I then placed the unit in front of my chest and moved it around, displaying my internal organs as they actually appear.

"That's incredible!" Misty exclaimed. "Is it harmful as X-Rays can be?"

"Not at all; as I said earlier this is actually a child's toy."

"May I try it?" she asked.

I handed it to her and explained that each detent you touch increases the viewing distance. "If you press your finger forward in the detent, your viewing area will move forward as well; likewise, pressing backward will reverse the viewing distance. Point it straight down and see what you can find." As she began experimenting she located an underground spring and an oil deposit. "Place your middle finger on the second detent," I said. As she did the entire viewing area turned bright yellow-orange.

"What's that?" she said.

"The Earth's molten-iron core," I responded. "Place your next finger on the last detent, and press slightly forward and tell me what you see."

"All I see are tiny dots of light. What are they?"

"That is the night sky on the other side of the Earth." Her mouth was wide open in disbelief.

"Can we manufacture these?"

"No," I said, "we don't have the necessary elements on Earth to do that; this will remain a one-of-a-kind device."

"What do you plan to do with it, Ral?"

"I will rent it out for exploration of oil, minerals, the ocean, and so on — and give the money I receive to charity. It is truly a shame we cannot duplicate this device; it would be a great diagnostic tool in the medical field and a huge help to law enforcement, fire fighting, rescue missions, and the military."

"Have you heard anything else from the Ar-Zians since this last visit?"

"Yes, I have saved the best news for last. On the first anniversary of Ar-Zian Day, this coming July fifteenth, just after dusk, they are going to show the Jubilee fireworks display over our planet. It will first appear over the United States and play continually for twenty-four hours, so the entire Earth will be able to see this spectacular display."

Misty said, "I have an article here dated January 8, 2024, by Stan Fredon of the *New York Daily Recorder*, and I quote. 'Mister Diamond has visited an advanced civilization on three occasions. According to him, they are 800,000 years ahead of our own; yet all he has brought back are a few toys and technology that by his own admission, is hundreds of thousands of years old. Where is the new stuff? The MID, NID, Life Center, or the technology to go anywhere in the universe instantly.' How do you respond to that type of criticism?"

"First of all, having visited worlds where the inhabitants are perfect in mind, body, and spirit, to see the display of greed espoused by Mister Fredon, makes me ashamed of being a member of the human race. The 'old technology' he speaks of will save millions of lives and countless dollars from this point forward.

"Secondly, the Ar-Zians have a very strict policy of not interfering with the natural progression of other civilizations. They have made an exception in our case, because they see what I was able to do for them as being extraordinary. They were possibly going to lose five lives, which they consider very precious, and that price would have been devastating for them. They chose to show their appreciation by giving us things we would not discover for hundreds of years or possibly never.

"Thirdly, let me ask you a question, Misty. When industry develops a new technology, what is the first thing the government wants to know?"

"I suppose, what are its military applications?" she said.

"Exactly!" I responded. "The Ar-Zians value life so dearly, they would never be able to live with the fact that a creation of theirs was used to harm another living thing. I'm sure the person who invented the hammer never dreamed it might be used to beat someone to death, yet those things certainly happen.

"Fourth, I was put in the unique position of representing some seven billion people of another species; I desperately wanted them to like us. When someone invites you into their home, you don't look around and start asking for things. They know our situation; if they choose to give me something, I would accept it graciously and leave it at that.

"Fifth, as we learned in school, the 'Periodic Table' is a list of chemical elements that comprise everything around us. Whether manufactured or naturally occurring, all things contain one or more elements on that table: a list of ingredients, if you will. With a few additions in 2018 and 2022, we now have a total of 119 elements, or ingredients, with which to work. The Ar-Zians work from a table of 534 elements. They are elements found naturally on their planets, other planets, asteroids, comets, and a few they have created themselves. Almost everything they create contains elements that we do not possess. Even if they gave us detailed instructions on how to build one of the machines they use, we would not be able to do so. Also, we don't have the processes in place to manufacture such devices. It would be like going back a few hundred years and giving our ancestors all the necessary parts to build an automobile. Without knowing how to weld or how wires conduct electricity, there is no way they would be able to assemble a working car.

"Lastly, I hope the Ar-Zians will be like a big brother to us, looking out for our well being. Scientists agree that it's only a matter of time before the Earth is hit by another asteroid, comet, or meteor. It has happened many times in the past and will happen again in the future. An object just a few miles across has the potential to cause the extinction of all life on Earth. I am hoping that maybe the Ar-Zians will place a few Probes in our Solar System to monitor our safety and intervene on our behalf should something be headed in our direction."

"How do you like the title of Mister Galaxy?" Misty asked.

"I don't really care much for it; I prefer Ral."

"You have to admit, though, you are the most popular man in the galaxy; after all, everyone knows your name on three planets."

"I may be the best known, but I don't consider myself the most popular."

"I hear that you are a shoe-in for the next Nobel peace prize; that has got to be incredibly exciting."

"I would not be able to accept such an honor if it was offered to me."

"You're kidding," she said. "Why not?"

"The Nobel prize is awarded to people who have made a significant contribution to mankind."

"You don't consider ending world hunger and entering into an era of world peace a significant contribution?"

"Of course I do," I said, "but I didn't do that…the Ar-Zians did. All I did was lend a friend a couple things he asked for, like loaning a neighbor your lawn mower. It could just as easily have been anyone else on the planet, but it happened to be me. If I were to accept the prize, it would be like being honored for winning the lottery."

Peter gave Misty the "wrap it up" signal, and she leaned forward to shake my hand. "Thank you, Ral, for a truly fascinating interview."

"It was my pleasure Misty."

"Cut! Great job, people," Peter said. "That was the easiest interview I have ever directed. . . . Thanks everyone."

In anticipation of the interview ending early, Tina and I had made arrangements for a small party at our house. We hired a bartender and had catering service from two different restaurants. We partied until around 10:00 p.m., and then Peter and the crew prepared for their departure the next morning. Misty had gone back to Sacramento around 7:00 p.m. I asked Carol if she and Parker could stay a few more days with us, and she gladly agreed. Early the next morning, we bid goodbye to Peter and the rest of his crew, who boarded a limousine to take them to the airport. Carol, Parker, Tina and I sat on the gazebo and had some coffee and breakfast rolls.

Parker said, "Carol tells me you have added more land to your original forty acres; how much do you have now?"

"We have a total of 120 acres, I responded."

"What do you do with all this land?"

"Mostly, Tina and I just enjoy riding around on our ATVs, and also do a little fishing, and of course Tina has her horses."

"Would you be kind enough to show Carol and me around?"

"We would be delighted to," Tina said. We all headed toward our garage where among other vehicles we keep a four-wheel drive Jeep. As Tina drove, I pointed out places of interest. "We have many winding trails and roads that go to our favorite spots," I said. "Up ahead on the right is one of four ponds on the property. We keep this one stocked with trout and other varieties of fish. When we have ill or disadvantaged children from the various charities visit us, they always enjoy fishing. There are lots of other things for the kids to do as well, such as hiking, horseback riding, and exploring the two cave systems on the property. There is a stream up ahead that the children and we enjoy tubing on."

As we went a little further, Parker pointed out a huge spruce tree that had died. "What a shame," he said. "I bet it was a beautiful tree at one time; it must cost a fortune to have something like that removed." I asked Tina to stop the car, and we all exited.

I removed a nondescript case from the back of the Jeep and said, "I am going to show you something that has to remain between us." I opened the case to reveal a short flashlight looking device. "Zo-L gave this to me when he learned the problem I was having with some of my trees dying. Spruce trees grow to about seventy-five feet tall and can cost upwards of one thousand dollars to remove." I pointed the device at the tree and said, "Look at the large branch on the bottom left; notice the yellow and purple points of light. The yellow one on the left stops at the surface of the tree, and the purple one extends through to the other side of the branch ... don't ask me how, light doesn't normally do that."

I pressed a small button on top of the unit, and the purple light cut the branch off at the trunk, and as soon as the branch and trunk separated, the branch disappeared. "I can use this device to trim a tree, cut it into firewood, or disintegrate it entirely."

Having said that, I shined just the yellow light on the center of the trunk and pressed the button again vaporizing the entire tree instantly. They were in awe. "Let me show you something else," I said. I reached inside the box where I keep my "Ar-Zian flashlight" and retrieved a picture. "The man we bought the property from was a bit of a hoarder. He would let anyone drop off almost anything here thinking he could eventually make some money off of the items. For that reason, we got a really good deal on the property." I handed the picture to Parker, he was surprised to see about 1.5 acres of old junk cars, farm equipment, appliances, and you name it.

"How did you get rid of all that stuff?" he asked.

Holding up the device, I said: "With this. As you can imagine this device can be used for evil as well as good, and that's why no one else must ever find out about it." Carol and Parker agreed.

As we drove further, a large three-story building came into view. "What is that?" Carol asked.

"It's the headquarters of The Ar-Zian.

"Oh the charity you and Tina started."

"Would you like to go inside?" I asked. They both nodded yes, and we pulled up in front. "I'll wait here," I said. I was glad I was not able to walk very far because of my surgery, as it is a little like bragging or showing off your good deeds. When they came out I could tell it had affected the both of them. We drove around the rest of the property for a few hours and than decided to go back to the house and take a nap before going out to dinner. We went to The Pit for dinner and hit the only nightclub in town afterward.... We had a wonderful time. Tina and I really loved being with Carol and Parker.

The next morning we all slept in late. Tina was the first one up at around 10:00 a.m. and started cooking breakfast. I rolled out around 10:30 to find Carol and Parker already having coffee in the kitchen. After breakfast, Carol said, "Parker and I would like to talk to you both about something."

"Is everything all right?" I asked.

"Could not be better," came the response. "After seeing all the wonderful things you and Tina have done for others, Parker and I realized what selfish people we have become. Sure we give a tithing to our church, but other than writing a check, we really haven't helped anyone. We have talked about it, and if you will have us, we would like to move to California and help with your charity. We could buy some property nearby, build a house, and be neighbors."

"You would have to agree to a few things first," I said.

They looked at each other with a puzzled expression then said, "Okay. What?"

"First of all, there is no reason for you to buy any property. You guys can live here with us; as you can see, we have plenty of room. If you did decide you want to have your own place, you can build here anywhere on the property you want."

"Oh, we couldn't possibly impose on you like that," Parker said. "Are you kidding?"

Tina chimed in, "You would be doing us a huge favor; it gets pretty lonely here with just the two of us. Please say yes!"

They smiled, stood up and came over and gave Tina and me a big hug. "What sort of timetable are you thinking about?" Tina asked.

"As soon as possible," Carol said.

Tina responded, "This is certainly cause for celebration. I'll get the champagne."

After spending two weeks with us, Carol and Parker went back home to make all the necessary arrangements for the move to California. Tina and I were beside ourselves with excitement ... especially Tina. In less than a month, they showed up unannounced at our front gate with only two small suitcases. Tina and I rushed out to pick them up in the Jeep and soon we were hugging like we hadn't seen each other in years. We popped some champagne and sat on the gazebo to catch up. "When is the rest of your stuff going to arrive?" Tina asked.

Pointing toward the two suitcases, Parker said, "That's it."

"You're kidding!" My wife said.

"Parker and I decided we wanted to start a whole new life together, so basically, we brought two changes of clothing and two toothbrushes.... We just may have to go shopping," Carol continued, as she reached out and touched Tina's arm. We toasted each other several times, talked for hours, and I thought to myself ... *this is absolutely fantastic*.

"Oh!" Carol exclaimed. "I almost forgot. Joyce gave birth to triplets, and I heard through the grapevine that she would not be going back to work; she is going to stay home and be a full-time mom. And the biggest news of all is that *Hard Facts* is going to offer Joyce's job to Misty, AND there is also a very good position open for her mentor Jane if she wants it."

"Man, this day just keeps getting better and better," I said.

We talked and joked for hours, poking fun at each other and ourselves. Parker asked if there were any German restaurants around. "Thankfully, not," I said. "Nobody likes German food anyway....Why do you ask?"

"I'm German," Parker answered, "and I thought it might be someplace different to try for dinner.

"Does anyone really eat German food?" I joked. "I mean, you've got bratwurst, knockwurst, and liverwurst. *Worst* is right in the name; what does that tell you?" Everyone laughed. Tina and I hadn't had this much fun with another couple since Arthur and his wife passed away. This was going to be a friendship that would last forever.

FINAL CHAPTER
PRELUDE

On the first Ar-Zian Day, the much-anticipated fireworks display took place. The entire world was treated to the most spectacular show anyone had ever witnessed. Everyone on Earth joined in the celebration; this was something that had never happened before and now it would be a yearly occurrence. The news media around the world was trying to figure out how to report the event. It wouldn't do any good to show recordings of something everyone had seen first hand, so they just showed scenes of people celebrating in the streets all around the world. People were hugging total strangers; everyone was well behaved. . . . It was an unforgettable day.

After many years Arthur and his wife Amy had passed away leaving their home to their great grandson. Tina and I were thrilled when Albert and his wife Jenn moved in, and we soon became good friends. They were like extended family; and we loved getting together to hear stories about their great-grandfather and great-grandmother. Tina and I always invited them over when our family members would visit, and we were truly as one family. They even referred to us as Nana Tina and Poppi Ral....We loved that.

Albert is a doctor, and Jenn is an emergency room nurse. They worked at the same hospital and ended up getting married. Tina's and my birthday were coming up, and we wanted to celebrate with our kids. We were getting older and knew we didn't have too much time left. We wanted to explain our will and all the other important matters to our heirs to avoid any problems when we died. We thought we would use our eighty-fifth birthdays to accomplish this task, as we always celebrated our birthdays on the four days we were the same age.

We recently had a lawyer draw up all the necessary paperwork and wanted to bring everyone up to date. Thanks to the Ar-Zians, Tina and I were in relatively good health other than suffering the ravages of old age. We never had a major disease or disorder of any kind. This celebration was just for our family, which included our kids, Bob and Robin, and the grandkids, Carol and Parker, and Albert and Jenn; all were considered immediate family as far as Tina and I were concerned. We didn't want to dwell too heavily on legal stuff; after all this was a celebration.

To accommodate everyone's schedules, we had the celebration a week early. Months ago Tina and I went over all the pertinent information with the kids and asked if they would like to take over managing the charity. They both looked at each other and hesitated. After an awkward pause, they explained that since both of them had children and grandchildren, they felt there would not be enough time to adequately run the charity and enjoy their families the way they felt they should. Tina and I could tell they were afraid they had disappointed us. We hugged them and told them that there was nothing wrong with that; in fact we were glad they were putting our grandchildren and great grandchildren first. Tina and I were secretly thrilled they passed on running the Ar-Zian. Being in charge of large amounts of money can tear a family apart, but we wanted to at least make the offer. We made sure the kids, grandkids, and all other family members were well-provided for including Albert and Jenn. We informed them that family was the most important thing to us. After all the legal stuff was out of the way, we really had a wonderful celebration.

The following week we had our usual one on one celebration, we were both eighty-five years old for a few days. It was afternoon on a cool day in November and raining slightly. Tina and I were sharing a bottle of wine while in the spa on our back deck. It began to rain a little harder, and we could see lightning off in the distance. We were toasting each other for all the wonderful memories we shared over the years, when suddenly there was a blinding flash and a horrifically loud noise.

Lightning had struck the water in the spa and ignited the deck on fire. It was a Saturday, and Albert and Jenn were both home. They immediately looked out their front door to see what had happened. They spotted smoke coming from our house and ran to our assistance. They saw Carol and Parker attending to us, and they both jumped into the spa, and they took over as Parker and Carol put out the small fire. They tried in vane to revive us and called for an ambulance; Tina and I were both pronounced dead at the hospital about half an hour later.

FINAL CHAPTER
UNDISCLOSED INFORMATION

In 2024, Clayton James was in his last year as President. The United States economy was doing well, and the national debt was slowly being reduced. The country was in the best shape it had been in many years. President James could not run for another term due to a serious illness from which he was not expected to survive. Jonathan Wilmington was elected president and during his term the economy began to tank, and the national debt began to rise once again. The next president, Carla Cain, was elected in November of 2028, and under her leadership things had gotten even worse. Despite her novel and progressive ideas, nothing was able to turn around this downward spiral. The U.S. was on the verge of economic collapse, the national debt was at an all time high, and our credit rating was at an all time low. Foreign countries would only do business with us on a cash basis, unemployment was the worst it had been in decades, and inflation was skyrocketing.

There were four people running for president in the election of 2032, but the people didn't really like any of them. President Clayton James had survived his battle with death and was now in his seventies.

People began to reminisce about the old days, remembering how great things were when Clayton James was president. A grass-roots movement was started to try to convince him to run again, but he didn't take the movement seriously due to his age. In the history-making election of November 2032, Clayton James was elected President of the United States by a write-in candidate vote. Everyone in the country was stunned; this had never happened before. The big question now was would he accept the post?

Presidential-elect James informed the news media via telephone that he would announce his decision after church service the following Sunday. Living on a modest ranch in Kentucky, former President James and his wife attended a small rural church in Shelbyville, outside Louisville. Dozens of news reporters were there from all over the world; there were more people outside the church than inside. After the morning service had concluded, the 165 parishioners filed out of the church. Clayton James did not want to detain anyone who might have other plans, so he gave them the opportunity to get a head start before the media frenzy began. You could hear a pin drop as the former president walked out and stood on the top step of the church. He looked out at the crowd and simply said, "I will serve." As everyone erupted in a giant show of support, Pastor Wayne Fox put his arm around President James, and they both re-entered the church.

The country didn't want to wait until January of 2033 for President James to take office, and current President Carla Cain could see the writing on the wall. She resigned on December 1, 2032, and President

Clayton James was sworn into office the same day. On December 17 I received a message via Orb from Overseer, and immediately contacted the White House, and I received a call back a short time later.

"Mister Diamond, how are you?" came a familiar voice.

"I'm fine, Mister President, and I hope you are as well."

"What can I do for you, Ralph?"

"Actually, sir, it's what I can do for you and our country; I need to see you as soon as possible, sir."

"I'll make the arrangements and get back to you, Ral; it's so nice to speak with you again."

Two secret service agents arrived at my home early the next morning, and I was on my way to Washington. I arrived at the White House around 3:30 p.m. local time and was then escorted to the Oval Office to await the president. He arrived a few minutes later, and we embraced, discussing how nice it was to see each other again. He motioned for me to sit down as he walked over to the chair behind his desk. He said, "I was a fool to think I might be able to get us out of this mess; it's going to take an absolute miracle!"

"Never stop believing in miracles, sir," I said. I reached for my wallet and removed a small memory disk. As I stood up, I gestured toward the TV and said, "May I?"

The president nodded, and as I inserted the disk the TV turned on. "This is a recording I made of my last communication from Overseer." I hit the play button and Overseer appeared and began to speak to me in Ar-Zian. At one point he gestured toward an image that appeared to his left, then he and the Orb disappeared; the entire recording was less than twenty-five seconds long.

"Was that an asteroid he pointed to?" The president asked. "Are we going to be hit by an asteroid?"

"No, sir, the Ar-Zians are offering us an asteroid."

The President slumped back in his chair in disbelief and said, "As I'm sure you are aware, Ral, NASA has been trying to figure out how to mine asteroids for many years now. The world is rapidly running out of elements for industry such as antimony, zinc, tin, silver, lead, indium, gold, and copper."

"Yes sir," I said. "When the Ar-Zians learned of our predicament, they sent out hundreds of Probes, searching for an asteroid with enough valuable content to make the U.S. self sufficient again. The one they selected is approximately 2.48 cubic miles in mass and contains everything you just mentioned in addition to cobalt, iron, manganese, molybdenum, nickel, osmium, platinum, and a whole bunch of other stuff not found here on Earth. There is enough valuable material there to pay off the national debt many times over, Mister President."

"But, Ralph, retrieving such an asteroid is way beyond our current capability."

"Actually, sir, the asteroid is currently sitting on the dark side of the moon, and the Ar-Zians are waiting to hear from me."

"What do you need me to do?" the president asked. "You need to select a secluded area where you would like them to bring the asteroid, and I'll sign for the delivery."

The President laughed and said, "Tell me more."

"Once the place has been selected, under cover of night the Ar-Zians will collapse a bowl-shaped area of ground large enough to hold the total mass of the asteroid. Next they will place the asteroid in the depression and break it into pebble-sized rocks, which will flow into the area providing easy access for mining. They will also cover the entire area with a thin layer of dirt to hide the contents."

"How long will all this take?"

"Just a matter of minutes, sir. They gave me a small sphere which we are to place in the center of the delivery spot, and they will take it from there."

"In Alaska there is a large semi-secret military base that should be perfect for this operation; it's surrounded by mountains and completely hidden from view; please excuse me, Ralph, while I make a few phone calls."

The President called one of his aides into his office and asked if he would escort me to a secret area below the White House. I was amazed to enter into a fully stocked bar complete with TVs and pool tables. I was led to a private area and was told the President would join me shortly. The aide motioned for the bartender, who quickly arrived with my favorite, Jack and Seven. About twenty minutes later the president arrived and sat down. He stretched out his hand to shake mine and said, "I can't believe this; please tell me this is for real."

"It is, Mister President."

"Everything is set; you just tell me when, Ralph, and I will go with you."

I contacted Overseer using the communications Orb he had given me to let him know of our plans. The President and I thanked him repeatedly and informed him we would fly to the destination point the next day. "Once we have placed the location sphere in the center of the drop zone, I will contact you once again; please advise us if that meets with your approval." We received the Orb back before the President even had time to order a drink; Overseer had approved everything.

The next morning, the President and I boarded a military helicopter with blacked-out windows and were flown to a nearby military base. We then boarded a military jet and were on our way to the Alaskan base. We waited for nightfall and were then flown by helicopter to the center of the drop site, where I handed the sphere to the President. He looked at me and said, "You are the one who should do this."

I looked back saying, "You're the President of the United States, and I'm just here to sign for the package, remember?" We exited the helicopter, and as he placed the sphere on the ground, it emitted a tiny beam of light straight upward.

"We had better be on our way, sir," I said, "Things will happen pretty quickly now." We flew to a flat spot on one of the nearby mountaintops to watch what was about to unfold. It was a brightly moon-lit night, and we could see everything perfectly. The ground began to vibrate as waves of energy emanated from the sphere. As we watched, we could see animals fleeing from the sphere in all directions.

I thought to myself, *how wonderful of the Ar-Zians to consider there might be wildlife hurt during this mission*. When all animals were a safe distance away, a giant depression started to form right in front of us; the ground began to tremor and groan under the tremendous stress. Even though the water table is rather high in the valley below, the ground compacted so tightly that not a drop of water was present in the depression. Suddenly, a gigantic asteroid appeared in the hole, which loomed more than a mile into the night sky. It broke into tiny pieces and with a deafening roar flowed into the huge hole, creating an atmosphere of sparks and intense heat that made the cold night air feel very warm. It completely filled the area to about one foot below the surface of the ground. As it glowed a reddish-orange color, dirt began to move from a large hill about five miles away and covered our newfound wealth from view.

A small glowing Orb landed on top of the now-buried asteroid and a brilliant beam of purple light shone on the bottom of the mountains on opposite sides of the valley. A large tunnel was being formed on each side to provide easy access for mining. They were half-circle in shape and about sixty feet wide at the bottom, large enough for two lanes of traffic and two railroad tracks. The president looked at me and said, "They don't miss a thing — do they?"

"No sir, " I answered. The entire operation took place in a very remote portion of the base in less than twenty-five minutes and was witnessed by only four people: the President, two military chopper pilots, and myself. A few weeks later the President announced that a large mineral deposit had been discovered in a remote area of the Alaskan tundra. The United States of America was soon back on top, the national debt was paid off slowly so as not to draw attention, and President Clayton James was revered as the greatest president of all time.

Tina and I attended two more Jubilees after the first; we told no one about these except Carol and Parker. We had been hounded for years after the first one, everybody from our own government to entrepreneurs and industry wanted us to bleed the Ar-Zians for everything we could. Several members of the government wanted to draft an act of Congress or a presidential executive order that would force me to petition the Ar-Zians for more advanced technology. I, of course, refused to do that, and as far as everyone knew there was no further contact between the Ar-Zians and me.

In fact, a number of things had occurred. A Probe was left at our house in another dimension to be used by us to communicate with Zo-L, Ra-L, and Overseer anytime I wanted. We would periodically send messages back and forth; it was like interstellar email. They missed us so badly, they insisted on us visiting and bringing our family. They had seen pictures of our son Bob and daughter Robin and wanted to meet them. We were glad to oblige, and our kids were thrilled to actually be able to visit another planet.

Tina and I had accepted the Ar-Zians' kind invitation to have our lives extended and come to live next door to Zo-L and Ra-L on PW-1. After the first Jubilee, they prepared two bodies cloned from our DNA but with the internal structure of Ar-Zians. We would not otherwise be able to survive on PW-1 for any extended period of time. Before they returned Tina and me home, we were taken to the Research Center on Ar-Z to show us our new bodies. We were both speechless as we were looked at ourselves: same height, much slimmer, beautifully colorful eyes; everything else externally was the same, and we both looked to be about twenty-five years old. We told them we wanted to live out our lives on Earth first, at least to a certain degree. They sent two small Probes home with us, one to monitor our health and another to communicate with them when we were ready to make the transition.

Several years later, Tina and I were starting go downhill health-wise. We knew it wouldn't be much longer before the decision was made for us that we would have to make the transition and move to PW-1. Tina and I called Carol and Parker over to the gazebo for a meeting. As they both sat down, I said, "You guys have meant the world to us, and your friendship over the years has been the most wonderful thing. As you are aware, Tina and I are getting up there in years, and we have made a very difficult decision. This is going to sound unbelievable, buts it's true. Overseer has prepared new hybrid bodies for both Tina and myself. We are going to live next door to Zo-L and Ra-L on PW-1. Our lifespan will be the same as theirs.... We will live about four thousand additional years there. Tina and I are leaving everything to you guys: the land, the house, all the income from sale of the gifts the Ar-Zians gave me, and the charity." I reached into my shirt pocket and pulled one of the Tina Diamonds.

"Remember these?" I asked.

"Oh yes," Carol said. "Those are the Tina Diamonds that Ar-Zians gave you in place of your salt pellets."

"That's correct; there are 19,607 more of them and a solid diamond oxygen bottle buried beneath that water tank. The only thing we ask is that you keep the charity going."

They were both astounded and didn't know what to say. They came over, and with tears in their eyes embraced us. "You and Carol are much younger than us, so I imagine you have many years left to really make a difference in the world."

Fighting back tears, Carol asked, "When will this all take place?"

"Very soon. I imagine; our last medical tests were pretty scary. The Probe that monitors our health has a kind of bar graph on its display. When it reaches a certain point it will let us know, and then travel to Ar-Z and let Overseer and the researchers know....Things will happen pretty quickly after that.

"Will we be allowed to be with you when the transition takes place?"

"Nothing would please us more, Carol," Tina said. Parker and Carol remained on high alert as the end time drew near. We spent the last few days together nearly constantly.... It was great.

The moment had arrived around 10:00 a.m. one morning as we were all enjoying each other's company in the kitchen. The Probe sounded the alarm and appeared right in front of the four of us. I said, "Message received," in Ar-Zian and the Probe disappeared. "It won't be long now," I said. About 5 minutes later, Overseer and two researchers showed up in our living room. Overseer came over and gave us a hug and said, "The time has come."

"If it is okay, we would like our friends to witness the transformation." We were all instantly teleported onto the waiting craft cloaked in invisibility behind the house. We were staring at the new Tina and Ral; to say it was spooky was the understatement of the century. Overseer asked if we were sure we wanted to proceed, "because once the transfer is made it is not reversible, and from this point forward you will have no further contact with Earth." We agreed.

The whole experience was like something out of an old Frankenstein movie. We were placed into a very narrow clear cylinder one at a time.... I went first. There was bright orange light accompanied by a buzzing noise, and the transfer was complete. Tina watched in horror as I collapsed limp inside the cylinder. She started screaming, and that was the first thing I remember hearing, as I opened my eyes in my new body and reached out and touched her on the shoulder. She spun around and realized I was okay, and gave me the biggest kiss I had ever gotten. I said, "It's your turn, honey."

After her transformation, we said goodbye to Carol and Parker .... It was incredibly sad. Zo-L and Overseer levitated Carol, Parker, and our old bodies to the spa and set the scene for our demise.

Tina and I entered another dimension and watched the whole thing take place. Carol and Parker were told by Overseer to stand at a safe distance and close their eyes and cover their ears. There was a tremendous noise and a bright flash as a bolt of lightening hit the spa. It was very traumatic watching our best friends witness our staged deaths. Being hit by lightning, we should have had burns or other signs of damage, but there were none. Our deaths were deemed to be from natural causes. It's amazing when you think of the wonderful changes that were made to our whole world, just because of one random act of kindness. Who would have ever thought that loaning someone two simple items could literally change the world forever? War had become a thing of the past; we may not all like each other, but we no longer try to kill each other. Unbeknownst to the people on Earth, the Ar-Zians have installed Orbs and Probes all around the solar system to protect us against errant asteroids, comets, gamma ray bursts, and things we know nothing about that could cause catastrophic consequences. Even things such as Polar shifts, ice ages, and climate changes will no longer be a threat.

It was wonderful of the Ar-Zians to hybridize our bodies so we could maintain most of our features. Our faces look just the same as when we were in our twenties, with the same feature proportions as before, except we have no hair ... anywhere. Our eyes are a combination of many different colors, and like the Ar-Zians, we have no white areas, and we are able to zoom in on objects both near and far. We have two sets of eyelids, one clear and the other one opaque. Our organs have been modified to accommodate the different atmosphere and gravity. We also no longer have a digestive or urinary system; we certainly don't miss those! And what a blessing it is not to have all the annoying insects of Earth; it's wonderful not having to swat flies or mosquitoes or to wake up in the morning with a rash or insect bites, and our new bodies never itch. Our arms and legs are the same as before, except we have much greater mobility since our joints have been replaced with cartilage. We can also rotate our heads a full 360 degrees...pretty cool. We are so thrilled to wake up each morning feeling absolutely fantastic. No pills to take, or having to depend on our morning coffee to shock us into existence. No aches and pains, no stuffy nose, no teeth to brush or hair to comb, no finger- and toenails to manicure, no dead skin flakes, nothing at all . . . just pure bliss!

Tina and I live right next door to Zo-L and Ra-L and will probably do so for another 4,068 years; we refer to our new existence as our "pre-heaven." We are pre-programmed to die the same time as Zo-L and Ra-L. I asked Tina to check the back of my neck to see if there was an expiration date printed on it. . . . There wasn't. Things are very different from Earth here. There is a deafening silence! No animal sounds; nothing that happens inside a dome can be heard outside and vise versa....It's spooky. We love when it rains; you can see the drops hit the dome top and slowly move down to the ground. It's weird because the dome wall is invisible from the inside, and the rain just seems to spread out in all directions rather than coming straight down.

One day as Tina and I were lying in bed it started to rain. It was beautiful to watch, but it was silent. "It's a shame we can't hear it," I said. Just as I uttered that, we heard the sound of raindrops. We quickly learned that we can select what we choose to hear. . . . That was great.

One very nice thing: There is no sadness of any kind. Everyone is very happy all the time. We still have all our memories, even the ones we had forgotten, and many we would like to have remained forgotten. It has taken us some time to adjust, as everyone here is perfect! We were so used to people having ulterior motives, lying, cheating, cursing, and on and on; it's wonderful not to have to worry about any of that. The days are twenty-four hours long and the nights eight hours. We were totally bored at first as there is really nothing to do here. No one has hobbies; there are no clubs — nothing to maintain, no stores or restaurants to visit ... nothing! Tina and I used to like to have a drink and sit out on the gazebo in the evening, but here there is no such thing as an alcohol beverage, or any beverages for that matter. We also enjoyed volunteering at church and other organizations and really miss doing things for others. Everyone here has everything they could possibly want, and no one needs charity of any kind. We were feeling useless and wondered if we had made a terrible mistake coming here.

Zo-L and Ra-L did their very best to help us adjust to our new bodies and surroundings. They had MID create all the games that were available and taught us how to play them. We also completed all the lessons that Life Center teaches everyone from first to last, so we would have a better understanding of how to live life on PW-1. They introduced us to all their family, neighbors, and friends, who made a habit of visiting and taking us various places. They were all so very kind, and we loved it when they would bring their children. We were not only having trouble adapting, but now we felt like we were a burden to others. We missed our church very much, as there are none on either Ar-Z or PW-1. Everyone is very spiritual, but they have no places of worship. We spoke to various people about this and were told that they consider it worshiping God whenever they see something beautiful or amazing. After all isn't everything created by God? Tina and I understood this principle and have always felt the same way, but something was still missing — There is nothing to pray for. Of course we would pray for the people of Earth, but there was never any feedback. Back home we always felt like we were helping others by praying for them, and it made us feel good as well, especially when our prayers were answered. Tina and I made it a habit to pray each evening before going to bed, although finding a subject other than praise was very difficult.

We were told by Zo-L and Ra-L that our old memories could be relived through our dreams. In fact we could control our dreams, a process known as "lucid dreaming." I had actually tried for months on Earth to enter a state of lucid dreaming, but was successful only once. I purchased a device, which was a sleep mask containing sensors and LEDs that was worn over the eyes at night. During the REM (rapid eye movement) phase of sleep is when we dream. The mask's sensors would detect the eye movement and flash the two LEDs repeatedly to let you know you were in a dream state. The idea was if you knew you were in a dream, you could control the subject matter and activity. Zo-L said all we had to do was to think of what we wanted to access, say it to ourselves a couple times as we entered sleep, and we should also be able to do it together. Tina and I were very excited, and rushed home to try it out.... It was incredible. We were able to relive anything that had happened in our lives, even as a child. This made an incredible difference in our outlook, and we were beginning to adapt more readily.

Tina and I were very avid scuba divers, and we asked our friends if there was any way we would be able to pursue that activity on PW-1. Zo-L answered, "After Ar-Z was hit by the asteroid 805,000 years ago, the atmosphere became very toxic, killing nearly all life on land. While rebuilding, we looked for every possible way to save lives in case of another catastrophe; the Research Center was formed and that became their main goal. Among a great number of technological advances, they perfected a simple procedure to allow us to breathe underwater. I'm not sure if there is anyone left alive who had the procedure, but I will check for you." Tina and I counted on our friends very heavily, and prayed we were not becoming a burden to them.

Zo-L and Ra-L came over to our dome about a half-hour later and informed us they had good news. "Although there is no one still alive who had the modification, it was proven to be perfectly safe and in no way interfered with living life normally and was totally reversible. I can have a ship here immediately to take us to the Research Center on Ar-Z, and we will be back before nightfall," Zo-L said.

Tina and I looked at each other, extremely excited, and both said: "Yes, please."

Overseer met us at the Research Center, as he was very concerned about how we were adjusting to our new lives; he had been informed of the difficulties we were having so far. The procedure was performed very quickly and was completely painless. We looked slightly different, as there were two small sets of gills on the sides of our neck. The Research Center has a large tank of water they use for certain tests they perform, and Tina and I were transported there to test out our new abilities. It was incredible! With our two sets of eyelids, we could close the clear one and see perfectly underwater without ever having to blink. Breathing seemed very normal, and we were ecstatic, to say the least. We could even communicate verbally underwater. We stayed in the tank for several minutes, and could not contain our excitement. We rose out of the water and hugged Zo-L and Overseer and apologized for being such a bother to everyone. I think they were happier for us than we were for ourselves.... It was beautiful! We insisted on going back to the Research Center so we could thank the people who performed the body modification. Everything was looking much better now! When we arrived home we were exhausted, mostly from the emotional highs throughout the day.

We were enjoying our new lives much more now that we had something to do. We went diving every day, and even though there were no fish, the plant life was spectacular, millions of plants that we had never seen before. The water was warm, and the oceans and lakes were shallow....We were truly in heaven.

After a few weeks, Tina decided she wanted to learn how to play the guitar. With her enhanced brain, she picked up the ability very quickly. I was a little jealous; it had taken me many years to be as good as she was now after just a few minutes.

We sang and played together for all of our friends, their family members, and neighbors; we were becoming quite popular. We were approached from time to time to play concerts, and with our fully enhanced brains we were able to play amazingly fast and never made a mistake. We had actually performed for more than two hundred million people on one occasion. These people care so much about the feelings of others; no one has asked for a guitar, and no one has asked to learn how to play as they would not want to steal our thunder so to speak. I'm not really sure they would be able to play, because they have only three fingers and a thumb with no real joints.

Tina and I decided to learn to play some of the great hymns and other songs we used to sing in church. With our new total memories, we were able to remember every song we had ever sung. Soon we were harmonizing and playing to over 200 songs: new, old, and many gospel favorites.

We asked Zo-L and Ra-L if they would get a few friends together so we could perform and get some feedback. Within two minutes their dome was almost completely filled. Tina and I began with "How Great Thou Art," one of our favorites and followed up with several others. We had to sing them in Ar-Zian, so they didn't really rhyme, but we still got the point across. Everyone came up afterward and told us how much that performance meant to them, and we were thrilled. I think we have found our calling and now had a way to help others.

Since there was no music on either planet, they have never heard of dancing, other than my referencing their acts of jubilation as the "Happy Dance." When I had a band in my younger days, seeing everyone dance was the main reason to play. Tina and I have always enjoyed dancing, so we thought we would try to teach the Ar-Zians how. It was going to be difficult. First of all everyone would have to learn English, so the songs would make sense to them. We approached Zo-L with our idea, and he passed the request along to Overseer. Within two days, everyone on both planets spoke perfect English, well, our version of English anyway. Since their skeletons are all cartilage without joints, they look like someone holding cooked spaghetti and waving it around. It was not a pretty sight. We didn't care what they looked like; we just hoped we could teach them something they would enjoy. They already did something that resembled a dance; the one I dubbed The Happy Dance, so that is where Tina and I would start. Together we wrote a very simple song that everyone could join in. We would sing a very short one-line refrain, stop singing, and we would all do The Happy Dance. We thought that since they all knew the words, they would sing along; we were stunned when they didn't. We later learned that they couldn't sing. Somewhere along the line of genetic engineering, they had all become tone-deaf; they could distinguish different frequencies, but could not replicate them vocally. It didn't matter to us because the idea caught on, and they just loved dancing. Little by little we introduced new songs and new dances, and always ended with a few hymns.

We were asked to play everywhere including several gigs on Ar-Z, and it seems Tina and I had become rock stars. We completely underestimated the inventiveness of the Ar-Zians, who quickly created a vast number of dances themselves, many of which took place in the air. Tina and I were thrilled, as we finally found several things to do and felt like we were contributing to the happiness of others.... That was very important to us.

We began experimenting with the flavors NID produced, to see if we could create some of our favorite dishes that we missed, like pizza, fruits, and different types of candy. It took quite some time mixing various flavors, but we came up with a whole array of things that became instant hits. Tina and I were quickly becoming real trendsetters.

We also started quite a craze with our dog Pudd. The Ar-Zians had all watched the encyclopedia DVDs we had given them, and they fell in love with some of the animals they had seen. The Research Center quickly created MID programs to create a variety of pets. Nearly every family has a pet now, thankfully, all of the furry, cuddly variety; otherwise Tina and I might request to be returned to Earth. They are animatronic devices with a capacity to learn any behavior. If they do something that draws a favorable response, they will repeat it and even alter the behavior. If you say "sleep," it will turn off and stay that way until you call its name. They are amazing; they don't eat, poop, misbehave, or bark. We have two of them and they really have made a tremendous difference in our lives.

Tina and I are now able to fly, which is our absolute favorite thing to do. We are so grateful to Zo-L and Ra-L for having introduced us to everyone in their family, plus all their friends and neighbors. They all know how hard it has been for us to adjust, and they contact us on a regular basis and take us to some of their favorite places. It has been one Ar-Zian year now, and we have completely adapted. If we get bored, we grab our guitars and go someplace we haven't been before and start playing. Before very long a large crowd gathers and starts dancing, and we couldn't be happier.

Tina and I are not sure if we have the capability to reproduce; however, we have made a conscious decision not to do so; after all, the Ar-Zian people are perfect in every way, as is their society. We didn't think it would be proper for us to pollute their gene pool. Living next door to Zo-L, I have been privy to all the latest information concerning our galaxy and the universe before they become available for all to view through Life Center. He told me that Probes have discovered over a hundred planets with intelligent life on them. Occasionally, he takes Tina and me on sightseeing expeditions around the galaxy....What an incredible thing!

Zo-L asked me to come over to his house one day, stating he had some information he wanted to share with me. It was a Probe recording from Earth; actually, it was a news broadcast. This was extremely unusual, as we were told before we arrived that we would have no contact with, or receive any information from, Earth after we began our new lives on PW-1. Zo-L likened this regulation to people believing that relatives who have passed away are in heaven looking down on them.

"If you think about it," he said, "how could you enjoy heaven if you were constantly looking down on all the chaos you recently left? You might see your grandson being murdered, or a friend struggling to fight off a life- threatening illness, and so on. That would defeat the whole purpose of heaven, if you were just to continue participating in your former life only at a greater distance. Your lifespan has been fulfilled on Earth, and now you are here to start a new one. ... Enjoy it and don't look back."

As I remembered that conversation, we arrived in his dome, and we sat down. He reminded me of all the times I had complained about the United States government and how fed up the people were with the incompetence and arrogant attitude of Congress. "Oh yes," I said, "it still makes me mad, even after all these years."

Zo-L instructed Life Center to play the Probe recording. It was a follow-up story started years ago by a small group of political activists and a hand full of celebrities. They formed a grass-roots movement to do away with the two party systems and the Electoral College in favor of a five-party system. The existing two parties never get along, each had their own agenda, and almost nothing was getting done for the good of the people or the country. The new proposal was quickly dubbed "The Enema Bill." The movement, no pun intended, gathered a phenomenal amount of signatures, over two-thirds the population of the country. The petitions suggested a five-party system that would break the deadlock that had been going on in Congress for decades. There were already a number of political parties in existence but with limited funding; very few candidates were ever elected to Congress and never anyone to the presidency.

The petition further suggests that some of the money saved by not having to fund war efforts be equally divided and distributed to the five political parties for campaign purposes. The goal was to make campaigning more fair, less time consuming, and less expensive, while giving each candidate a fair chance at victory. No longer would the Electoral College have an influence on who was elected; it was by popular vote only. Each party would have to account for all of the money it received, and it would be illegal to fund raise or accept money from any other source. The news media was all over this story, and with their oversight and public pressure, the measure was brought before the public in a special election.... It passed with an amazing 97.62 percent approval.

Negative campaigning was now a thing of the past; no party would waste valuable funds trying to discredit the other candidates; it made more sense to espouse what you would do for the country. No longer would political action committees and special interest groups have any influence on the outcome of an election. Campaigning was decreased from months to just a few weeks. The change was considered to be one of the greatest political achievements the United States had ever accomplished and was even compared to creating the Declaration of Independence.

ABOUT THE AUTHOR

Born at a very young age in Westerly, Rhode Island in 1944, my family moved to California in 1953. I brought my parents along to drive the car and my older brother Gene to drive me crazy. After graduating from Long Beach City College in 1964, I spent two years in the aerospace industry before moving on to Xerox Corporation where I worked for over thirty-three years. Now retired, I have proudly been doing nothing since 1997. This is the first book I have ever read or written, so hopefully you will have purchased it before discovering my lack of credentials. I hope you enjoy it; I can truthfully say it's the best book I've ever read.